By Emma Copley Eisenberg

The Third Rainbow Girl

Housemates

HOUSEMATES

HOUSEMATES

A Novel

EMMA COPLEY EISENBERG

HOGARTH | NEW YORK

Housemates is a work of fiction. Names, characters, places, and incidents are the products of the author's imagination or are used fictitiously. Any resemblance to actual events, locales, or persons, living or dead, is entirely coincidental.

Published in the United States by Hogarth, an imprint of Random House, a division of Penguin Random House LLC, New York.

HOGARTH is a trademark of the Random House Group Limited, and the H colophon is a trademark of Penguin Random House LLC.

LIBRARY OF CONGRESS CATALOGING-IN-PUBLICATION DATA
Names: Eisenberg, Emma Copley, author.
Title: Housemates : a novel / by Emma Copley Eisenberg.
Description: First edition. | New York, NY : Random House, 2024.
Identifiers: LCCN 2023035446 (print) | LCCN 2023035447 (ebook) |
ISBN 9780593242230 (hardcover ; acid-free paper) |
ISBN 9780593242247 (ebook)
Subjects: LCGFT: Queer fiction. | Novels.
Classification: LCC PS3605.I8278 H68 2024 (print) |
LCC PS3605.I8278 (ebook) | DDC 813/.6—dc23/eng/20231106
LC record available at https://lccn.loc.gov/2023035446
LC ebook record available at https://lccn.loc.gov/2023035447

Printed in the United States of America on acid-free paper

randomhousebooks.com

1 2 3 4 5 6 7 8 9

First Edition

Book design by Susan Turner

For the housemates

So last spring Berenice Abbott and I decided to go out and see a little part of America. We thought that America was worth seeing, was worth loving, was worth writing about and worth photographing.

—Elizabeth McCausland

You can fuck
anyone—but with whom can you sit
in water?

—Ilya Kaminsky

PART 1

I.

WHERE I LIVED THEN, THERE WAS NO PHOTOGRAPHY, NO MOVIES, no books, no art of any kind.

It was enough to make me wonder why I had ever spent so long on it. Art! It had once been my whole day. My whole experience of living.

People talk about how time moves slowly, but I had the opposite problem that season, a period of great depression that began in 2017 and lasted three years. During that time, I was always turning behind me to see where the morning had gone, the day, the month, the year. I watched videos of capybaras pushing their noble noses through various bodies of water or of beavers whose webbed hind feet slapped the concrete as they walked, semi-upright and pigeon-toed, with carrots wedged between their small, articulated hands and their toothful mouths. There was one overambitious beaver in particular who I loved to watch as he continuously lost a single carrot from his hand/mouth bundle and stopped to pick it up, only to lose it, or a different carrot, again, moments later and slightly farther on in his travels. You would think at a certain point that the beaver would learn, that he would let one carrot go in service of retaining the rest and his general well-being. But no. He never learned.

I felt like that beaver: the more I tried to take on, the more I dropped—emails for example, just simple offers of contact or meaningless photography work. I had my Social Security checks to cash, I had my house to move around in, and I had my body to feed—the only carrots I could carry. I also liked watching videos people had recorded of themselves walking around their neighborhoods in Philadelphia, videos in which nothing happened but their feet scuffing pavement and the world going by. In this way only, I left my house.

A whole day could pass just in avoiding my office closet with its film and negatives that belonged to me as well as its books and papers that belonged to—what should I call her? I'll call her what they called me in her obituary, written almost fifteen years earlier in the paper of record: "housemate." Other things they wrote in The Housemate's obituary: *aged 54, acute myeloid leukemia; there are no survivors.* I resented this last part not just because I felt that *I* had survived her, but also because it made her sound alone when she was not. She had friends didn't she? And former students, who loved her too.

You might be asking why I sank into such a Miss Havisham-esque state during that season when, as I've said, The Housemate died long before and to this I say: I don't know. Sometimes it just works that way. For many years you are fine, and then whammo, you are not. There was the 2016 election, yes, and the general state of the world, and the fact that I had dramatically decreased my work as a photographer, thinking, I am nearly seventy years old and it's time for me to enjoy my life. But none of this explains the way I *felt*.

I felt like a stuffed animal that had lost its stuffing. I spent my time tending to other closets of lesser importance, taking out all the contained objects and sorting them into categories according to their use and usefulness to me. As I worked, I listened to the news, or sometimes—the only art I could tolerate—to musicals. I was especially partial to Sondheim, particularly *Into the Woods,* and particularly numbers that featured The Witch. *Careful before you say, listen to me,* I would sing along with her. *Children will listen.*

Next I put all the useless-to-me things into boxes and called the thrift store on the avenue to send someone to pick them up. Finally, I bought new things from the everything website in order to absorb the space freed up by the things I'd just gotten rid of. This was an important step and a step that I savored; the only thing that brought me joy. In the story of an object and me, no time was ever so good as when its digital likeness and that of many others of great similarity were lined up vertically and auditioning to be mine. I scrolled slowly, considering. I took great pains to select the exact right scrubby sponge, the exact right set of black shoelaces, the perfect knit winter hat. I read all the reviews.

When the new things were delivered, the device my friend's kid had set up in my kitchen made an ominous sound which was really just the sound of another living person doing a job they were underpaid to perform, a person I would never speak to or meet. After that sound was another—the real sound of a truck or van starting up again and driving away down my street toward the avenue. It was in this manner, too, that I made groceries appear at my door.

I still live on this same street, a two-way where the cars go too fast despite all the stop signs and the houses are attached in rows with porches you can look down. I live in West Philadelphia, a shtetl most people have only heard of in the context of its cameo in the credits of a TV show starring Will Smith or because it contains the campus of an Ivy League university with a destructive hunger for real estate. I have lived here for much too long, so long that to fetch a half gallon of milk or go to the bank involves five to seven emotionally gutting interactions.

Normally I can handle this, but that season I just couldn't. It wasn't just that I was afraid to run into people I used to know, but rather that I felt the neighborhood to be a graveyard of my past lives. Here the fancy yoga studio which used to be a camera store where I'd chat with the scruffy owner about lenses and buy film when I was still working as a photographer. Here the house that once belonged to a colleague of The Housemate's in the English department at the University, a woman with excellent taste in sweaters and ceramics and who, at parties, would serve cheddar cheese and rosemary crackers on the most beautiful rectangular trays. Everyone at those parties knew that The Housemate and I were an item but that didn't stop them from looking at us out of the sides of their eyes, whether because we were lesbians or because she was a professor, though not mine, and I a graduate student, I can't say. We were exactly the same age anyway; she had been one of those wunderkinds who'd graduated high school at fifteen. Let's give them something to look at, The Housemate would say, holding up a loaded cracker and awaiting the opening of my mouth.

There the building containing the first apartment The Housemate and I ever shared. There the fancy grocery store which used to be a soul food restaurant where The Housemate and I would go for long conversations about projects we wanted to do together. There was a black dog with a flat snout who liked to lie on its checked floor in slants of sun.

We could pick a little operation, nothing but a Ferris wheel and a funnel cake stand that moves from town to town and follow them, she said to me in that restaurant once, while leaning down to pet the dog. She had an idea which was new then but is old now which was to record people's voices speaking and have that be the result of the work instead of a book. The tapes she made on those trips are still in my office closet to this day.

And so on.

It's funny, in a non-haha kind of way, considering everything that came after—how the pandemic would force us all into confinement, alone in our homes—that I was ahead of the curve by several years during that time, creating the conditions of isolation for myself. So it was a fluke in a way, very unlikely and totally by chance, that I was even out of my house for long enough to see Bernie and Leah that day in the coffee shop.

Why did I follow them back to their house? Was it only because they were so beautiful and so young? No, comes the answer. It was also because there were two of them and they had that map.

IT WAS ABOUT A YEAR into my artless season, May of 2018, when I woke to a terrible pain in my back and a leak in my moka pot. No matter how I screwed and unscrewed the thing, water dripped out and the coffee would not burble up to where I could get it. I watched some videos, first about moka pots and then about other things. I looked on the everything website but the new pot wouldn't arrive until the following day. Plus walking, I knew, was the only thing that would resolve the back issue. I loitered in the vestibule of my house for what might have been an hour, futzing with the ribboned laces on my shoes in hesitation. Then, suddenly, I whipped open the door and was outside.

It was hot, the world having apparently skipped spring and gone straight to summer. The tree my neighbor had planted in a bucket was now too large for the bucket and the church had changed its flags. At the avenue, I took the dreaded turn left, eastward toward the University. After a few blocks of seeing no one I recognized, I felt emboldened and slowed my walk, breathing through my nose. I kept my eyes straight ahead and when I reached the anarchist coffee shop, I decided to chance it, getting in line behind a bosomy person with a thigh tattoo of a rat eating a piece of pizza. The tattoo peeked out from where her pants (very short) ended and her socks (very tall) began.

Light streamed in through the dirty mottled glass windows and the plastic flower chains that hung from the metal coffee-can light fixtures danced and blew around whenever the door let in the wind. I kept looking over my shoulder as the new people came in, but they were all strangers. The little barista behind the counter with her hair in two antennae and her pierced septum was taking her sweet time making a kale smoothie. As she blended it, I looked around the coffee shop and I saw them.

There are different words now, better words that I am still trying to get used to using, but all I can say is that one of them looked like a thin girl and the other one looked like a fat boy.

They were two white kids, sitting next to each other on a bench seat in the dark back corner of the coffee shop where two cinder block walls painted red met at a right angle. In front of them was a flimsy aluminum table, and on top of the table was a map: not a book that you flipped but a wide piece of creased paper that you spread. I listened as they talked a little bit—interrupting each other and pointing out the flaws in each other's thinking—and I saw immediately that they loved each other in a way that I recognized because I had lived it: way more than sex and way less than life.

I ordered a black coffee as quietly as I could, which I was given in a ceramic mug to stay, a thing I hadn't done in years. I took the aluminum table next to theirs.

Where would we even go? the girlish one—Bernie, I would learn—asked. She spread both hands apart on the map and I wondered what cities and towns each of her fingers were touching. She wore a thin white T-shirt that showed the texture of her skin through its fabric. It was much too big for her, which only emphasized the smallness of her neck and the slope of her shoulders. Her head, though appearing at first much larger than her neck, was actually in proportion, it was only a trompe l'oeil—a trick of the eye.

Her eyes? Large and a little uneven, the left one being slightly more open and angled down than the right one which was tilted slightly up and showed more of the eyelid. Her nose? Long and thick, like a triangular piece of paper folded in half. Some people's eyes and nose and mouth are clustered together in the middle part of their face, but Bernie's face was the opposite; her features were spread out so that there were no blank areas and each quadrant of face had something interesting going on in it. Her hair—to her shoulders—and eyebrows were light brown but her eyelashes were darker and very long, which kept the light off that whole part of her face, giving the impression of darkness and of luster.

We'd go wherever we want, the boyish one—Leah—said. She was not looking at the map but rather looking down at Bernie, since she was so tall, possibly six feet. The line of Leah's torso in profile was pleasantly curved, with her belly in its T-shirt extending past the vertical line made by the open button-down she also wore. Her big right hand held an iced beverage in the air, then brought it to her face where she sucked on it through a bent metal straw. As she spoke, drops of condensation flowed down and fell on the map.

Bernie brushed them off. I don't mean to be an asshole, she said, but do you really think that you and I could do a project like this? I studied those people in college. They had grants from the government. They had assignments from magazines. They were already famous artists in their fields. They had years.

Evans and Agee were out only eight weeks for *Let Us Now Praise Famous Men,* Leah said. She stabbed the straw around in the ice, sucking up the foam and the remaining liquid.

Evans! I thought, and saw not so much his actual 1936 black-and-white photograph *Corrugated Tin Façade / Tin Building, Moundville, Alabama*—a large and lovely mound of dirt in front of the eponymous and strangely shaped tin-clad building—but rather a reproduction on a thick paper postcard that I'd bought at a museum in New York when The Housemate and I had gone there together on one of our Saturday day trips. She hadn't liked the photograph much, and told me so, but I'd tacked it above my desk anyway, pushing the pin into a soft part of the window trim. She'd also disliked Agee, a strange writer whose words could garble your mouth with their moisture.

Bernie leaned forward, used her elbow to push up a section of the map into a single accordion fold, and rested her head against her hand. I could see then that the map was a map of Pennsylvania, the state we were in.

I don't have eight weeks, Bernie said.

Leah searched for someplace to put down her empty glass, settling eventually for the floor by her feet. When she turned my way for the first time, I saw that her face was round and ruddy and pink. Her blondish hair was cut short but not in the fashionable way in which the hairs stood up vertically; these hairs lay down horizontally, eddying in circles over her head and ending at her ears with a little flip.

Leah turned back to Bernie. How long do you have? she asked.

Bernie considered this. I'll lose my coffee shop job no matter what, she said. I could probably swing three weeks from the library if I tell them about Daniel Dunn dying.

I perked up at this too, another name I knew. But died? I pulled out my phone and typed in his name. Lo and behold it was true.

Photographer Daniel Dunn Dead at 71.

I clicked, and Bernie and Leah's conversation, though continuing, went quiet as I read.

Daniel Dunn, the article began in earnest, *one of the most influential photographers of the twentieth century whose legacy was tarnished by multiple accusations of sexual misconduct and by financial ruin, died on Monday at his home in Mifflin County, Pennsylvania. He was 71. His ex-wife, the sculptor Michelle Kleinman, said the cause was alcohol poisoning.*

Daniel Dunn (1947-2018) was an American photographer best known for his large-format color photographs of unremarkable American landscapes taken over the course of several road trips in the 1970s. Dunn is frequently credited with establishing color photography as a legitimate medium in the world of fine art photography following the decades-long domination of black-and-white.

His accolades. The now-famous artists he taught. *With his images that married an obsession with the visuals of everyday American life and a sharp eye for documenting crucial national political and cultural moments, Dunn is sometimes said to have single-handedly erased the notion of photography as an elitist art world medium and returned it to the hearts and living rooms of ordinary Americans.*

After founding and chairing the prestigious photography program at Croyden College in Sleepy Hollow, New York, for 28 years, Dunn was, until 2017, a full professor and chair of the Department of Fine Art (Photography) at Evergreen College in Huntingdon, Pennsylvania. But his accomplishments were tainted. I skipped over the next few paragraphs, as I'd already heard all about Dunn's misdeeds the previous year when the friend had sent me the article, just one of many old art world men who'd finally gotten busted after years of impunity.

It is believed that following his departure from Evergreen College this past winter, Dunn vacated his longtime home and studio in the small college town of Huntingdon and had been living in the secluded cabin home where he was raised.

Contacted this week by The Times, Evergreen acknowledged

the allegations and suggested they played a role in Dunn's departure from the college.

"Though our investigation into the December 2017 Title IX complaints is still ongoing, we were very disturbed by the conduct alleged by the complainants and accepted Professor Dunn's immediate resignation."

But almost immediately after Dunn parted ways with Evergreen, he was back in the public eye, this time for his disastrous financial decisions. On Jan. 12 of this year, Dunn was sued in the Supreme Court of Pennsylvania for nonpayment by a company that had loaned him $7 million. There was also a lawsuit from Philadelphia-based company True Color, claiming that Dunn had not paid more than $400,000 in bills for photography services rendered over the past 12 years.

According to close colleagues and business associates, Dunn's financial difficulties began in the mid-2010s, in tandem with both increased demand for public exhibitions of his work and the health troubles of his mother, the late Eileen Dunn. Dunn spared no expense shuttling from installing gallery shows in far-flung locales to hospital beds to see his mother, even bringing Mrs. Dunn to Paris for an extended stay at L'Hôpital Présidentiel, a French medical facility said to be conducting promising experimental trials of treatments for aggressive late-stage cancers.

According to Benjamin Pogden of the Jack Bowles Gallery, which represented Dunn until recently, Dunn and the loan agency had been able to reach a settlement in the months before Dunn's death through the sale of Dunn's properties—a loft in SoHo and a stately flat in Paris—as well as through a few lucrative sales of his most famous work to international investors less bothered by the hit to his reputation. Recently, prices for Dunn's work in the United States have plummeted.

It is not known whether he continued to make photographs in the recent months or if he was trying to raise further funds to pay his debts.

"I don't know what he was working on," said ex-wife Kleinman, "but he said he was still working."

"He was always friendly, always said hello," Mr. Jacob W. Yoder told The Lewistown Sentinel in an article remembering his next-door neighbor. "But he told me he was done with all that photography stuff."

THREE WEEKS IS GOOD, LEAH was saying, her head tipped back and resting against the red wall. Three weeks is enough.

There was silence between them.

Just to be very clear, Bernie said, the kind of photography I do, it's not like, oh cool, snap that. It's fussy. It's slow. You can wait hours for the light to change.

I know, Leah said. Large format. I've been reading about it.

Plus I'm out of practice, Bernie said. So I doubt I'll make many pictures.

That's fine, Leah said. Still, you're driving me. That's not nothing. I'll see things I could never see without you.

True, Bernie said. She picked at the map, folding and unfolding a corner.

And what about Dunn's house? Leah asked.

It's only a couple of hours from here.

So I guess we go there first?

OK, Bernie said.

OK, Leah said.

Leah was looking at Bernie's face again, so I did too. Bernie had sunken eye sockets and thin wrists and her forearms were bare. She looked cold, thoroughly chilled, and I shivered just to think of it, of what it must feel like to be in her body. My mind rolled instead toward Leah, the warmth of her, her bigness. I wished to cuddle up next to her big belly which was straining against the fabric of her T-shirt. Even then, at the beginning, when I barely knew them, I could see this difference in temperature.

When they stacked their woven plastic baskets and put their cups in the brown bus bin below the cream and almond milk station, I too rose from where I sat. I lingered, pretending to look at the vegan peanut butter bombs until I heard them jingle the door open, and then I darted through after them. I kept my distance as they walked east along the avenue toward the half-occupied state senator's office and the vape store.

Leah was the more distinctive walker, jutting her legs out from the hip, a little bowlegged, then rolling her feet from outer toe to inner heel, and moving her arms with each step like an enthusiastic power walker. The ass of her pants was loose and moving, and the back of her shirt showed lovely indents where the flesh folded over, making small triangles at the place where the backs of her arms met her trunk. Bernie, no-hipped, walked without much movement side to side but rather kept her legs stiff through her knees, almost kicking her feet out in front of her like a zombie, one hand in her pocket and her head down. Her small ass cheeks appeared into roundness then disappeared into flatness, one then the other. As I followed them, watching, I pretended I was in one of my videos. I pretended I was only doing what thousands of people do all the time, every day. I was only a camera: recording.

Bernie and Leah turned left onto the side street that held the music studio and the dry cleaners then right onto a tree-lined street where they stopped in front of the second house. Bernie turned first and Leah followed, up one set of steps, clearing the landing, and then up the second set of steps. As Bernie crested the last step, her foot caught and she tripped and Leah lurched forward in a flash, grabbing Bernie's arm to steady her such that they reached the porch at the same time, where they stood for a moment laughing and making large self-deprecating hand gestures.

I saw in the way that Leah looked at Bernie and Bernie looked at her feet that Leah loved Bernie more than Bernie loved Leah. I thought of a quote from one of The Housemate's favorite books which I still keep on a downstairs shelf. "There are the lover and the beloved," Carson McCullers wrote, "but these two come from different countries."

Bernie and Leah had both been smiling as they stood on the porch but when they got to the house's big front door, they weren't anymore. As I stood on the street corner under a sign marked NO PARKING HERE TO CORNER watching them unlock the door, an intense desire was born in me to know how their trip—very grand by the sound of it, and how was Bernie connected to Dunn?—would turn out, and more broadly what would become of them. What did they want out there and where *would* they go? Would Bernie ever love Leah equally, or would they be alright, just as they were, in this imbalance?

If I am being honest, this project of tracking Bernie and Leah was born from selfish interests too. I suppose I wanted to know, too, if it would be different for them than it had been for The Housemate and me. To be an artist in America, and a woman, and gay, in love with another gay woman artist who is up against the same things? Much has changed, but not everything has. Would they be able to be both separate and together, arguably *the* thing that The Housemate and I had never been able to solve?

Bernie and Leah disappeared inside the house. I thought for a moment I had dreamed them up. But no. The wind blew across my face. I felt it. The curtains moved in the big picture window of the house. I saw them. They were really in there now, the two of them, really living. I could come back tomorrow, I knew, and the next day, and look at the house's brick walls. But I could never get inside that house.

Except then I *was* inside it. I closed my eyes and slid right through a crack in the brick and into their living room. There was Bernie and there was Leah. I could hear their voices and feel their shadows moving through that dark, dark space. I don't know how I did it exactly, that first time, except to say that it felt like the way taking a good photograph used to feel, and like how my friend says giving birth was: it was me who did it and it was not me, and the second the process was complete, any sense of how it had been accomplished was gone.

But I have a sense, a sense that grows stronger as I write this, that I saw it all that day and that I was no longer alone. I saw their past and I saw their future and maybe even times before and after that. And I could return there—I did, again and again—to that corner outside their house, and make the leap into their lives whenever I wanted. It has been this leaping that made all the difference.

II.

THE DAY BERNIE MET LEAH WAS BRIGHT WHITE AND DYING. IT was a Saturday in January so the block's many trees, roots wrecking the sidewalk as they grew, were bare, their branches lolling in the wind. There had recently been a fire at the old apple factory building that burned for days despite the best efforts of those responsible for its extinguishment, so the smell of ash still hung in the air.

They met because of the house, a three-story Victorian managed by a suburban rental company, that sat on the white end of a block that marked the edge of gentrification. To the east, intrepid white queers bundled their tiny offspring into snowsuits and strapped them into all-terrain baby carriages. To the west, Black women knocked and stood in doorframes with the storm doors open, talking. To the south was the avenue, a commercial corridor that connected this neighborhood on one side to the University via expensive pizza restaurants and local pet stores and the co-op grocery store and a sprawling green park that hosted a farmer's market and on the other side to the suburbs via Ethiopian restaurants, hair salons, and car dealerships decorated with strings of multicolored flags.

To the north was the subway Bernie had taken to get here, a train that went both below and above ground, hurtling by murals that conveyed messages of love and color and caution.

Bangs combed and wearing a cheap blue blazer that was too big for her, Bernie stood in front of the house's huge door with its great pane of glass and horizontal brass mail slot. Attached to its neighbor on one side but separated on the other by a damp alley, the house's front garden, which sloped steeply, was a graveyard of limp hostas and its porch a parking lot for bikes.

Bernie had never heard of a housing interview, but the person she'd been emailing with assured her that it was important to make sure she was "the right fit—for everybody's sake."

Four Swarthmore grads, looking for a fifth housemate, the ad read. *Looking for someone with excellent emotional processing skills and ability to engage in open dialogue and proactive communication. We use a chore wheel to make sure labor is distributed equitably. Must be into Jigger the cat, most important member of the household, haha, and antiracist. Queer preferred (we all are).*

When things had soured with Bernie's first housemate, a girl from college, over cleaning (Bernie didn't do any), there had been another girl named Sheila from Bernie's job at the coffee shop with a room open in her rowhome in South Philadelphia. There were dive bars and cans of watery beer paired with shots of well whiskey and cigarettes put out in large planters that toppled over onto fingers, sending the unlucky to under-resourced emergency rooms. There was breakfast ordered in at three in the afternoon, for too much money, in large, sweating Styrofoam containers, eaten while watching movie trailers about the end of the world. Several months passed this way.

Did Bernie care about photography during these months? Occasionally, when she was dancing in a bar that she had not paid to enter, Bernie would notice the light bouncing off the mirrored walls and feel a feeling. Or, going to work, standing in the subway car, the walls of the tunnel would be moving away from her in such a way that could have been crucial to look at later.

But mostly the answer was no. No she didn't look, and no she didn't care. She cared about her own face (cheeks so round, eyes so small) and her own coat (not warm enough) and her bank account and about the faces and coats of the people to whom she served coffee in the mornings and the effect that these things had on the tip jar/her bank account.

It is possible, I have found, to love something but forget about it for periods of several years or even longer when your mind is filled with a special kind of blankness or a particularly loud sort of noise. Sex can do it and so can grief. Also raising a child, I've heard, or caring for the aged, two things I never did because I was afraid of exactly this kind of forgetting. But, I think, even if forgotten, the thing you love is always there, running in the background. It takes energy to forget something you love that much, in a way that can leave you feeling perpetually tired and unused.

Once, during those pre-Leah months, Bernie was out walking when she saw a camera lying in the street, just off the curb. It was nothing special, the opposite of special really, a black-and-silver plastic and nearly hollow battery-operated film camera.

She went to pick it up and held it in her hand. It was shining wet and nothing happened when Bernie pressed the big silver power button or the flimsy wheel that was supposed to turn the thing from OFF to AUTO. But when she pressed and held down the button marked OPEN the film compartment did, revealing a dried-out and exposed roll of Fujicolor film. Just the words on the roll's label—FILM FOR COLOR PRINTS, PROCESS CN-16, C-41 were enough to kill the rest of that night and her next morning, hours Bernie spent in bed, sitting cross-legged and touching each part of the camera with her index finger. She held the camera up and looked through the viewfinder; it fish-eyed her room badly. But then Monday came and, withdrawing the camera from her coat pocket as she walked to the subway, she threw it in a trash can.

Sheila, the housemate, joked that they paid their rent to a Russian mob wife, but then one day the woman really had shown up on their stoop in a white suit with the news that a cousin was moving to America and they were moving out.

Ah well, Sheila said. It was good while it lasted.

West Philly, with its old deciduous trees and earnest leftist infighting, had not been Bernie's first choice, as she preferred the hard-drinking and emotionally suppressed culture of her previous neighborhood, but as the move-out date approached and she sent reply after reply to roommate wanted listings with no result, she began to see the situation somewhat differently.

BERNIE RANG THE BELL, THEN rapped sharply on the pane. She heard a person approach the door, then stop. In the long pause that followed, Bernie perceived the anxiety of whoever was on the other side; their hesitation palpable, their heavy breathing audible.

The door opened. Big smile, both hands waving. Plump face framed by a haircut that seemed made for an old-fashioned hat to sit on top of it—a trapezoidal duke's hat perhaps, in a deep color, or a round page's cap with a feather in it. Her forehead was wet. Her name, she said, was Leah.

Come in! Leah said, then stepped back so Bernie could.

She spoke loud, so loud that it was jarring, but also winning. Bernie had never been one to make fun of those who tried very hard at life, as she herself was also such a person.

Leah leaned forward, pulled the big door closed, and locked it. They stood in the small vestibule looking at each other.

Bernie, said Bernie, pointing to herself.

I know, Leah said. I mean, I figured.

Leah shook her hair out of her eyes like a boy in a swimming pool. She was big. Big breasts atop big stomach atop thighs in men's khaki pants, big long legs that terminated in round-toed soccer sneakers—black with white stripes. Cheeks like huge apples that shone in the weak overhead light. Nose a little pointy and downtrodden. She wore a red hoodie, the zipper of which was sliding down and revealing interesting freckles on her neck and chest.

Well, Leah said. Shall we?

Bernie followed Leah into the dim living room which connected to the dim dining room via a large cased opening. Light filtered in weakly through the alley side windows and several gooseneck lamps, all plugged tautly into the same outlet, made futile attempts at illumination. A shiny exposed brick wall ran the length of the dining room and on into the fluorescent-lit kitchen, which Bernie glimpsed through a narrow door. Small bits had come unsealed from the brick wall and tumbled down onto the dark hardwood floors, which shone aggressively even in the absence of light.

The house was like a body whose blood didn't circulate well. Energy pooled in certain places and didn't move. Years later, Bernie and Leah would meet the woman who grew up in this house. Yes, the woman would say. It was always this way.

The dining room's oval table and chairs were mismatched, but not in a fun way; some were square and made of blond wood while others were dark, rounded, and ornately carved. Leftover protest signs made of cardboard and Sharpie had been hung on the walls with push pins or placed in the windowsills—THIS PUSSY GRABS BACK and BLACK LIVES MATTER with a sharp fist made of lines; TRANS IS BEAUTIFUL.

Have a seat, Leah said. I'll get the others.

It occurred to Bernie then that this was a house in which beauty and meaning were opposed, in which objects were only valued if they fulfilled a functional purpose or conveyed a message. The way an object acted upon the eye or any other part of the body did not matter here. On the inside of an open closet door was taped a matte-pink poster of an anatomical heart, its various chambers and veins colored in green and yellow tones. This poster could have added beauty to the space or continued its beauty, but frameless and bubbling in the middle from the placement of the Scotch tape, it did not. It wasn't that they didn't know beauty, Bernie saw, it was just that they did not care for it.

Meow meow, said a warm black-and-white lump of cat who appeared at Bernie's shins and then bumped her head against

Bernie's anklebone. Bernie's pants were slightly too short and her socks had slunk down into bunches so the cat's velvet fur was shockingly soft against her bare skin.

The cat lifted her small face, closed her eyes, and began to purr in Bernie's general direction. She had one clipped ear and one regular ear and a white marking on one side of her snout like a fat letter L which gave her face the overall charming and bizarre look of the Phantom of the Opera wearing his mask. The cat turned her substantial rump on Bernie then, exposing her pink asshole—all the more prominent against her lustrous black fur—and flopped onto the floor, where she hoisted her opposite leg into the air and began to lick herself vigorously from primordial pouch to clawed back paw.

I see you met Jigger, Leah said.

There was that smile again. No teeth, but a joy all through the forehead and eyes. The three housemates, who had filed into the dining room behind Leah, all laughed.

Leah had written the ad, but it was her girlfriend, Alex, a tall white girl with flat olive-colored limbs and brown hair gathered in a small knot at the nape of her neck, who took on the role of lead questioner once all the housemates had been introduced and settled themselves and their mugs of chamomile and Lemon Zinger along the two long sides of the rickety dining table. Bernie sat alone on the table's short side with her back to the front door, a thing that made her jumpy and paranoid. Her father believed he had been shot in the back in a past life, and this information, if it was information, had been passed down to Bernie.

Leah and Alex sat on Bernie's left. To her right was Violet, tall and narrow with short dyed platinum blond hair and black roots, and then Meena, who wore an electric-pink mesh tank top that showed off her substantial arm muscles, and looked moist, as if she had just come in from the rain.

They were both Asian; Violet East, and Meena South. There had been exactly two people of color in Bernie's central Pennsylvania high school: siblings, a boy and girl, whose parents ran the Mexican restaurant despite emigrating from El Salvador. Bernie had shown up to Evergreen so idiotic and tongue-tied about race that when she'd opened the door to her double and found Karen Chen from Pittsburgh and her parents, both pharmacists who explained how their friends' son had come to the school, been premed, and then become a successful doctor, as Karen would no doubt also do, Bernie felt she was being put to some test and was determined not to fail.

You can say Asian, Karen had said eventually, growing tired of Bernie's endless hemming and hawing. You can say Chinese. It's not a slur, it's just what I am. Or Chinese American. Whatever.

OK, Bernie said. Thanks for the tip.

You're welcome, Karen said. Will you stop being weird about it now?

Yes, Bernie said. I mean, I will surely try.

HOW DO YOU FEEL ABOUT public education? Alex asked now.

Good? Bernie replied.

Charter schools? Alex continued.

Good?

Hmm, Alex said, writing this down on a yellow legal pad.

Alex is a journalist, Leah said by way of explanation.

You say that like you aren't a journalist too, Alex said.

I'm not, Leah said. Not really.

Right, Alex said. You're much too complicated to be boxed in.

Exactly. Leah smiled.

Mommy and Daddy are fighting, faux-whined Violet.

Leah and Alex turned and smiled at each other, and Leah patted Alex's skinny knee.

How do you identify? asked Meena.

Like my pronouns? Bernie answered.

Yup, but also like any other words you might want us to know that describe your identities, like *working-class, disabled, butch, femme, witch, poly, pansexual, sapiosexual, bottom, top, boi, stud*—

Jesus, Meena, you can't say *stud,* interjected Violet, rolling their eyes at Bernie conspiratorially.

Really? Meena said.

Really. White people and Asians should not say it because it's a word that comes from the Black community.

Hmm, Alex said, writing this down.

I am a woman I guess, Bernie said. Actually I prefer the word *girl* to the word *woman* if I'm being honest.

Ugh preach, Meena said.

I use they/them pronouns, Violet said.

OK, Bernie said.

And I'm nonbinary but I don't really care about pronouns, Leah said. I mean they are great, everyone should be called what they want to be called. But just for me personally.

OK, Bernie said.

What about social justice? Alex said. Approximately how many hours per week would you say you spend working to mitigate the effects of racism, sexism, transphobia, homophobia, or classism?

Or fatphobia, Leah added.

Right, Alex said. That too.

Well, when I was younger, in college maybe, Bernie said. But now I work a lot so I don't have a lot of free time.

And you're a photographer, Alex said.

We googled you, Leah said.

I, Violet said, did not google you.

We looked at your photos of the river, Alex said.

Ancient history, Bernie said.

They were interesting, Alex said. Not a lot of people in them. A bit cold maybe. Almost clinical? Like for an architecture magazine maybe? As if they were old or from the past?

Alex, Leah said.

It's not a bad thing, Alex continued. I just mean that they don't look like they're from today. They don't look modern.

They're timeless, Leah said. As in, they could be from any time. I liked them a lot and I have to look at a lot of photographs for my work. That one of the little house with the Confederate flag mowed into the lawn but kind of faded and that big bird in the tree? It felt like it was about the political statement the flag was making and also not about it at all, just a photo of a house in a beautiful place with a strange-looking bird. It felt like it was trying to zoom out on that house and put it in a context, in a broader place, wherever that place was.

Central Pennsylvania, Bernie said. Where I'm from.

Well I liked *that* one, Alex said. That one had a message at least. A takeaway.

Violet looked up from their phone which they had slid out of their thigh pocket.

Leah knows things, they said to Bernie. About art.

Not really, Leah said. I'm getting my PhD in media studies, I won't bore you with the details. But for extra money and because I'm interested in it, I also work for the city weekly paper. Mostly I just fact-check but I do a few reviews of shows now and then, when they let me, and some other short things. Mostly it's a lot of reading press releases and double-checking the spellings of people's names.

Violet's attention was back on their phone now, their thumb swiping powerfully.

Volunteering? Alex continued. Principled consumption? Ethical giving? Reparations?

I like animals, Bernie said. I used to work at a shelter. When I was in high school.

Oh that counts, Meena said.

Does it? Alex said.

I think so, Leah said.

THIS IS WHERE WE KEEP the cups, Alex said. This is where we keep the beans, the rice, the tofu, the cheddar cheese, the apples, the tubs of peanut butter, the compost, the plastic bags, though we try to use as few as possible, the mousetraps—

—I know it's terrible, Meena cut in, but we came to a group agreement to use them last year after that mouse on Leah's toothbrush.

Violet leaned their hip against the counter and made faces at Bernie as Alex gestured to each item, each face a little different and a little mean.

The kitchen staircase to the second floor—once used by servants! Alex informed Bernie as they climbed it, Leah, Meena, and Violet in tow—ended at a hallway with a door on its left.

Best light of anywhere in the house, Leah said.

The room was nearly round on two sides and divided into many small walls, but Leah hadn't lied. It did get good light, south-facing and strong. Three large windows made a bay that looked out over the back garden—a barren slab of cement but for a few brown vines, two white plastic chairs, and a string of globe lights missing several bulbs. A built-in wood armoire adorned with curlicues separated two small closets. Gone was the haphazard feel of downstairs. Empty, just wood and bones, this room was classical—a classic.

Bernie could imagine herself living against this background. The room felt right, like the right place to change her life. She imagined that she would be enormously productive while living in this room, taking photographs on the streets of Philadelphia and then coming back here, tired and emptied out, so the room could fill her up again.

I'm next door, Leah said, coming in and gesturing to the closed door that had once connected the two rooms but which was now covered with a sheet of Styrofoam insulation coated in a silver material, roughly cut.

Our old housemate was a fanatic about noise, Leah said. Not that it helps much, unfortunately.

Here, Leah said. See it from my side.

They moved into the hallway and then into the small room across the stairway. It was painted a warm white and a thick linen curtain fell across the lone window. Her bed was crammed into the corner—small, possibly a twin, and brass, resembling a doll's bed that Bernie had circled many times as a child in an expensive doll accoutrements magazine. Leah's pillows were a burnt-orange color that matched the edge of the turned-back flat sheet. The comforter was plush and clean white except for the snoozing black half-moon Jigger made in its center. Jigger opened her eyes and raised her head up, annoyed.

Leah's bedroom smelled like something, like weed but lighter and sweeter. Sage, maybe. On the left wall facing the bed was a pleasing arrangement of framed drawings, prints, and photographs, including a narrow vertically hung broadside of a poem printed in pretty serif lettering on thick deckle-edged paper.

America, the poem began. *By Leah McCausland.*

Oh, Leah said, don't read that.

Violet leaned through Leah's doorway.

I'm down the hall in what used to be the front parlor, Violet said. We three would share the bathroom on this floor. Meena's room is at the top of the stairs, the only one with roof access.

I grow tomatoes, Meena said. And there's a kitchen on our floor too, but no one uses it.

The whole group, Bernie included, moved into the bathroom which was windowless and strangely large. Hairs dotted the porcelain around the sink knobs and globs of toothpaste had collected on the mirror. Somewhere along the tour, Alex had taken her hair down, but she moved now to put it back up, winding a stretched-out elastic around and around a thin fistful of hair until it formed its nub again.

And Alex is upstairs in the front over Violet, Leah said.

Lucky me, Violet said, making accusatory eyes at Alex and Leah. Praise be for noise-canceling headphones.

Oh come on, Leah said, bumping Violet's shoulder with hers. We don't do anything you haven't done a thousand times louder and much later at night with Lucy Vincent and, shall we say, some others?

Violet smiled widely and flicked their eyes side to side like, *guilty*.

How long have you two been together? Bernie asked.

Almost exactly three years, Violet answered for Alex and Leah. It was winter of senior year. I'll never forget it because we had to have a four-hour dorm meeting about how your dating would affect the "broader social dynamic" and I nearly died of hunger and boredom. But I couldn't leave because it was snowing.

It was not that long, Leah said.

It was that long, Meena said, which shut everyone up.

BERNIE AND LEAH STOOD IN the front doorway again, back in their original positions—Bernie on the porch and Leah in the vestibule.

So you let us know and we'll do the same, Leah said.

Bernie wondered about Leah then, this person who was on the one hand so like everyone else and on the other not at all. It felt good to wonder about someone, a thing that had not happened to Bernie in a long time.

I'll take the room, Bernie said. I mean, if you'll take me.

Leah smiled. You have my vote.

What does it feel like, standing in the moments that will mark your life? What Bernie felt was unclear. There was maybe a certain something, a certain spice of change. This day was different, had been brought about differently—not as a result of the actions of others but by things she herself had done.

Meow meow, said Jigger, who had stepped out onto the porch and was now rubbing against Bernie's shin.

Oh no! Leah cried.

Bernie scooped Jigger up in her arms and was shocked by the cat's lightness; she was just bones and fluff.

Give her here, Leah said, and Bernie did, holding the cat out to Leah like a baby.

Bernie had a feeling then. It was a feeling like, *don't go*, even though she was the one leaving.

III.

JIGGER WAS KNEADING LEAH'S RIGHT BOOB, SPREADING LITTLE pinpricks of pain into her dreams. She was in Alex's bed, and even with this going, even with Alex big spooning her, Leah could not stop thinking about Bernie's photograph of the house and the bird. It was still there in her mind. It flashed off, like someone closing it between the hard covers of a book. But then they always opened it again.

Alex moved Jigger out of the way with a gentle hand and pushed on Leah's belly with her whole hand, as if testing a firm balloon to see if it would pop.

Where will you run? Leah asked.

The river trail probably, Alex said. But I can't go too long because I've got to go down to the stadium later, and that will take hours.

Alex was working on a story about the striking concessions and custodial staff at Wells Fargo Center. She was a journalist for the real paper in town, the *Inquirer,* and though she'd started as an intern, now, almost three years out of college, she had an actual paid job, with a focus on labor and labor organizing, with an actual desk and her own telephone extension, and a blue check next to her name online. This was the core difference between Leah and Alex—Alex knew what she cared about and what she wanted to do with that caring on a day to day, hour to hour basis, whereas Leah did not. Alex had gone to Columbia journalism school ($75K) straightaway after they'd graduated from Swarthmore in the spring of 2015, while Leah had spent the year puttering around the New York City apartment where she'd grown up.

Exciting, Leah said. Will Scabby the Rat be there?

Oh I don't know, Alex said, rolling onto her back. It was still dark outside but a slant of light from the streetlamp on their block was always finding its way into Leah's eyes.

Leah had recently become obsessed with the inflatable rodent-shaped balloons that striking workers often propped up in the beds of large pickup trucks parked outside their contentious places of work. The balloon had red eyes and fangs and a winding, thickly appealing tail.

I wonder where Scabby is made, Leah said.

A factory somewhere probably, Alex said, where everything else inflatable is made. She got up, opened a drawer, and began pulling on a pair of baggy gray leggings.

But are there multiple Scabbys, Leah continued, all slightly different, with different eyes, noses, and tails, or are they all identical, a template of an exact Scabby that is endlessly and perfectly reproduced?

Leah, Alex said.

What?

It's a symbol. It's about being a coward, someone who is willing to take dirty money. Who cares what the balloon looks like?

Leah had no answer. Alex put on first one thermal shirt, then another, then pulled her hair up into a tiny topknot.

But Leah cared. Inflatable Scabby the Rat did something to her that the idea of labor organizing did not.

ONE FLIGHT DOWN IN HER own room, Leah locked Jigger out (meow meow) and tried to go back to sleep, but Bernie was already awake and making a racket. Through the wall that now separated her room from Bernie's, Leah heard Bernie pushing cardboard boxes across the floor, perhaps even kicking them with her feet. Though hearing was not quite the right word for the relationship of sounds passing back and forth between her room and Bernie's. It was more like seeing or sensing; they were that present and close. This had been true with the previous housemate too, but the difference now was: Leah was listening.

Leah had a feeling then, a feeling she had been having more and more that winter: a strong sharp feeling of wanting to move, of wanting to be shoved through some rip in the fabric of life. What kept coming back was an image of an old ziplock bag containing cold sauce—tomato or similar—getting squeezed by some fist until one of the corners burst and the sauce came splatting out. But did Leah want to be the sauce that splats, the fist that squeezes, or the bag that bursts? Didn't know.

It is said that there is nothing more painful than living with an untold story inside you but it was Maya Angelou who said it and the word she used was not pain but agony. Leah had no agony like Maya Angelou had it, for it had been Jewish, upper-middle-class Manhattan for Leah before it was intense queer West Philadelphia, but it was nonetheless true that Leah had something inside her, that it was untold, and that it made her mean. On the outside, she went to her friends' fundraising events and shared Alex's articles online with adoring captions and refilled the filtered water pitcher when she emptied it. But inside, she was cranky all the time, just bored and sharp.

The dog howled then, a white-and-gray husky, with huge light eyes, that lived next door. Afternoons when she was the only one in the house, Leah had seen the dog too, in its small concrete yard next door, just circling and circling, growing ever more agitated. It would run up its wooden stairs, then down its wooden stairs, then up them again. Whenever the dog paused, it was a pause of movement, of vibration, rather than a pause of true rest.

Getting up from bed a second time and padding downstairs to the kitchen, Leah felt like that dog. She took up residence at the oval dining room table, reading the news and then reading social media about the news. It seemed that each day that year brought some new catastrophe that directly exploded the lives of several specific groups of people, though which groups was constantly changing: one day it was immigrants in Arizona, the next trans people in North Carolina. When Alex came back from her run, she touched Leah's shoulder lightly, just the surface of her finger pads brushing Leah's hoodie, as she passed. Leah then read the news that social media had created, which started the cycle all over again.

Technically, as both a student of communication and a person trying to communicate in writing, all of this constituted work. Constituted living. Yet it did not feel like living. It felt like scratching around. Leah had a thing she liked to do while reading the internet which was to scratch her scalp and let the waxy stuff accumulate under her fingernails. Then she would dig it out with her other hand, careful to keep the white half-moon clumps whole as she extracted them, and let them fall on the floor.

Sebum was the word the internet provided for this stuff, but that was so unhelpful. Approximately one time out of twenty when she googled something was the result actually satisfying. For example, you couldn't google why the sky looked bluer today than it did yesterday and understand. Even if you followed this train of thought to a "science made simple" article about the more basic question of "why is the sky blue" the answer was no more clear. The explanation provided only led to more questions. What was a "gas molecule" and what was "argon gas" and what were "light waves" and how could light possibly travel in this way, in a form that could be measured and quantified? Click on one of these unique terms—gas molecule say—and less and less was revealed. A gas molecule, from what Leah understood, googling it again now, was a kind of particle which made up the "gas system" and could also "move freely within a container." What system? What container? How free was free?

Leah was not free in the papers she wrote for her PhD program classes and she was not free at the alt weekly paper where she worked either. She wrote mostly bullshit for both. There was nothing wrong with what she wrote, per se, her words did no tangible harm. But both academia and journalism were morally bankrupt enterprises from the start, if you wanted to see it that way, which Leah more and more often did.

Bernie came through the kitchen door into the dining room then. She wore baggy jeans and a small, white long-sleeved T-shirt which exposed a sliver of midriff. She looked, in the looseness of her limbs, the heaviness of her eyelids, and the sag in her shoulders, asleep while upright.

Morning, Leah said, lifting her chest flesh off the table, scooting in her chair, and sitting up a little straighter.

Bernie raised a hand in greeting and kept on walking, through the living room and into the vestibule and then back again, having retrieved a pair of dirty white sneakers. She sat on one of the couches to put them on.

The dog howled again.

Oh good, Bernie said. So it is real. She put on the first shoe, her eyes open wider now.

It's definitely real, Leah said. Been happening for a while. I feel bad for that dog. Huskies are sled dogs!

Bernie nodded and put on the second shoe. She sat that way, both feet on the floor for a moment. Hey, she said, turning to look at Leah. Could you do me a favor?

Probably, Leah said. I mean, depending.

Bernie stood and came back into the dining room. Could you smell me? I know that sounds weird. My boss at the coffee shop told me I smelled, but I can't smell anything.

It's hard to smell yourself, Leah said.

Exactly, Bernie said.

Leah stood and took a few steps toward Bernie who was already lifting her arm in the air like she had an urgent question. Leah leaned down and brought her nose closer. Bernie's armpit smelled like a regular person's, no more, no less, but the smell itself was strange, unexpected somehow. The smell did something to Leah, activated something in her body. It was as if before the armpit, Bernie was an idea, but now, after the armpit, she was real. Besides Alex, who else's body had Leah gotten this close to in the past year, years even? Leah could think of no one.

As Leah was withdrawing her nose, she noticed that Bernie's neck and hair also smelled, strongly, of coffee and chemical vanilla, which Leah reported to Bernie.

Well that seems fine, Bernie said. She looked around as if searching for something she had lost, or perhaps that was just how she looked at a room.

Can I ask you something now? Leah said.

Bernie nodded. Her hair had a halo of flyaways.

How did you get your photos so sharp? You can see every leaf.

Large format, Bernie said.

Aha, Leah said.

Four by five. She put her hands to her cheeks and pushed up on her cheek flesh. Well, I'm off, she said.

Bernie wasn't even fully out the door before Leah was googling again. Camera words. Technical words. But what she took away was this: Bernie used a very big, very slow camera that took expensive film, and had mostly, with a few notable exceptions, been used by men who were now either very old or very dead. It was called four by five because the film was, rather than a roll, individual sheets that each measured four by five inches. So far, Leah thought, so good.

AT ONE OF THREE COMPUTERS reserved for fact-checkers, Leah dialed the number she'd been given.

Yes hello I am calling from *Philly Paper,* we're writing a piece on the fifteenth anniversary of—yes. I am wondering if you ever met—yes, you did, great. And I have winter 2000. April? I would describe that more as spring. OK.

The other two fact-checkers sat at their computers and were flirting again, loudly, such that Leah had to put a finger in her other ear to hear the man on the phone.

Ah OK, Leah said. Yes. And would you say she was, quote, charming? Great. OK. Yes, this is standard practice, it's to make sure everything we print is true. You too. Goodbye.

The boy fact-checker negged the girl fact-checker—Wow, who chews on their pens like that?—and the girl laughed—Shut up, shut up!!

The two of them flirted and talked, talked and flirted, interminably throughout this and every afternoon. They were both Temple undergrads, a fact which caused Leah to feel ancient, and idiotic, though it was their incompetence and lack of favor with the managing editor that allowed Leah to write as many articles for the paper as she did.

A few weeks before, the managing editor had called the two of them into her office and, leaving the door open to Leah's great satisfaction, told them that they talked so continuously it was impossible that they were getting any work done. Leah had typed slowly so as not to drown out their chastisement.

WHO WAS THAT? THE GIRL asked now in the same flirty voice she usually reserved for the boy, as if she'd forgotten to switch.

Leah told her the man's name. For the museum anniversary piece, she said.

Cool. I'm done with the McLatchy check, the girl said. There wasn't a single mistake! I'm shook.

That's because I already checked it, Leah said. I put it in Stephanie's box for her to send to copyedits.

Oops, the girl said. Well no one was here when I got here and I wanted to be useful.

Oy, Leah said.

Leah knocked on Stephanie the managing editor's open door but she was on the phone and gestured for Leah to sit. The last time Leah had sat here, she had told Stephanie that a profile of a dockworker said one thing, but the dockworker said another. No one is the authority on their own life, Stephanie had said, waving her hand.

Supposedly, this was fine. It was considered bad form to show what you wrote to the person you wrote it about, as that made it less "objective" and thus less true. Further, to write anything here, Leah had learned, she had to get Stephanie or another editor to approve her idea, to see it her way. These editors were people who had once loved words or wanted to be writers themselves, but now most of them just wanted to be left alone and for their lives to be made as easy as possible by facile ideas that would generate clicks and move them a slot or two closer to elusive, impossible job security.

Also, in order to say yes to an idea, they wanted a predetermined argument, a takeaway, and the mapping out beforehand of the "framing" Leah's piece would take, plus a list of people who she would interview. But how, Leah wondered, was she supposed to know who she would want to talk to for a piece before she wrote it? This seemed backward, like trying to furnish a room before you knew its dimensions. And if at any point they decided they no longer saw the piece the same way Leah did or they just didn't want to deal with Leah anymore (she had a reputation for sending a lot of emails and turning in drafts that far exceeded the agreed-upon word count), they could just say they'd changed their mind and kill the story so that it never ran.

Most of the articles that Leah's housemates were reading and talking about in the kitchen were also clearly a product of this system. Either they made arguments about "justice" and "representation" that were so flatly predetermined and simple as to make Leah want to crack a pencil in half or they were written in gesturing and floaty theory-ese that was outrageously divorced from the relevant concerns of being a person. Either they purported to know everything, tackling all the problems at once and offering vague, useless answers, or they tackled nothing, risked nothing, tried for nothing.

But books were no better. Most of the books that lined the front window of the volunteer-run bookstore on the avenue were either practical guides to overcoming compulsory monogamy and white supremacy or neatly contained novels about pretty people struggling to fall in love, or stay in love, or have a child, or lose weight (a shocking number of the books lefties loved revealed a plain hatred of fatness), or lose weight after having a child. The viral book reviews, shared in their housemate group chat, were almost always written by viciously smart Brooklyn-based writers who panned any book they deemed too ambitious or emotional—offensive on principle it seemed—in clipped, sarcastic prose. Only smallness of scope and affective numbness were aesthetically acceptable.

Sorry, Stephanie said, once she'd hung up the phone. Crisis in advertising. What can I do for you?

Leah explained the situation with the girl and the double fact-check. That's why it wasn't in your box, Leah said.

Idiots, Stephanie said. No offense. I mean, not you. You're fine. Speaking of. Pitch me something? We've got a hole in the issue for the sixteenth.

Oh, Leah said. Well, I've been thinking about a history of Philadelphia and southern New Jersey vis-à-vis Indigenous peoples and how they're still present in the area but invisible and there's one shelter in North Philly that caters to that community and it—

The plight of the Native Americans? Stephanie said. Been done a hundred times.

OK, Leah said.

Leah often wanted to write about things that happened all the time or had been happening for a long time, but editors rarely, if ever, wanted that, preferring instead to ask why this night was different from all the other nights, why on this night we dip our pen into the well of bitterness not once but seventeen times. Editors did not want truth that had been true a long time, they only wanted things that had recently become true. They wanted the exception to the rule, the new way of thinking about something, the iconoclastic take, which was not how Leah's brain worked.

Maybe a piece about Sasha Millionaire then? Leah said.

Remind me, Stephanie said.

She was a Black trans woman who—

Oh right, murdered.

Well actually she went missing last year, they're not sure if she's dead or not, but her case was horribly mismanaged and her family has said that the police won't even return their calls about the case—

No, Stephanie said, reaching into her purse and pulling out a tube of something that turned out to be tinted lip balm, which she applied with a finger.

It's a worthy topic alright, she said, very sad and an important issue, very timely, transness and all that, but it's not a great story. Maybe if they find her body? Narratively, you know, it's better if she's dead. What else?

Well, there's this lesbian haunted house, Leah said, remembering a press release she'd seen come in to the paper's general inbox. I think it's supposed to be about how lesbians are scary? Maybe there are ghosts?

Ooh, Stephanie said. I like it. But who would you talk to?

WHO WOULD LEAH TALK TO, and who was Leah to talk? On the trolley back to West Philly, she sat in a one-seater listening to music that was at once a little ambient and a little sad. Could she do any better? She could not. Had she pushed back on Stephanie? She had not. Was she out there, hustling, writing a thousand pieces she really cared about for free and pitching them everywhere, as Alex was always suggesting? She was not.

Leah saw then that she had a new email. It was from her departmental administrator telling her that her application for summer research funds had been approved. Approved! But what to do? What to spend that time and that money caring about?

Leah searched Bernie's name, and again clicked on Bernie's website.

"With big thanks to Prof Daniel Dunn," read one of the artist statements. Leah googled Daniel Dunn.

Originally using a 35mm camera, Dunn ultimately switched to the 4 x 5 large-format camera for which he is now almost exclusively known. At age twenty-six he became the youngest photographer ever to mount a solo show at the Museum of Modern Art. His photograph of the sacred site at Shanksville, Pennsylvania, where Flight 93 went down on September 11, 2001, appeared on page A1 of *The New York Times* and has been anthologized in best-of photography books and textbooks more than 100 times[citation needed] and earned him a MacArthur "genius" grant in 2004.

Early Life

Dunn was born Daniel Winslow in rural Mifflin County, Pennsylvania, to Arthur Winslow, a dairy farmer, and Eileen Dunn, a schoolteacher. At age five, Eileen Dunn's brother gifted Dunn a darkroom kit for children and a small 35mm camera with which Dunn made his first photographs. Shortly after this, Winslow abandoned the family, causing Dunn to take his mother's last name. At age fifteen, he dropped out of high school and took a bus to New York City, staying with the same uncle who had gifted him the camera. Dunn's career began the following year when he approached the then-curator of the Museum of Modern Art without an appointment. The curator received Dunn and purchased a set of three photographs, his first sale.

To click on the "Sexual Assault and Harassment Allegations" section, as Leah did then, was to read sentences sourced entirely from a single 2017 *New York Times* article:

On December 15, 2017, in the wake of the #MeToo movement, three female undergraduates whom Dunn taught at Evergreen College in Huntingdon, Pennsylvania, filed separate Title IX complaints alleging sexual misconduct by Dunn.

When this came to light, several alumnae of Croyden College's prestigious photography BFA and MFA program located in the Hudson Valley region of New York, which Dunn founded in 1984 and chaired for nearly three decades, also came forward with allegations against Dunn.

"While a student at Croyden," said Guggenheim-winning photographer Wendy Felfenthal in a statement through her gallery, Space 371, "Daniel Dunn pressed his clothed genital area against my body in a suggestive way. I was shocked and disturbed."

Stacy Wu, a photographer best known for her innovative portraits of celebrities and art world figures, tweeted in support of Felfenthal and added her own experience: "I was 19 and a sophomore. Daniel Dunn told me to close my eyes and then took my hand and put my fingers in his mouth and sucked on them. He said it was to teach me something about my pictures, but what was that supposed to teach me? He also told me that I should use 'the whole exotic Asian woman thing' for professional advancement."

Andrew Gooding, one of the Los Angeles Times' "15 Young Black Visual Artists to Watch" and who is nonbinary and uses the pronouns "they" and "them," told The Times that Dunn had once unbuckled their belt, removed it from around their waist, and then asked Gooding to slow dance with him.

"It was very odd," Gooding said. "Not exactly sexual, but definitely not appropriate. On the other hand, he made me the photographer I am today. Like literally taught me how to see. I don't know what to think."

In response to widespread outcry among current students and parents at the left-leaning college an hour outside of New York City, Croyden College has commissioned a law firm, Baylor & Truxton, to investigate these statements by former students.

Their report is not yet complete, but an employee from Baylor & Truxton, who requested anonymity for fear of reprisal, told The Times that the allegations of misconduct against Dunn go as far back as 1984, the year Dunn founded the Croyden program, though they "seem to be clustered around the years 1997 to 2003." Dunn and his ex-wife, the sculptor Michelle Kleinman, divorced in 1999.

The source further offered that while there had been no formal Title IX allegations against Dunn while he was employed at Croyden, it had apparently been "an open secret" that Dunn employed unorthodox teaching methods and that, under the auspices of an artistic education, he had routinely taken undergraduate and graduate students for excursions to the homes of his friends, to off-campus restaurants where alcohol was served, on wilderness hikes to secluded destinations, and once for an overnight stay at the Four Seasons Manhattan. Many of these activities were said to have had "romantic and/or inappropriate undertones or to have violated Croyden College's policy on the transportation and supervision of students," but the firm had yet to turn up any "specific instances of sexual assault that would meet a legal standard."

Dunn left Croyden for the position at Evergreen College, a small liberal arts college with an idyllic campus in rural central Pennsylvania, in 2012, according to a Croyden spokesperson, "To pursue new artistic avenues and be closer to his mother who was ill with pancreatic cancer."

Dunn, responding to the 2017 accusations, told The Times that "everything my students have said is true. My intent was only ever to make those I taught better artists, but I see now that my attempts were misguided and easily misconstrued."

Leah imagined sixteen-year-old Daniel Dunn, feral and talented, appearing at the famous art man's office. The gall of it and the risk, the bravery and the entitlement. It made her ill with contempt and wonder. She felt a whoosh of terrible energy in the brain space between her ears. Whoosh was the right word because it felt like flight, like movement, like wind, or liftoff. It was like whatever had been damming her up that season had been removed and now the feelings were sloshing freely through her body.

Someone was screaming. Something was trying to break through, was banging on the pane yelling, Let me out! Go, someone was saying. Go now. Go today.

Who were they? Were they, for instance, America, the absurd dreamers and failures of this wide, wide country? Were they the rural queers, the drag queens and kings performing in gay bars in the small and midsize cities of the American South, Midwest, and desert states? Or were they the coal miners, the dairy farmers, the gravediggers, the honeybee farmers of Pennsylvania, Maine, West Virginia, Wisconsin, New Mexico, Wyoming, and other close by but wild places? And why did she think that these people, whose lives she knew nothing about and could not possibly understand, were calling to her, Leah McCausland? Didn't know. But she did.

Something was missing from her mind, she was becoming more and more convinced; some vital piece. It felt like there had to be another way, some other way of communicating true things and being understood that didn't involve exploiting people or selling your brain for money or employing the clickbait-creation techniques she so hated. But what was it? Didn't know.

For she did want, really, really want—was *yearn* too strong a word? It was not—OK, Leah *yearned* to communicate and to be in the room where the big communication was happening. To really communicate was to commune, the internet told Leah, aka to converse or talk together, usually with profound intensity, to share or interchange thoughts, feelings, ideas, or sentiments, talk over, discuss, to be in intimate rapport, to have in common. A commune was also the smallest administrative division in France, Italy, or Switzerland, or a close-knit community of people who shared common interests. Association. Fellowship. Cooperative. Kibbutz. Municipality. Village. Neighborhood. Family.

Leah put her phone away. She could feel it all rising up within her still, a thing that had been coming for a long time and wouldn't be shoved down much longer. It was want and it was curiosity and it was fear and it was ambition, pure and acidic, that sloshed through her thighs and sloping shoulders and belly. It made her fingers tingle. She shivered.

As the trolley car rose up out of the dark tunnel and into the light of the avenue, Leah wanted to go away from here, away from this city. She didn't know how exactly, since she had never learned how to drive a car, but she had money in hand now. She didn't know what the story was but she had a hunch that Bernie was a part of it. Maybe they would find a story out there and tell it. And it would matter. A big story on a big scale. A national scale, an American scale, a story big as Texas. Leah would eat and eat the story until she contained the story, until she was sick with truth and then she would tell it so blazingly well and with such unabashed force and nuance that no one would be able to look away. People would want to profile her, to take her and Bernie's picture on the steps of the house. She would be so young and so fat and so gay but also so talented, like Truman Capote maybe, except she wouldn't flame out or drink herself to death. Starting tomorrow, she would take her vitamins along with her antidepressants and go on a walk and drink a gallon of water every day. She would live for years, maybe even decades. She would live so long.

IV.

SHE JUST TOOK TO PHOTOGRAPHY, I IMAGINE DANIEL DUNN WOULD say to me if I could die temporarily, find him, and interview him in the afterlife. *It was like she just got in the car and turned the ignition on and all I had to do was say, "Drive."*

See the place where Bernie is from: twenty-six acres of spruce, hemlock, beech, sugar maple, and a winding one-lane blacktop barely wide enough for two cars to pass each other without resorting to the ditch. Her mom trained horses in a round pen in their back field. Pickups with horse trailers attached wore away Bernie's asphalt driveway over the years, leaving gravel and then dirt. In spring, the worms came out, inching down the driveway in their funny way: kinked then straight, kinked then straight.

Bernie and Daniel Dunn would never have met if Bernie's mother had not dropped out of high school in Baltimore to go back to the land, and if Bernie hadn't also been lazy and uninformed about her college applications with two parents who didn't care, applying only to schools she'd driven by but that weren't Penn State—too much cheering; too much blue-and-white apparel, and what was a Nittany Lion anyway?

It was late, maybe ten o'clock that Friday night of her junior year at Evergreen College when Bernie sat in the computer lab making an advertisement for a fake horse care company. She was trying to make these horses channel her mom's horses but instead they looked like sausages, linked and listless.

The laser printer whirred then stopped; a man walked through the bank of computers then stopped.

Those horses, he said, are beautiful.

He stood at the left edge of her peripheral vision and an old feeling rose in Bernie then, a feeling of something forcing her hand and her automatic response to that kind of pressure: no, she felt, won't, shan't, you can't make me. How many times had a man demanded a moment, broken a reverie, brought about the removal of headphones during the best part of the song to ask for a quarter, a pen, the time.

Thanks, Bernie said, not turning to look. But they look like sausages.

No, the man said. They're horses.

Now she looked. He was a white man with deep lines carved both horizontally and vertically into his forehead, creating the impression of a tic-tac-toe board. Plus, a shaved head and a short graying beard. Yet he gave the overall appearance of fitness, of having done a great deal of laborious outdoor-based activity, a man who could, like Bernie's brother and his friends, frame out a wall or pull out a ditched sedan with a truck and a winch. Dirty green sweatshirt, dirty black jeans, clean black canvas shoes. Pointy ears, like a masculine elf, or Bruce Willis.

You a fine art major? he asked.

No, Bernie said. Graphic design.

Kind of a waste, he said. Isn't it?

No.

I just mean graphic design is for serving other people's visions. Art is for your own.

How do you know I have my own?

Call it a hunch, he said. Those horses. You drew them and scanned them. I think you want your hands involved.

Maybe, Bernie said. She looked down at her hands, which were thin and dry; her eczema was acting up. She itched across her palm.

I've got a few spots left in my 101 class if you want to jump ship.

He showed Bernie where to register for his class in the college system. Introduction to Photography, D. Dunn.

Maybe I'll see you there, Daniel Dunn said to Bernie. He had both hands in his pockets now and the elasticized bottom part of his sweatshirt had ridden up a little, pooching out the fabric around his middle. His YKK gleamed.

SIT THERE, DANIEL DUNN SAID when Bernie showed up, indicating a small metal stool that lurched perilously every time Bernie shifted her weight.

Great photography documents, he said. It tells the truth. It doesn't depict. It doesn't advocate. It doesn't spectate. It is neither overly generous nor overly nihilistic. It has hope but it is not sentimental. It does not react against. It is neither inherently moral nor inherently amoral. It does not judge. It does not pity nor does it exalt.

He showed them Alfred Stieglitz, with his dark swaths of prairie sky and up-close pictures of interlacing hands. Don't do this, he said.

He showed them Diane Arbus—drag queens and possibly trans women with their mouths open very wide captured from below so the camera looked up into their mouths; little people photographed head-on. Don't do this either, he said.

He liked the work of a straight white American man named Walker Evans. He liked the work of straight white French men Eugène Atget and Henri Cartier-Bresson. He liked the work of a straight white Ukrainian man named Weegee, and that of a white American lesbian named Frances Benjamin Johnston and that of white gay man Minor White and White's student, a Chinese American man named Baldwin Lee. He showed the class slides of photographs by these people, people whom Bernie had never in her life heard of, but whose photographs nevertheless made her feel feelings, feelings that might be best summarized as: you can do that, something great, with some combination of your two automatic eyes and your two dumb hands? Some of the photographs were black-and-white and some were color but they were all sort of quiet, nothing showy, no great pyrotechnics. Just people and places, faces and cars and signs and street corners and open fields. There was one in particular of a muddy motel parking lot up against a squat swath of green lawn, the sky looking as if it had just stopped raining but was about to rain more.

Bernie interrupted. Whose is that?

Mine, Daniel Dunn said.

It's like this, Daniel Dunn said, toward the end of that first class. Just look at the thing you want and then take a picture that shows that thing how it is. Don't let it get changed, that's all. Make it look with the camera how it looks to your eye.

What now? Bernie asked, at the end of class.

That green cabinet, Daniel Dunn said, pointing. Pick a camera, any camera.

Only two remained—both black boxy things with three knobs bearing the words CANON AE-1 in large lettering. One looked busted from being dropped too many times; Bernie chose the other.

Wait, Daniel Dunn said. He pointed at another cabinet that had lost its doors and contained stacks of little orange boxes labeled KODAK 35MM.

Film? Bernie said. It simply hadn't occurred to her.

I can see if another student who got a digital camera will switch with you, Daniel Dunn said, though his tone said: *If you are a fool.*

No, Bernie said. She looked again at the camera. It looked back.

Bernie walked straight to the fine art library on campus. When she put Daniel Dunn's name into the computer catalogue search box, many books came up. In the stacks where no sun ever shone, some of his books were fat, and some thin, but the two Bernie checked out and took home to her room were his road-trip books. She particularly liked one photograph that showed a diner without people, just the long clean expanse of a shiny white vinyl counter, red spinning stools with silver metal bases, a sugar dispenser, a napkin dispenser, and an ashtray. Glass cases for donuts or hot dogs or sandwiches, a single booth with olive vinyl upholstery, racks of paperbacks on either side of the front door, a gumball machine empty of gumballs that blocked out the word—CLOSED. Meaning the other side said OPEN. Slung over the booth was a single jacket—suit, most likely. Here was the church, here was the steeple. But where were all the people?

There were clearly people, there was clearly life—there was that jacket, that OPEN sign, the cars going swiftly down the street outside the diner's windows and glass door, smudged with handprints. The photograph itself was the life, whoever it was that had stood there and taken it was alive and so that made the picture alive.

This diner photograph, Bernie read in the book, was made with an enormously heavy and clunky camera that was used by all the photographers Dunn liked. Also himself. She read more and learned how this kind of photography was ridiculously difficult and prohibitively expensive to practice and thus hardly ever used anymore. It was dying, the internet said. Was basically already dead. Yet all the words that were used to describe it—*muscular, all-encompassing, rarefied,* and *the ultimate challenge*—sounded to Bernie like synonyms for God. *No you can't,* the book told her. *Yes I* can, she told the book. *Watch me.*

Bernie watched as Daniel Dunn stood in the college's darkroom—just a kitchen really, similar to the one she worked in for her on-campus job, with metal sinks and metal prep tables, but modified to be lightproof—doing a demo for her and the two others in the class of twenty who had opted for film. She watched as he wound the test strip around what looked to be a large metal spool—the developing reel—which then got plunked into a metal canister—tank—with a black plastic top through which chemicals—developer, fixer—were poured in and then poured out.

Daniel Dunn had been right: she did want her hands involved. She liked touching everything—the strong wire of the reel, the cold surface of the tank—and she liked the way the chemicals smelled—like vinegar, like metal. And when, having swished the liquids in and out of the tank by herself for the first time, then washed her film and hung it up to dry on a line with clothespins and fallen asleep for several hours on a couch someone had dragged outside the darkroom for precisely this purpose; when she woke, groggy and still half-dreaming, plucked the roll from the line and brought it out into the light and held it up to a lamp and there were blotches and lines, blobs and squares, squiggles and accidents of chemicals and technique, all darks and lights and middle grays, she saw that she had recorded, no, that she had rendered, no, that she had *made,* trees and rocks and street signs and classrooms and campus food delivery trucks. She had made them all.

The first photos Bernie presented for critique that first semester were of her dorm room desk—that particularly institutional kind of shiny orangey wood. There were ten photos of the surface of her desk and three of her blue carpet.

It is about the now, Daniel Dunn said, looking at Bernie's efforts. It is about being who you all are—he gestured to the students sitting high on their uneven metal stools—at this particular moment. It is all here: the pressure to get a college degree in the face of mounting irreconcilables in the argument about whether such a degree is satisfying let alone financially viable, and the pressure for college to be the best years of your life. Your future is uncertain, and you can't go back to where you came from aka your parents' houses and this place you are now—this institution of higher learning—is nothing but an ugly desk and a blue carpet.

He really said this, spoke the words with sonorous confidence, pacing forward and back. It was so accurate, giving words to that for which Bernie had no words, that she felt a bit robbed, plundered even.

Now Jennifer's work, Daniel Dunn said, is exactly what I

was talking about when I was referring to how a photograph can be changed to look like what we think of as "art" but which is really just capitalism. Is this a blog? Is this an advertisement? Are we selling purses? Are we selling sneakers?

Jennifer was tall, her ponytail secured with a purple elastic that was also a bow, and she sat next to another girl with a similar ponytail. She studied her photographs with neutral eyes as Daniel Dunn spoke about them, and bit her nails.

Bernie waited until Daniel Dunn had packed up his papers and slung his floppy black canvas bag over his shoulder.

When do we get to do large format? she asked when he came out into the hallway.

Never, he said.

When then? Bernie asked. Advanced?

No, Daniel Dunn said. I'm late, but you can walk with me to my car.

He held the door of the academic building open for her and she went through it, out into the sunshine.

I don't teach it, he said, squinting at her. It's not for students.

She hated him then, really hated him. Who says this? Who, with knowledge, when asked, will not give it to someone else? He was not inherently generous, she saw then, he did not have generosity of spirit, the thing her mother had once said was the single most important quality a teacher of horses can have.

Why? Bernie asked Daniel Dunn.

They were crossing the wide green now.

It took me years, he said.

I have years, Bernie said.

Exactly, Daniel Dunn said. Why rush?

You said yourself my pictures are good.

They are, he said. The best I've seen in a long time. But large format is a whole other ball game. It's painstaking. I still make mistakes. It's so slow. It takes hours. Days even.

They passed a bouncy girl in athletic shorts who pointed at Daniel Dunn with her index finger and cried out his name. He waved to her and said her name back.

It's a thing of the past, Daniel Dunn continued. For old-timers like me.

Not necessarily, Bernie said. Haven't you heard? New is out. Old is back.

Oh yeah? Daniel Dunn said. They had come to the faculty parking lot. We'll see, he said.

He didn't give on the large format point, but he did email Bernie separately from the rest of the class and invite her to go shooting with him so that she could watch him work the big camera if she liked. She did like. All that verdant summer between her junior and senior years, he drove her around in his car, an old black Saab that smelled of cigarettes, and asked her questions. He wanted to know her opinion on everything—this TV show, that kind of jeans—and he wanted to know everything about her. How old was her brother? (Four years older.) Did they have a good relationship? (More or less, though he opted to bury his money in the ground rather than give it to any bank, he said, not because he was Trumpy but because he was so free.)

As they had these conversations, Daniel Dunn was doing at least two other things—driving and looking. He was driving slow and he was turning his head left and right to look at houses, guardrails, trees, branches, ditches, culverts, road signs, seasonal flags, holiday wreaths and décor, sun, clouds, and light. He was stopping them, rolling them slow onto a grassy turnout or washed-out logging road, pulling a U-turn in a well-kept driveway and then ducking down to a service road or overgrown boat launch. It was an odd thing to be asked big questions by someone who was only ever paying you half his attention, but half of Daniel Dunn's attention was still a good amount of attention. A lot, even.

Whenever he stopped the car, Daniel Dunn, always dressed in black jeans, white socks, dirty sneakers, and a green canvas bucket hat, stood in the road to extract the camera bag, a dark piece of cloth, and a tripod from the back seat. Then he unzipped the camera bag and lifted the camera out and onto the tripod. From where Bernie stood, also in the road, the camera looked like two black squares the size of pieces of sandwich bread separated by black accordion folds attached to two feet that connected, at a right angle, to a single rail.

Daniel Dunn slung the dark cloth over his shoulder, picked up the whole camera/tripod setup, and carried it down into the grass. He looked into one of the black squares, which seemed to be the back of the camera—a piece of glass gridded with lines. A few more times did he pick everything up again and put it down in some new place. Many, many times did he take the dark cloth from his shoulder and pull it over his head and face and most of the camera, leaving only the front square of the camera uncovered.

From underneath the cloth, its creases undulating like a very slow ghost, Daniel Dunn turned knobs that made parts of the camera move forward and back, then knobs that made other parts tilt up toward the sky or down to the ground, stretching the accordion folds. Then he emerged, the cloth over his shoulder again, walked a few feet forward and held a small black plastic thing that resembled an ancient cellphone up to the sky.

They discovered they were from the same part of rural central Pennsylvania, just one county away. They knew the same gas stations and parking lots and scenic overlooks and high schools, even if they had gone to them decades apart. The land didn't change, the gas stations didn't change, not in a span as short as forty years.

That was just after my dad walked out on us, Daniel Dunn said.

Me too, Bernie said. I mean, the same with my dad.

Neither had to flesh out the details to be understood. Daniel Dunn's father not only walked out, Bernie learned, but had also liked to bring other women around the house to meet and torment his mother and once showed Daniel Dunn his gun and fired it, unloaded, into Daniel Dunn's mouth. It was all very *This Boy's Life,* and Bernie found herself daydreaming and sometimes dream dreaming—she often fell asleep in Daniel Dunn's car as he drove them back to campus—about the movie someone would someday make about Daniel Dunn and about her, Bernie, his androgynous and talented assistant. They were like father and son maybe, or boy and boy.

Aha, Daniel Dunn said. A fast reach down to the film bag, then a pop to the front to close the lens, the jamming in of the film holder, the slick retraction of the slide—I'm being careful not to bump the camera as I do this or I'll have to focus all over again!—then the cocking and releasing of the shutter, so slow and so fast.

Quick, he said. Across the road, or we'll lose the light.

Daniel Dunn was obsessed with "losing the light," a phrase he said so much that Bernie began to fear its utterance, for it always signaled the end of the working day. Lose the light, he said, lose the picture.

One day after they'd lost the light, Daniel Dunn drove Bernie to the cabin where he was raised, an hour away from the college, took her into a small freestanding shed, and showed her a pile of logs he'd recently split.

You know they are ready to burn when you tap them with your finger and you no longer hear an echo, Daniel Dunn said. Try.

They all sounded the same to Bernie.

What percent of the total love you need should you be getting from romance, do you think? Daniel Dunn asked after a long silence, from his corner of logs.

I don't know, Bernie said. Thirty? Twenty-five?

That little? Daniel Dunn said. I think, when I was married, I was trying to get seventy, maybe eighty percent. That's probably too much.

Definitely, Bernie said.

What is it like? Daniel Dunn asked then. When you go on a date with another girl?

Bernie had said nothing to Daniel Dunn about being queer, but it was true. She had just been taken out for burritos by a tall women's field hockey player with a wide pale mouth and had plans for more.

Depends on the girl, Bernie said.

Daniel Dunn laughed then, a boyish snicker that made him cover his mouth, and Bernie was filled with a feeling so large and good it knocked all the thinking out of her. To make him laugh!

WE LIKE TO THINK THAT all teaching is basically the same—algebra, world history, psychology, photography. Someone has knowledge and someone else doesn't. Someone is paid and someone else pays. But it is not. The teaching of art is a particular thing with a particular ability to give life and to inflict damage. This is not about an older artist who destroys the career of a promising young female student with his weakness and lust. This is instead about what it means to have been taught what constitutes good art by someone who does not believe in your full humanity and it is about what you do with that experience—forever—once you have lived it. In short, there may be people who go to algebra to learn how to live but I don't know any of them.

Slowly, Bernie became able to predict which of her photographs Daniel Dunn would choose for critique. In his office with its windows that would not open, he would look at Bernie's contact sheets and select the best two. He liked the ones that contained more magnitude or suggested bigness, and the ones where Bernie had achieved dark, almost true blacks. He liked interiors. Hated trees.

That one, he would say, circling a frame in red pen as the sheets sat on his desk, in between taking calls from various lawyers and creditors and hospital collections agencies. As he paced the office, his head tilted to the right to hold the phone between his white ear and his red T-shirted shoulder, Bernie took to holding the sheets up and pointing to her guesses.

One time after a correct selection, he pushed her lightly on the shoulder and then pointed at her with his index finger.

That fall, Bernie and her roommate, Karen, watched the 2016 presidential election returns come in with the other students on her floor, in a large lounge, painted mint green and mopped so recently it still smelled of antiseptic. Someone had baked a chocolate cake from scratch, with a layer of frosting thick as a thumb; someone had bought cheap champagne from the liquor store on Main Street. But as eight o'clock turned to nine and then to ten, the students put their cups down and stopped drinking from them and the cake was never cut. Karen went outside and then there was a scream, a sound Bernie had never heard Karen make before. Bernie watched the pixels materialize into headlines on her phone from under the thin blanket while Karen slept, snoring uneasily. In the morning the sky was a terrifying shade of dark purple, reddish as a wound, and spitting lazy rain.

The only class she had that day was Daniel Dunn's, so she went. Someone was crying, softly. Someone dropped a pencil onto the floor and did not pick it up.

When Daniel Dunn came in, he didn't speak for a long time, and then he did.

Today is a very bad day, he said. I'm not going to lie to you. I am old and nothing like this has ever happened before in my lifetime. This is not normal. This is not OK.

Whoever it was who was crying cried louder now, then covered their mouth.

That's it, he said. If you want to go, you can. If you want to stay here, you can. I'll stay.

Most of the students left. Bernie stayed. Jennifer and her friend stayed.

Over winter break after Bernie had taken Daniel Dunn's introductory and intermediate classes but before she had taken his advanced one that spring, he began to email her about things other than going shooting, though they still did that too. At first, the emails were links to photographers she might like, to artist fellowships and residencies in faraway places like Wyoming and les Calanques, France. Then, they were bits of his thoughts, pieces of his dreams.

I dreamed I was a little boy and my mother's spinster sister came over to borrow the sewing machine but instead my mother gave me to her. She dressed me in all black and when I asked her why she said it was so the angel of death wouldn't find me—some Amish B.S. When I asked why the angel of death would be looking for me, she said my name, she said, Daniel, the angel of death will always be looking for you.

Bernie did not respond to these emails, but they made her proud. During critique, she no longer stood with her hands in her hoodie pocket but now sat on any available table, swinging her legs. She sat on the broken stool, spinning circles and tapping her toes on the ground for balance. She ate loud foods during class—green apples, Doritos—and tossed their cores and bags forcefully into the empty trash can. She sometimes played games on her phone—Candy Crush, a vintage version of Snake—as Daniel Dunn railed against the other students—derivative, lazy, disingenuous, hiding.

After several months, the links and recommendations and dream descriptions were entirely replaced with *(no subject)* emails with images from his new project attached. His mother was very ill and he was doing a series about her sick, dying body. Bernie's hard drive became clogged with big zip files which, when unzipped, revealed seventy images, ninety, one hundred and eleven.

It's like nothing you've ever seen in your life, wrote Daniel Dunn, *her body becoming concave, not just losing fat but losing its very aliveness, its life force.* In fact it *was* like something Bernie had seen in her life, as her maternal grandmother had died of lung cancer in their living room when Bernie was eight. But Bernie did not tell Daniel Dunn this. Something had happened and now Daniel Dunn wanted only to share with her rather than receive her sharing.

Some weeks later, Bernie was in bed when Daniel Dunn's mother finally died. The emails came in pop pop pop, 9:41 P.M., 9:47 P.M., 10:03 P.M., 10:26 P.M., 2:03 A.M., all of them *(no subject)* and turning her inbox bold.

It was awful, Bernie.

Her face became purple, then draited of all color.

She was lost, called out, kept calling for my father, then my brother, Marty. Ma, I tolc her, it's me, it's Daniel. She kept calling Marty. Marty, Marty's dead, I tell her. Dead? She sad. Dead, I says.

Around three that morning, there was a crash that came from the direction of Bernie's dorm room window. Karen sat up and hugged herself with both arms.

Bernie leapt to turn on the light. A stone the size of a golf ball lay on the blue carpeted floor. The window was broken; a jagged hole let in the night air. Some small shards of glass had landed in the seams of Karen's thick yellow duvet.

What the fuck, Karen said. She looked at Bernie with huge eyes.

Contrary to her parents' wishes, Karen was not studying to become a doctor but was instead studying history. Bernie had overheard her telling her boyfriend, a nice boy who came around a few times a week, about the concept of turning points—moments in wars or social movements that changed everything that came after. Bernie spent a long time picking the pieces of glass out of Karen's duvet, and cut her palm at the base of her pinkie in the process.

Bernie! Daniel Dunn called, from outside.

I'm sorry, Bernie said to Karen.

Bernie licked the blood from her hand, pulled on her sweatshirt and sneakers from where they were piled at the foot of her bed, and was soon pushing open the cold metal bar of the building's front door. She stood on the light-flooded square of concrete outside her dorm, momentarily blind. She smelled the smell of grass and of fertilizer, a smell that would forever remind her of being young.

When her eyes adjusted, Daniel Dunn stood in the grass in the semi-dark. His jeans were wet from the knee down, as if he had waded through a shallow river. His hands were at his sides. His palms were open.

Bernie, he said.

It was too big a rock, she said.

I know it.

How did you find me?

Daniel Dunn made a fist with his right hand, used it to gesture to the side of his head, and then slowly knocked the fist against his head.

There's too much in here, he said. Trees and hands. Why do they always take pictures of trees?

Bernie crossed her arms over her breasts and closed the distance between them. She felt the water from the grass absorbing into the fabric of her loose leggings and making them heavy.

Daniel Dunn wanted to go sit on the swings that hung

over a pit of sand inside an alcove of trees. Bernie had once seen a boy and a girl making out on these swings, the boy pulling his swing far over to reach the girl's.

Daniel Dunn ejected his words so quickly and with such force that Bernie knew they came from somewhere that was not his brain and that he wouldn't remember them tomorrow. She alone would carry this memory.

My head has too much, Daniel Dunn said, his sneakered feet making deeper and deeper grooves in the sand pit.

So you said, Bernie said.

I need somewhere to put it all. I wish there was somewhere to put it all, some order, some way to make it all make sense.

Make what make sense?

My life, I guess, he said. My feelings. My family. All of it.

Aren't your photographs where you put it? Bernie said.

Maybe fifty percent. But lately that hasn't been enough. I need somewhere else. No one wants to hear the things I want to do. I'm an old white guy and I'm not rich anymore. No one will call me back. No one will respond to my emails. Documentary photography is no longer enough. It's too passive. It's too boring.

Maybe you are passive, Bernie said. Maybe you are boring.

Mean, he said.

Honest, she said. The truth. Isn't that what you always say? If no one is responding to the work it's not their fault, it's yours?

After Daniel Dunn cried into the book made of his palms on the swing set and into the thick fabric on the knees of his blue jeans and apologized several times and Bernie did not say it was OK, she turned to look at him. At his long nose, the way his neck did not make a straight line down into his back but hit a bulbous form, his back hunched in a stoop from so many years of carrying cameras.

A sweet wind blew and Bernie shivered. Give it to me, she thought. Give me what you know.

I want you to teach me large format, Bernie said. To use the big camera.

I told you, Daniel Dunn said, wiping his nose on his shirtsleeve. I don't teach it to students.

Bernie paused.

You threw a rock through my window, she said. My roommate woke up. You must have called and asked for my dorm room. Someone would have made a record of that.

Daniel Dunn raised his head and looked at her. Smiled.

Listen to you, he said. Bernie the gangster. Who would've thought you had it in you?

I would've, Bernie said.

THAT NIGHT, HE DID TEACH her.

What else, Bernie? Daniel Dunn asked. They had gone out shooting and were back in the car now, heading home.

When do we develop them? Bernie said. She was used to the gloves and goggles and signs on the college lab's wall, the drawings of the stick figure's face and eyes and the water running down from them. Hydroquinone, monomethyl para-amino phenol sulfate, and phenidone; also sodium carbonate or borax—the active ingredient in ant poison. These chemicals, Daniel Dunn had told the class, were highly toxic if ingested; less than a tablespoon of the bath used to bring a photograph into this world could take a person out of it.

Color film? Daniel Dunn said. No. Haven't done my own

color developing in years. I send it out to a guy in Philadelphia. I'll give you a bunch of film and a camera to use. Shoot it and leave the negatives in the mailbox at my house. I'll include them when I send my own stuff out to be processed. Anything else?

I guess that's all, Bernie said.

But it wasn't. Now it was she who was emailing Daniel Dunn, at all hours of the night—*But how do I know? What do I do when? What do I do if?*—and he who was responding with short sentences. He loaned her the Arca-Swiss camera they had used to shoot that night and gave her two cardboard boxes filled with Kodak large-format film, each yellow box thick and perfectly unused like a box from a luxury card game, ten sheets each, more than she could possibly shoot in a semester, let alone a short lifetime. She dropped off her taped yellow boxes by the metal door of Daniel Dunn's garage and he left the developed prints back in there too, in thick brown paper envelopes. The day she held her first color prints in her own hands: no good, obviously, but holy wow. This continued through the rest of the semester until graduation.

The day before she left for Philadelphia, she called Daniel Dunn and he didn't answer, so she went to his campus house with the loaned camera and the remaining film. She was about to leave it outside his garage when he opened its door.

Bernie, he said. What are you doing? His eyes were red and dry, like he'd been sleeping, possibly even here, in this garage.

Your film, she said.

Keep it, he said.

Your camera? Bernie said.

Keep it, he said.

I'm going to Philadelphia.

Good for you. You can drop your used film off in person, I'll give you the address. I'll keep paying for it.

Why? Bernie said. Why would you do that?

Don't ask questions, Bernie, he said. Just say thank you.

Thank you, Bernie said.

You're welcome, he said. Anything, he said, for my sexiest student.

Bernie laughed then. She would always, for as long as she lived, regret that laugh.

What? he said. You don't know you're sexy?

Not really.

Then you're dumb, he said. Really fucking dumb. You have that allure that people who are just singular have, people who can be no one else but themselves. It's sexy. Not to me, obviously. But to women, I presume.

She blinked.

Can I give you some advice? he asked, then did not wait for her answer. Don't ever let making pictures become your whole life. If you do, it will eat you alive. Get a hobby, get a wife, get religion, go outside, get in nature. Something. Anything else.

The wind blew his hair back from his face and he closed his eyes for a moment too long. He might have been a little drunk, or very.

OK, Bernie said.

I'm tired, he said, and stepped back into the garage. Go on now. I'll see you, Bernie.

So she went. All that first fall in Philadelphia, she went out to shoot nearly every day, she dropped off her tape-sealed yellow packages and picked up her brown envelopes in person to and from Dunn's guy. She went to shows. She met people. Emails were sent and emails were received.

Then, just before Christmas, it all came rushing out. The Title IX complaints, two of them made, Bernie felt, though she would never know for sure, by Jennifer and her friend. In some strangely physical way, Bernie could no longer touch Dunn's big Arca-Swiss camera. She put it in its case one day and just never took it out. She put her changing tent and loupe and dark cloth and tripod in a gym bag and zipped that up too. She put all the unused film in a box and taped it up.

Some people said that after Daniel Dunn left the college, he went to Brazil, others Cartagena, others Italy, others that he was in Alaska photographing puffins. Still others said that he stayed in his house on campus, that he had never left, that he had never gone anywhere at all.

V.

IN THE HOUSE, THERE WAS ALWAYS A SPECTRUM AND NO ONE wanted to be on either of its ends. Alex was the most dogmatic about not ever running the heat above sixty-two degrees. It was generally thought that Violet was the weakest in this regard, being the only one who failed to cover their windows with their allotted plastic sheets (Alex did it for them with a hair dryer one day while Violet was at work), but this may not have been so, as Violet complained but never actually touched the thermostat, whereas Meena and Leah had both been known to bump against it accidentally with their elbows.

There was nothing worse than being wasteful in the house unless it was being rich. All of the housemates except Bernie were somewhat rich, and thus not truly like the people who lived in other group houses along the avenue. Those people lived communally to save money rather than to prove some political point, or were squatters, bringing home leftovers from their jobs at the anarchist coffee shop to place into their sidewalk-level mutual aid fridges.

Violet was actually, unequivocally rich. Their grandparents, who had been aristocrats in China, emigrated from Taiwan and started an auction house for East Asian art that advertised on billboards along I-95, so they counteracted this fact by being a professional organizer for the rights of mushroom farmers and never calling their mother back. They had a trust fund, they confessed to Bernie one night in the kitchen.

I get a portion of the interest, Violet said. They were drunk and Bernie was standing in the light of the fridge. Not even the principal, they went on, leaning into the island and opening up a tunnel of space between shirt and skin. They were wearing a black sports bra or possibly a binder.

The money just keeps growing back, Violet was saying. They looked off into some distance, as if in resigned wonder. Isn't that crazy?

Bernie pictured a lizard continuously regrowing its tail and agreed that it was.

There had never been a time that Bernie could remember when she had not struggled with money, when she had not dreaded checking her account balance and paid attention to the cost of milk and eggs. No one in the house had debt from college except Bernie. Meena and Violet had clearly grown up in immigrant houses where money was discussed often, as they never discussed it, whereas Alex and Leah were always discussing it, as if talking about money was the most interesting and unexpected thing in the world. Alex was particularly excited about a group called Rich Kids for Revolution, in which "young people with inherited wealth" met to discuss how they could pool their money into an amount significant enough to create real change for a worthy cause.

The next meeting is Thursday, Alex said to Leah one day. You going?

Of course, Leah said. I want to put in my vote for the mural program.

You're gonna vote for the murals? Alex said. I can't believe you'd do that over the halfway house for previously incarcerated people.

The halfway house will find other donors, Leah said. Its worth is obvious. There's no institutionalized support for the arts in this country, so informal giving circles like ours are the only way they'll survive.

Bernie could hear them talking in Leah's room as she went into the bathroom. Everything traveled. Every creak in the old floors, every clank of the old radiators, getting hot or getting cold. The closing or opening of every door, no matter how slowly. The sound of Alex coming down the stairs at five in the morning for her run—neither rain nor snow nor sleet nor dark of night, etc.—was more effective for Bernie than any alarm clock. Meena was a loud masturbator, which she tended to do around midnight on Saturday nights when she was on the phone to Nepal with the housemate who had previously occupied Bernie's room and was now Meena's girlfriend.

Leah was almost always in the house, Bernie soon figured out, as Leah only had class twice a week and only went into the office a few days a month. In practice, this seemed to mean that Leah lacked any real schedule or daily organizing principle. When Bernie saw her, usually around dinnertime, Leah was almost always disappointed in herself.

Didn't even start working until after lunch, Leah would say, standing in front of the sink eating a microwaved burrito. And miles to go before I sleep!

Some mornings when Bernie was brushing her teeth, she saw Leah coming down the stairs from Alex's room, raising a hand to Bernie before disappearing into her own room, but whether zonked on sex or sleep it was hard to say.

Sometimes Leah cried. Bernie could hear it through the wall, mostly between the hours of nine and ten o'clock at night, but sometimes later. Usually Leah would cry, then she would go to the bathroom, run the water, and head upstairs to Alex's room. Bernie wondered why Leah didn't cry in Alex's room if she wanted to cry and Alex was her girlfriend. Bernie wondered what Leah had to cry about, though she knew enough to know that everyone had something. Leah had grown up in a nice, brainy Jewish family with two parents who both had good jobs and the means to send her to fancy private school and keep large, thin dogs. There had been a succession of them; Bernie had seen the pictures. The same dog, over and over again, dying and then being reacquired.

IN HER ROOM ONE NIGHT, while Leah's computer keys were going like mad next door, Bernie googled Leah. Many of her pieces for the weekly paper were indeed, as she had said, quite boring.

New Show by Germantown Artist Exposes Complicity of "Woke" White People read one headline attached to a Leah article. "I hope these works will expose the complicity of white people who consider themselves 'woke'" was a quote from the artist in the article. *City Says It Will Commission Murals by More Artists of Color. But Is It Just Talk?* read another. "I think it's just talk" was also a direct quote from someone interviewed in the piece.

But scrolling down farther, there was an article Leah had done for the paper the year before called simply *The Purple House,* in which it seemed Leah had interviewed and then written about a woman in Southwest Philadelphia who lived in a house that she had painted completely purple—purple doorknobs, purple window boxes, purple planters made of tires, purple chain-link fence.

"Why so purple?" Leah had asked the woman, and then the woman just talked, movingly, for many paragraphs, about leaving North Carolina for Philly during the Great Migration, and a woman in a purple dress she'd seen when she arrived.

Another night, through the bedroom wall, Bernie heard a sad Scottish band blare into Leah's room then get quickly cut off, jacked into headphones. Leah was hard-flipping the pages of a book and was still flipping them when Bernie passed her door to go to the bathroom. There was a rectangle of light coming from under Leah's door into the hallway, as if Leah's brain itself were making the room glow.

On Bernie's way back, Leah's door was open and she was watching something on her computer in the dark, headphones on. She wore a white T-shirt and black basketball shorts, and sat back in her office chair. Her hands rested on top of her stomach and she twiddled her thumbs.

The first time Bernie saw a butch woman, standing in the Walmart parking lot in her hometown, she felt confused, slapped. There she was—if she was a she—a man's back but different, the shoulder blades too high, the arms too—what? Thin? Narrow was a better word. Long ponytail with the hairs pulling themselves out of their elastic, as the woman—if she was a woman—stretched a blue tarp to cover a truck bed full of split logs. Little waist with those divots where a rust-colored T-shirt bunched up, no ass, jeans big through the knees and pooling tight in ripples around the ankles, lace-up brown work boots with the big toes like all the boys at school wore.

When she had come around to close the tailgate, Bernie thought: she is going to see me. The woman's shirt rippled in the wind. The sun came out and the woman squinted into it and at Bernie. See me, Bernie had said, inside herself. Look here, look now, look my way. But if the woman saw Bernie, she gave no sign.

The feeling Bernie had now, looking at Leah, was not that, but it was similar. See me. Look my way.

And then Leah did. She turned and waved at Bernie, was about to open her mouth, but Bernie waved back and scuttled quickly to her room.

BERNIE HAD NOT FORGOTTEN ABOUT the poem hanging on Leah's bedroom wall that she had not wanted Bernie to read. One weekend evening when Bernie knew Leah was out with Alex at a potluck and Violet was out who knew where and Meena was upstairs in her room playing guitar, Bernie slipped into Leah's room and read it.

I believe, the poem began. Bernie had expected the poem to begin with a sly reference to polyamory or a labored image of a die-in staged on the steps of some nationally significant building. Not with plain individual feeling. Leah believed in huge adjectives and nouns apparently, in love and loss and compassion and sacrifice. On the whole, the poem was not very good, Bernie didn't think, it lacked the energy and quiet power of the piece about the woman with the purple house. But one line—"or is it just that I am addicted to America" stuck around in Bernie's mind a long time. On Monday morning when she took the dark trolley into Center City with the other people who either open the world or close it down, she was still turning that line over in her mind.

Bernie's first job was under the ground, where no sun ever reached, at a coffee kiosk in Philadelphia's central train station, from six in the morning until noon, five days a week. The kiosk sat in the middle of a wide, highly trafficked corridor that connected disembarking suburban commuter rail trains to Philadelphia's subway system, causing a great flood of people to stop at or part around it.

The other white girls with brown hair who worked the front counter with Bernie lived with their fiancés or mothers and bought expensive yarn from the twee yarn store on South Street which they made into intricately patterned mittens and purses and posted to social media to shockingly large followings. The most skilled of the staff, a Black butch lesbian, worked the espresso machine out of view, churning out perfect flat whites and red eyes. She was trying to save up enough money to get her last six credits from Temple so she could move out of her grandmother's house and propose to her girlfriend. Unlike Bernie, they all had concrete responsibilities and plans.

Despite making his livelihood from it, Bernie's boss seemed to hate the city of Philadelphia. He did not understand, he was often saying, why the city was so crowded and so poor, but he also seemed to have no interest in finding out the answers to these questions. He lived in Cherry Hill, a New Jersey suburb that consisted solely, according to his remarks, of large grocery stores, malls, car dealerships, and good schools. There were a lot of white Philadelphians who existed this way, Bernie was learning, people who grew up in or near the city and worked here still, who claimed Philadelphia for its baseball or its football, for its food and its history, for its scrappiness and its unhinged mascot, but did not actually live in it.

After the coffee shop, Bernie took the train north and east alongside I-95 to her second job at a small public library in Kensington, a northern neighborhood in Philly that had once been an unremarkable mostly working-class neighborhood but was now often remarked upon either for its proximity to a more affluent area that was home to artisan woodworking studios and small-batch ice cream shops or for its open-air heroin markets.

Bernie sat at an empty child-short table and waited for children, any children at all who might wander in from the street and need help with their homework. To kill time, Bernie drew on a piece of computer paper stolen from the librarian. Not many children came, but adults often did, seeking a place just to take a little rest. Several times, though Bernie had never seen it with her own eyes, someone had been nodding out in the library bathroom and the librarian had administered them Narcan. The librarian, who had grown up in the neighborhood, wore cardigans in bright colors and was slowly losing her hair, the white line of her part growing ever wider.

Kensington was a word Bernie heard growing up, even a hundred and fifty miles away. It was a word said around fires in the woods and it was a word said in hospitals. Bernie's brother said it every time she talked to him, about someone else in their town. People said it if they wanted to get high, make money, make amends, or die. Bernie did not take this kind of dying lightly. Many, many, many people she knew had died this way, saying the word *Kensington* and then coming back to her town or saying it without ever leaving. Her social studies teacher Mr. Freeman died saying *Kensington,* plus a boy who lived down the road she'd briefly thought was beautiful who started a band made up exclusively of bass guitars.

Sitting in a window seat and hurtling west back home one night, she saw a mural of the American flag unfurling, and Bernie remembered Leah's poem. It was difficult to say what feeling, if any, Bernie had for the flag anymore. When she was a child, it was a friendly prop that presaged the arrival of a pleasurable holiday, similar in impact to glimpsing the Christmas tree stand in their attic. But now, the flag felt to Bernie like something that was supposed to be hers but wasn't, like a sweatshirt from a school where you'd had a bad time. Or even more primal than that maybe, like a picture of a parent from whom you're estranged.

I fucking hate this country, Bernie had overheard Alex say to Meena one night in the kitchen.

But Bernie didn't hate America. That was exactly the problem. The more suffering that transpired in America, the more Bernie felt American, as if she were cut out to be part of a place that suffered. It was like belonging to a fantastically dysfunctional family from which she knew she would never be free.

Bernie headed to Jaffa, an Ethiopian restaurant a few blocks from the house, a thing she did many early evenings before heading home, though she could not really afford it. She liked to sit at the bar and sip a wheat beer under the TV, where men were sporting against a green background, while the regulars, a mix of white neighborhood old heads and young men recently emigrated from Cameroon and Mali, talked and joked with each other and jumped up to hug each other at important athletic moments.

When you grow up in a place as beautiful as Bernie did and then leave it, you can spend your whole life looking for that kind of beauty again. As she walked from the subway to Jaffa, Bernie was looking and Bernie was finding. There is a way in which the city and the country are made of the same raw stuff, so much more the same than either is to the muted suburbs, which can feel like living with your ears stuffed with cotton or a perpetual sinus infection.

The sky was purple and the trolley groaned by, straining the overhead wire. The cars and bicycles raced each other down the street, drivers slapping their arms against the outside of their doors in displeasure. On the corner were the two halal places and the mosque and people were coming out from evening prayer. They stood on the sidewalk in lively clusters, holding steaming food in aluminum containers. Down the block, the anarchist coffee shop and the social justice bookstore were closing up. A young Black man in round wire-framed glasses and an older white woman with her dull hair in two braids were talking, passing a white plastic bag back and forth. The sidewalks were strewn with friendly trash—a Kit Kat wrapper, a squashed can of energy drink, a tract for the Working Families party. People were walking up the stairs to the big Queen Anne–style Victorians on the avenue which had been split into apartments, retreating into their homes for the night. They held their children's hands and parallel parked efficiently. They drew their shades and locked their doors.

At the Vietnamese convenience store, Bernie bought the cheapest banh mi hoagie and ate half of it sitting on the loop of an unoccupied bike rack, the fabric of her jeans the only thing separating her skin from the cold metal. When bits of cilantro and pickled daikon and carrots fell out of the sandwich and onto her coat, Bernie picked them up and stuffed them back into her mouth with the tips of her fingers.

Sister sister, said a Black woman in a thick scarf wrapped several times around her neck. Can you help me get something to eat?

No more cash, Bernie said, but I have the other half of this sandwich. She held it out to the woman, still wrapped in its white butcher paper and masking tape.

What kind?

Tofu.

Oh no, the woman said, shaking both palms at Bernie. No, no, no.

The bathroom door at Jaffa was light metal with a hole in it where the doorknob used to be. As she peed, Bernie inspected the graffiti—IF YOU WERE HERE, I'D BE HOME BY NOW; FUCK THE POLICE; EDDIE LAZARUS IS A RAPIST. Several arrows pointed to this last one saying YES and HE SURE IS. Someone had inserted a caret before FUCK so it also said ASS FUCK THE POLICE and someone else had written THIS IS HOMOPHOBIC with an arrow pointing to it.

Bernie wiped. Her vagina burned slightly, and she greeted it again as a long lost—what? Friend? Acquaintance, more like. When she wasn't touching her vagina or using it directly, she forgot about it. It did not speak maybe. It had no voice.

Bernie walked through the dark front room of the restaurant—empty tables beneath mirrored walls. A shelf ran around the perimeter just below the ceiling, holding framed photographs of the kings and queens of Ethiopia and Eritrea. In the mirrored hallway, Bernie touched her palm to her cheek. How strange it was to be inside a body, a floating and complex person with many different ways of feeling and then to look into a mirror and see yourself reduced to only one thing, the same physical face over and over again. Her cheeks were heavy, even plump, like a chipmunk or a fat baby who had never grown into its face. The skin around her eyes was dark purple and dry. She checked her teeth, which were shamefully crooked, and ruffled her dirty bangs. Good enough, good enough.

Bernie slid into a seat at the bar. The man who was always drinking seltzer and doing the crossword was drinking seltzer and doing the crossword. The bartender with her big, pretty jaw and tiny wrists wore a black V-neck shirt that revealed a collarbone tattoo of a fish hanging dead on the line and a wide, hollow space between her breasts.

Bernie ordered a beer and when the alcohol hit she felt tired, so tired. She put her arms down on the bar and rested her head on them.

Wake up, wake up, Daniel Dunn had often said to her when she fell asleep without meaning to in the passenger seat of his car. *You'll sleep your whole life away.*

Turning her head, Bernie saw Violet at the other end of the bar. They were standing with a group of tall white and East Asian queers. Bernie knew she should not want Violet, that wanting Violet was like wanting to win the lottery: if you bought a ticket, you made the pot of want larger, which decreased the chances of you personally ever getting what you wanted. Was it objectifying Violet to compare them to a pot of money? Possibly. But Bernie had the sense that Violet had waited all their life to be objectified and was now enjoying it. They were one of those masculine queers who had not worked as a little girl but they were working now, damn were they working.

Violet lifted their chin at Bernie then, and Bernie sat up and lifted hers back. Later, Violet passed Bernie on their way out to smoke on the bar's overgrown back patio and asked her how it was going, moving too fast to hear any answer. Bernie looked at Violet's straight back in their leather bomber jacket and at their little ass as they walked away. What the hell, Bernie thought. I'll buy a ticket. I'll buy ten tickets. Sign me up. I'll take those odds.

BERNIE HAD PROMISED HERSELF THAT she would try, now that she was in a new place, so try she did. Once a week, on Sundays, Bernie took up the big rectangular bag with its padded handle that contained the camera that had once belonged to Daniel Dunn and the small square shoulder bag that held its film, preloaded into the holders just in case, and took the train or the bus somewhere with the intent of making one or two exposures. She went to the park where you could see the oil refinery across the river. She went to the Divine Lorraine, that opulent building that had been left to urban explorers, and tried to take a different picture than the sepia-toned one you saw on postcards of Philadelphia at craft fairs. She looked at a plaza of Vietnamese restaurants and grocery stores that the city had slated for demolition but then hadn't demolished.

She practiced focusing, using the light meter, adjusting the exposure speed, closing the lens before putting in the film holder. She even cocked the shutter, pulling the little lever back with her thumb. But she could not touch the lever again with her index finger to release it and take the picture. Often, people approached her when she had the camera out. They wanted to talk, they wanted to comment, they wanted to ask and to know. How does it work? Where did you get it? What do you see when you look? Can I see?

So Bernie stayed in practice. She stayed ready. She walked around and looked at things and thought about photographing them but then did not photograph them. The ideas came and they went. Fundamentally, the camera was heavy and Bernie was tired.

BERNIE WAS EATING SOUP AT the kitchen island one Saturday night in April when the door to the basement slammed and Violet came up through it, waving at Bernie as they strode on toward the front door.

Excited voices. A loud call. Come in, come in!

Violet reentered followed by a very tiny adult person with a bright moon face and a large bow in her hair that sat off to one side. She wore a piece of black velvet fabric draped over her shoulders and secured over her chest with a rhinestone pin. Silk gloves.

Oh hi, she said, taking Bernie in. I'm Lucy Vincent. She extended a gloved hand.

I don't usually look like this, Lucy Vincent said, pointing upward at the bow in her hair and downward at the cloak and what was underneath—a taffeta party dress, white stockings, and black patent leather Mary Janes.

Yes she does, Violet said.

Lucy Vincent bobbled her head and then closed one eye in a mock gesture of deep thinking.

Alright, she said. I suppose my quotidian style does have a certain American Girl doll flair to it, I grant you that. But this is actually a costume, not my real clothes.

Lucy Vincent is an actress, Violet said.

Oh, said Lucy Vincent, waving her hand dismissively. It's just a very small production at the theater over on the avenue. The one next to the church that's also a synagogue and down from the anarchist coffee shop? But it's fun and keeps me out of trouble. What are we drinking?

Violet opened the fridge and pulled out two longneck beers.

To the living room? Violet asked.

It's such a beautiful night, Lucy Vincent said. Let's sit out back, I need a cigarette.

It's freezing, Violet said.

Oh boo hoo, Lucy Vincent said, and took Violet's hand.

In her bedroom, Bernie opened the window and stuck her head outside. Violet was dragging the two white plastic chairs across the concrete enclosed on three sides by chain-link fence. To the right was a small yard that belonged to the young Black man who lived in the basement apartment underneath another queer group house. Bernie had seen him out there sometimes, smoking weed and sitting with his ankle resting on his knee. He played good music, which leaked out from his apartment into the night air, music that Bernie had not heard in a long time—Robert Johnson, Muddy Waters, Loretta Lynn. Country music.

There was the sound of the back door off their kitchen opening and closing, the sound of Violet's voice and bottles clinking. Bernie should withdraw her head she knew, but she didn't. She watched as Violet placed the two chairs close together in the yard, and watched as Lucy Vincent took one of the offered beers, sitting down and crossing her small legs in Violet's direction. A low laugh.

What?

Nothing.

What?

Talking too low to hear.

Bernie pulled herself back inside the room. Her body felt old, ancient and crumbling. Cracks seemed to be forming in her neck and lower back a la a Disney cartoon of dissolution. If she could only stop sleeping on her stomach. But then she'd have to stop cramming cheddar cheese before bedtime and drinking beer and who would she be then? It is a slippery slope, eliminating pleasure: once you eliminated one pleasure from your life, the rest would have to follow. Pretty soon you'd be sleeping on your back like a corpse. Not dead yet. Alive.

Bernie's phone vibrated, and it was a 212 number calling again—New York City. She had been getting more and more of these lately, spam calls that flipped her stomach about fake car loan payments, or three-second voicemails in Mandarin. She blocked the number as she had done with the others; a game of technological Whac-A-Mole.

Good for Violet and Lucy Vincent, mazel tov, felicidades, etc. Bernie opened her laptop, which was at 15% battery. She made no move to fetch the charger, which was downstairs plugged in next to Meena's salt lamp. Bernie did this sometimes: taking no action, watching as a small problem became a bigger one.

It was quiet on the other side of the wall; Leah must have been out. Bernie lay back on her mattress and stretched her legs up the wall. She was not surprised from an intellectual perspective when she saw the email titled *May Rent,* but she was surprised from an emotional and financial perspective. Bernie's share was only $550, but she currently had $607 in her checking, now $601 after the craft beer from the bottle shop down the block which was perspiring to warm in her hand. With tips, the coffee shop paid around fifteen dollars an hour and the library twenty-two so all of that could have been more or less fine if her minimum student loan payment of $147 per month—she would pay Evergreen back what she owed it in approximately thirty-five years—had not also existed.

The computer exhaled heat onto her thighs as she scrolled through the classified ads website.

Community. Female leg models wanted.

What made a good leg? Bernie wiggled hers, up there on the wall. They were slick and barren and felt reasonably attractive, if somewhat bulbous in the calves and ankles. She was always letting her leg hair grow very long and then shaving it. Who could decide? Who could possibly know what it all signified? Everyone in the house let their leg and armpit hair grow long except for Violet who claimed to be genetically incapable of growing body hair, like a dolphin. Bernie didn't care really, but every now and then she would look down at her hairy legs and not like what she saw. This was her own hang-up, Bernie knew, something to be gotten over, as she had already gotten over so much. She had once been a football player's girlfriend in central Pennsylvania. There was nothing to changing your life, it turned out. You just put a toe in and fell.

Leg model, Bernie thought, and headed to Google Images to search it. She might not have seen the article at all had she not already been googling things, but she was googling things and so she did see it.

Photographer Daniel Dunn Dead at 71.

The article was right up at the top of Bernie's screen, in the "news" section. Next to a photograph of him in a cream-colored cotton T-shirt was the headline: *Dunn's color photographs created an American iconography. But his career was tarnished.*

A memorial service will be held later this month in the Little Levels Presbyterian Church in Lewistown, Pennsylvania.

RAISE YOUR HAND IF YOU'RE surprised Daniel Dunn drank himself to death, Bernie said to the crowd assembled inside her head. No one raised their hand.

Her computer dead now, Bernie sat quietly for a while, doing nothing. Then the hallway light went on and the double doors to Violet's room came together in a wobbly smack, and Bernie expected to hear Lucy Vincent's giggle again. But there was no giggle, only a single set of footsteps approaching Bernie's door. Then a knock.

Hey you, Violet said. I saw your light on. Can I come in?

There was nowhere else, so Violet sat on the foot of Bernie's low unmade bed. Bernie leaned back, resting her head against the wall.

Somewhere outside, a car went by, its muffler shot, clanking. So what, so Daniel Dunn was dead. Somewhere out there, there was one less person in the world.

It's Lucy Vincent, Violet said. I just need someone's advice. We used to go out and it was a whole thing. No one else in the house will talk to me about her because I already put them through it a year ago and they told me I was crazy to be spending time with her again. I really liked her though. And then she dumped me for this guy. Alf. He's directing the play she's doing. I've seen him at Jaffa and he's super hot, in that very classic sort of bro-y way? But apparently he's also super sweet? I don't know. So now she says she wants me back. But she's still seeing Alf and wants to keep seeing him. It would be a poly thing, open you know, everyone would know. We would all communicate. But I don't know. I got pretty burned last time. But I mean, Violet said, sort of rolling their eyes. She's fucking gorgeous, I mean, you saw her.

Hmm, Bernie said.

What, you don't think so?

Sure, Bernie said. She's pretty.

Not your type?

Bernie shook her head.

And what is your type exactly?

I don't really have a type, Bernie said. I like all kinds of people. But tall is good. Like you.

Oh, Violet said. They smiled. I mean, I also like that Lucy Vincent is fun, vivacious, I like how much she talks. I like how much she knows about the world, that she's cultured and all. She went to high school in New York down the street from Leah.

So what? Bernie said. You're cultured.

I'm an Asian kid from North Jersey. But I know some things, yeah.

You know quite a lot of things it seems to me, Bernie said.

Violet looked at Bernie a long time. What about you, Bernie? What do you know?

Nothing, Bernie said.

I don't believe you.

It's true.

Violet nodded, licked their lip slightly, and looked down at their hands, one on each knee.

You don't run around like the rest of us, constantly going here or there, to or fro, to this thing or that. You're, I don't know, steady.

Maybe I'm boring, Bernie said.

I don't think so, Violet said. Violet stood and sat down closer to Bernie, yet still on the edge of the bed, and with their back slightly to her.

I should go, Violet said. Let you get some sleep.

Alright, Bernie said.

Bernie scooched forward so she could put her feet on the floor and Violet turned. Now they were sitting next to each other. Violet's head was down, their long neck bent and very white like a swan's.

Some people are so beautiful it sort of hurts to look at them because you know that they will always be that beautiful and that they will never, ever belong to you.

Violet lifted their head and stood, so Bernie did too. Violet put their hands on Bernie's waist, then slid their fingers through her belt loops and tugged her pants, ever so slightly, upward. Then they leaned down and kissed Bernie. It was a very flat kiss, not bad, but firm, and wide. Bernie's mouth was closed at first but then it was open. Violet kissed Bernie's top lip once, twice, right, left, then repeated the same process with her bottom lip. Violet took one side of her face into their palm and kissed across Bernie's other cheek until their lips met their own hand at Bernie's ear. Bernie wondered if this was Violet's routine, if these were the steps, if they were running through the choreography.

Bernie, Violet said, into Bernie's ear.

Maybe it was the vibration or the heat of Violet's breath or maybe it was her own name in Violet's mouth, but Bernie jerked hard then, as if air had been pumped and pumped into a balloon and then the balloon had been shot out of the sky. In the year she had taken off between high school and college to make money, Bernie sometimes made balloon animals for children's parties, so this image did not come from nowhere.

Violet squatted down a little then knocked their face up so their mouth met Bernie's and their hands reached behind and across Bernie's back. The tide had shifted and it was a strange tide, it felt strange to ride it.

Bernie did to Violet then what she had imagined many times doing to Violet. She lifted Violet's hoodie off. She unbuttoned the buttons of their cotton shirt one by one.

Violet wore a small black binder with thick white piping around the edges, but when that came off too, Bernie saw that they had a tattoo—a purple cabbage flower that sat on their sternum, its leaves growing outward in ever-widening layers of magenta that spread over their triangular breasts. When Violet turned, she saw that on their back between their shoulder blades, they had another tattoo of the same cabbage, but seen from behind now. Five thick overlapping leaves held together by a jetting nub, as if the physical stuff of the cabbage were lodged inside their chest.

A part of Bernie wanted to ask—What's with the cabbage?—but it was a very small part of her, much smaller than the part of her that wanted to touch the skin that held the cabbage. Leah would have asked, Bernie knew. But Bernie was not Leah.

Violet sat on the bed, then leaned back onto the pillows.

The rest of their chest was very white, their stomach impossibly thin—Bernie could see every rib—and very soft. She had expected their body to be harder somehow. Bernie gathered Violet's small breasts, one in each hand, and rubbed each of their nipples between her thumb and forefinger, feeling them rise.

Oh, Violet said, jerking and hitting their head against the wall.

What did Bernie feel? She felt Violet's spongy damp pubic hair on the tips of her fingers as she rubbed the whole length of her index and middle fingers along Violet's cunt. Bernie felt tired, sleepy. She closed her eyes. With her other hand, she felt the goose pimples on the back of Violet's thigh. She heard Violet breathing, Violet breathing harder and then the creak of someone walking up the kitchen stairs and then down the hallway in a pattern that sounded so much like Bernie's mother—the setting down of the ball (arthritic, painful) and then the laying down of the rest of the foot, bone by bone—that Bernie stopped for a moment to listen. It was Leah.

What? Violet said.

Nothing, Bernie said.

Bernie had fucked that woman from the Walmart parking lot. But it had not been easy. She had gone back every week, not just on Sundays, cutting high school gym class to sit in the parking lot, even math a time or two. But when she had done it, finally and at last, when she spotted the truck in the parking lot again and invited the woman to take a walk in the state park and the woman said, *Now?* and Bernie said, *Yeah,* and the woman said, *OK,* and they walked for a bit and then stopped and the woman laughed in a mean way and said, *You didn't really want to just take a walk did you?* and Bernie said, *No,* and the woman pushed Bernie against a tree and insinuated her leg between Bernie's legs, and used her left hand to pull down the neckline of Bernie's T-shirt, what had Bernie felt? Wind, pine needles, a vision of the future. She was inside her body, she was not outside of it watching it as so many people said they tended to be. No. She was far inside. Making a sandwich. Channel surfing. Standing at a hotel counter. Ringing the bell.

AROUND TWO IN THE MORNING, long after Violet had come and gone, Bernie woke to laughing. Then loud breathing coming from Leah's room. It was Leah and Alex. Bernie could hear the coming together of their faces, the coming together of their stomachs. She could hear the pulling apart and the return, the slap and the silence, the shifting of weight and the encouragement. The friction and the wetness.

Bernie pulled her underwear down and then kicked the pretzel it made to the bottom of the bed and then onto the floor. She had not taken it off while Violet was there; Violet had tried to touch her but Bernie had declined—I'm good, she'd said. Now, she opened her legs wide as a butterfly—elementary school, gymnastics, flutter your knees, flutter your knees—and touched the pile of sensitive skin and nerves.

Oh god, oh god, oh fuck, oh fucking god, Alex cried out.

As Bernie came too, she did not cry out, but she did cry. This had been happening a lot lately. As she came, they were all there in the room. Her house was there, and their washed-out driveway and its worms, and the back room, cold in the winter and full of tack and saddles and Bernie's winter clothes. Her mother was there and her brother was there and her road and her school were there, and all the people who died in motorcycle accidents and car accidents and of saying *Kensington* were there and Daniel Dunn was there now too.

It was all there: the dark dark night, her dark dark heart, and the undeniable fact that when this time came, the hours between eleven at night and four in the morning, hours she used to spend lying awake as a kid watching game shows and failing to sleep; when these dark, lost, and timeless hours came now, when pleasure came, when she released her body, when she released her grip on the moment, just for a second, just to feel relaxed because she was tired of gripping, what came pouring out was water.

VI.

NONE OF THE PEOPLE AT THE MUSEUM THAT DAY EMPLOYED THE same technique to throw the empty orange pill bottles into the pool of black water. Leah watched as the photographer and her band of activist assistants threw these bottles, labeled OXYCONTIN, into the reflecting pools surrounding the two-thousand-year-old Temple of Dendur at the Metropolitan Museum of Art to send a message of shame. Shame on the family who had made the opioid crisis possible and shame on the administrators and the art people who continued to take the family's money.

In the video, Nan Goldin lifted a bottle out of her tote bag by its bulbous white top, then gripped it with her whole hand and hurled it, end over end, until it skidded across the water, while next to her, a man pulled a bottle out of his bag by its orange base and gracefully chucked it underhand, producing a pleasant plop.

As she watched, Leah thought about what it might be like to throw one of those bottles herself—the rush of wind from winding up and the snap of the wrist at the release. She had played too much basketball as a child, particularly the game where you lined up behind the free-throw line and tried to get your ball through the hoop before the person behind you could sink theirs.

The video was something Leah admired very much, but it was not exactly what she wanted to do. Leah was not an idiot. She knew that her idea was not a very sophisticated idea, that in fact it was a very old idea. At many different, culturally significant points of enormous upheaval, a duo of photographer and writer had driven around America for an extended road trip to make a record of it as it was then, with both photographs and words, before everything changed again. The idea was, fundamentally, that the sum of the two forms was larger than either form ever could be alone. The photographs were not illustrations of the sentences and the words were not captions for the images. Bernie's big, strange, slow way of photography was so different from everything Leah hated, so away and outside it all, which could only help things, help her write well and openly as she was capable of doing but rarely did.

Days were running short though if Leah wanted to act on this idea over the summer—it was May already. The time was nigh to talk to Bernie about it, but the right moment kept not presenting itself. Bernie almost never lingered in the common spaces, preferring to be out of the house or in her room with the door closed, an impulse Leah understood very well, and broaching such a thing in the hallway as they passed each other in the early morning after Leah had been up late bickering with Alex was unthinkable; likewise when either of them had just come from peeing.

There was a way, Leah knew from the college dorms but had forgotten, that when you got to know someone by living alongside them, you knew them both very well and not at all.

On the one hand, you heard the noises they made as they shuffled, half asleep, down the cold hall. You saw their little foot, encased in a dirty white sock, tapping to some tune on their headphones as they stood at the stove, frying a grilled cheese. You saw the white crust left on their toothbrush and how long they would wait to get a new one—forever, in Bernie's case; the bristles were as turned up at the ends as a sixties hairstyle. You saw the hairs left on their horsehair hairbrush—so much hair they were losing, shedding even, like a cat, like Jigger in the summer. You saw them hold Jigger close to their face and kiss her on the top of her small head, both Bernie and Jigger closing their eyes in pleasure. You saw the color of Bernie's shit where it was left behind in stripes on the toilet bowl.

But on the other hand you never knew why they were awake in the night—small bladder? Small fears? You never knew what song they were listening to on those headphones and why it made their foot tap, if they liked to dance or didn't, if Jigger was the first cat they'd ever loved or just one in a string of many and what they did all night every night in that room with the door closed. Except for that one night when both Violet and Bernie had made a great deal of sexy sounds. This didn't necessarily mean much, as Violet had fucked everyone a time or two—Alex, Meena, and most of their other friends from college. But there was something about the idea of Bernie having sex with Violet that unsettled Leah, that had disturbed her that night to the point of texting Alex and asking her to come down, a thing that Leah almost never did.

One Friday afternoon in early May, Leah was sitting at the oval dining room table munching cereal and preparing to leave the house for the art show she'd successfully pitched to the paper when Bernie came home earlier and looking a little stranger than usual. Paler maybe, or oilier, like she hadn't showered and didn't intend to.

Bernie ran her fingers over their mailboxes but came away with no mail. She sat down heavily at the table but kept her backpack on and her hands wrapped around its straps. Leaned back in the seat.

Long day? Leah asked.

Something like that, Bernie said. Violet home?

I don't think so, Leah said. It's Friday, so they have their constituent meeting and then traffic is usually really bad coming back from Kennett Square.

Right, Bernie said.

You OK?

Fine, Bernie said. What are you reading?

It's a press release email, Leah said. For a show I'm seeing tonight. I'm going to write about it. It's a haunted house of sorts, but—

Can I come? Bernie asked. I love haunted houses.

She wasn't looking at Leah, but was still clutching the straps of her backpack and staring now out the front window at their street.

Well it's a lesbian haunted house, Leah said, not a normal one, just so you're aware. In Kensington.

Fine by me, Bernie said.

Bernie still had not looked Leah's way. She was covering her eyes now, kneading them with the butts of her palms.

I could drive us, if you want, Bernie said.

In Alex's car? Leah asked.

Yeah. I know Meena does that sometimes.

Sure, Leah said. It would be a lot faster. If you don't mind.

Thank you, Bernie said, already rising.

Bernie drove them, in Alex's boxy green Volvo station wagon, up Front Street which was dark in the shadow of the El tracks above. When she was driving, Bernie was still and focused, but when she had to stop at a stop sign or a red light, she fidgeted, kept messing with the rearview mirror, kept touching the gear shift, or moving her seat forward an inch then back an inch. It was the first really warm day of spring, cloudy and sunny at the same time, and women wore rumpled sundresses, smoothing out the wrinkles against their thighs with the palms of their hands as they walked.

They passed the last stop on the El that Leah had ever heard of and continued north. A turn down a wide diagonal side street took Bernie and Leah past a small green park with a white-columned building at its center. Around the edges of the park, people were sitting and standing around a low wall; many were sleeping on the wall. Two sides of the park were lined with a tangle of camping tents, temporary shelters made of blue plastic tarps, and piles of sturdy trash—scavenged lumber, heaps of green and clear plastic bottles.

This is terrible, Leah said to Bernie, turning her head to keep looking as Bernie drove by. I had no idea it was still this bad up here. All the articles I've worked on about drugs in Kensington recently said that the mayor cleared the encampments. Distributed millions for treatment, clean needles, and grassroots prevention programs. Rates are going down, they say.

I guess not, Bernie said.

Wow, Leah said. Wow, she said again.

The building where the lesbian haunted house was being put on was sharp red brick, long and rectangular. It had once been a factory that made metal pipes. People had assembled on a ramp leading up to the entrance of the building and as they got closer, Bernie heard loud jangling music playing from a large boom box that propped open the door at the front of the line. The people in line giggled. One couple, a tall man and a short man, held each other, the short one opening his jacket so the tall one could come into it.

The line was moving, they were almost at the front now. A person with a white face of makeup wearing a wig with frizzy brown bangs, a black leather jacket with a sheepskin collar, a black leather newsboy cap, and a sign around her neck made of cardboard and string that said I SHOT ANDY WARHOL appeared in the door.

OK, Valerie Solanas said, then moved down the ramp counting one two three four five. You five, she said, making a cutting motion with her hand behind Bernie's head. The group included Leah, the couple ahead of them in line, and their friend.

Come on, Valerie Solanas barked, in character, and the trio laughed. Bernie and Leah did not laugh.

They were ushered into a lobby and then farther into a long marble corridor lined with green metal lockers.

Over here, said Valerie Solanas, quickly quickly, don't dawdle, I don't have all day. Again the trio laughed.

What are you laughing at? said Valerie Solanas with a total dead face, and they quieted right down.

OK, here's the deal, Valerie Solanas went on. Welcome to the lesbian haunted house. In this haunted house, you will see many evil lesbians, do you understand? I am only one.

Who else? baited the short queer, batting his eyes.

Stop asking so many questions, Valerie Solanas said.

The short queer and his tall boyfriend laughed.

Now, said Valerie Solanas, as I was saying. You will see many evil lesbians in this house who are conspiring to overthrow society, though they all disagree on how this should be done, of course. I personally think it is best to kill all men, but others do not agree. Some think we should start a new agrarian society, a commune in the country, where men are not allowed. Still others think it is about eliminating the artistic and intellectual contributions of men, simply erasing them from libraries and archives. You will see many possibilities. These things may produce feelings in you. I cannot protect you from your feelings. You may be touched, things may touch you, is that alright? It is perfectly OK if not, you just have to tell me now.

Valerie Solanas pointed to each of the group. Yes, the men said in turn.

No, said the girl with them.

No? confirmed Valerie Solanas.

No.

OK, one no.

Yes, Leah said.

Yes, Bernie said.

Valerie Solanas pulled out a walkie-talkie and spoke into it. I've got a no here. Uh huh.

She backpedaled a few steps, peeking her capped head behind a black velvet curtain. Then she held the curtain back and motioned for the group to enter.

Quickly, she said. Quickly.

Inside was a large circular room, no windows. A sort of French death music was playing, sharp grating violin sawing, then light flutes, then the strings came back sad and quick, and built and built and built back to the grating again. In the center of the room on a rotating disk was a pile of black Styrofoam graves, each with the name of a lesbian bar which once was open but now was closed. It was a heap, tall as several people.

A cry went up from behind Leah and she turned to see the trio exclaiming and jumping back from a low, dark structure, adorned with starfish and seashells, from which a fat voluptuous woman was emerging. She had a shock of white hair and wore a strapless black gown that ended in enormous purple-spotted stuffed fabric tentacles. Every few seconds, the tentacles sort of twitched then went slack, lolling about on the floor.

Ariel, the woman called, clutching a large yellow shell necklace at her throat. Ariel, you whore, is that you?

Ah yes, said Valerie Solanas. Ursula the Sea Witch is one of our most despised residents, yet very popular to take photos with. Would you like a photo?

The trio nodded and squealed and Valerie Solanas, in a show of exhaustion, closed her eyes and waited for someone's iPhone to be placed in her hand. But instead, the friend handed over a small silver point and shoot digital camera.

What the fuck is this? Valerie Solanas asked, examining it. Oh actually I know what it is. My mom had one of these when I was kid.

It makes the photos a little more special, the girl said, makes them stand out on my feed. I love the nostalgia of the way they look, all overexposed and blurry.

Whatever you say, Valerie Solanas said, lifting the little camera so she could look at its large rear screen. She pressed a little button and the camera diddled to life with a little chirp.

Leah too had been in possession of one of these cameras, had used it in high school and early college. You took the picture, connected a little cable to the camera so you could upload it to your computer and then posted it to the original social media app. Unimaginable now, except these people were doing it.

Say "Lesbian erasure"! cried Valerie Solanas, and the trio mumbled it back, laughing, while the picture was taken.

And you two? Valerie Solanas said, pointing at Bernie and Leah.

They looked at each other. Leah gave Valerie Solanas her iPhone and then she and Bernie moved to stand on either side of Ursula. Leah rested her hand loosely on Ursula's bare back.

Valerie Solanas took the picture and handed the phone back to Leah. The picture looked nothing like either Bernie or Leah, though Ursula looked more or less like what she looked like in life.

Now come along, said Valerie Solanas.

But Ursula was holding Bernie's arm.

No, no, no, Ursula said. You're staying here with me.

Ow, Bernie said.

Valerie Solanas and the trio moved on ahead without them.

Don't leave me here, Ursula said. Her makeup was beginning to run with sweat and she wasn't smiling. It was unclear if this was a part of the performance or something personal, meant just for Bernie. She tugged on Bernie's arm. Bernie tried to pull her arm back, but she was caught, held. Ursula smiled; her lipstick, which had been applied to the skin around her mouth, rippled and cracked.

You're hurting me, Bernie said.

I'll die if you leave me here, Ursula cried again, quite convincingly.

It happened fast, and Leah might not have been brave enough to do it anywhere else. She put out her hand and Bernie took it and Leah pulled hard and Bernie pulled hard and then Bernie was no longer held by Ursula the Sea Witch. Bernie's hand was warm and dry. Leah felt Bernie's skin and felt Bernie's hard thumb on the back of her hand.

Are you alright? Leah asked.

Bernie's eyes seemed very small and very red. Yeah, Bernie said. Thanks.

There was Ellen DeGeneres, wearing white dress pants, a white dress shirt, vest and bow tie, and white satin top hat, rolling around in a sea of fake money. Every so often she got up, sat in a red armchair, held a microphone made of papier-mâché into which she uttered nonsense words and more money rained down upon her from a fishing net suspended above. As they watched, she got down on the floor on her back, rolling from side to side in the green bills and kicking her white-sneakered feet into the air.

There was Camille Paglia, sitting in a chair in a white room, writing and saying nothing.

There was Abby Wambach in a room full of posters of herself in soccer gear, glugging from a giant bottle labeled VODKA and kicking a cardboard car with her foot.

My favorite, Valerie Solanas said, as they passed Aileen Wuornos in an orange jumpsuit, pacing around in a cage and calling out, Tyria! Dawn! Anyone!

They passed through a library with large cardboard books on wooden shelves, the names—AUDRE LORDE, OCTAVIA BUT-

LER, ADRIENNE RICH—written on their spines in big black letters.

Huh, Leah said, noticing a spine that said ERNEST HEMINGWAY. She pulled it out and jumped back into Bernie's elbow as the small plastic heads of snakes popped up and then came to rest hanging over the book's edges.

Finally they came through a corridor covered with light-colored gauzy fabric and flashing white strobe lights. It was the end.

You have done it! said Valerie Solanas, flapping her arms, though they did not go all the way up, constricted as they were by her leather jacket. You have survived the lesbian haunted house! Now get out!

BERNIE AND LEAH TOOK SEATS at the bar of a dive beneath the El tracks. Outside was light and inside was dark to a degree unattributable to the weather. Illuminated chili peppers dangled down the columns at each of the bar's four corners, and delicate iron bars covered the windows. A few chairs to Leah's left sat a straight couple on a first or second date. The man was asking the woman what kind of music she liked and the woman was saying that she didn't know exactly so the man was suggesting bands and imitating their music with his mouth.

I liked it, Bernie said, once they'd ordered—a draft beer for Bernie, a craft beer for Leah. Leah wondered if Bernie was worried about money; she seemed always to be opting for the slightly cheaper version of any thing.

I liked it too, Leah said.

Leah was scooted up all the way against the lip of the bar, her chest flesh resting on its edge, her thighs creating a wide surface on which to rest her legal pad with several pages flipped over.

It woke me up, Bernie said. I feel *awake*.

Totally, Leah said, writing down *awake*.

It made me laugh, Bernie went on. When Ursula grabbed me? I felt scared. And when you took out the Hemingway?

That scared the bejeezus out of me, Leah said. It was fun to be scared, have any big feeling really. I haven't felt that way in a long time at any exhibition or reading.

Sounds like you've been seeing a lot of really boring art, Bernie said.

Leah laughed. I guess so.

The plunge had to be taken, the day had to be seized. What was the worst Bernie could say? Only no.

The last thing that really did anything for me like that was you, Leah said. Your photographs. I've gone back to them a bunch of times. The one with the bird? The one with the hill? Sometimes I look at them in the morning when I wake up or just before I go to bed. They're really good, I think. You're really good.

That's nice, Bernie said. That's nice of you to say.

It's the truth, Leah said. Are you making more? I've seen you leave the house with your camera a few times. I've wondered.

No, Bernie said.

Oh, Leah said. Can I ask why?

It's complicated, Bernie said. I read your poem. In your room. The door was open, sorry.

That's OK, Leah said. It's not very good, I know.

Bernie said nothing.

I don't think I'm cut out to write original things, Leah said. I think I'm better when I'm responding to things other people have made.

The purple house piece? Bernie said. That was really good.

You read that? Thank you.

It's the truth, like you said. Why don't you write more like that?

It's complicated, Leah said, and smiled. Is it complicated for you because of the big camera you use?

That's part of it, Bernie said. And you need a darkroom. Or somewhere to get the images processed.

Sounds like a lot of pressure, Leah said. On each photograph.

It is, Bernie said.

You could do like that girl did at the haunted house, Leah said. Use another kind of older camera.

No, Bernie said. It's not the same. There's never been a digital equivalent for large format, and there probably never will be. The level of detail and the cumulative impact. The way it works on the body. The fiddling and using of the hands, the way you never, ever know how the picture is going to turn out until the very end. That's what got me interested.

Hmm, Leah said. But could taking pictures with an easier camera be the next best thing, or a way to think things through? Like journaling for me, or making notes maybe.

I hadn't thought about it quite like that, Bernie said. Actually though, before I used the big camera, in college, I used to do this thing where whenever I noticed I was looking at something, just like noticed the act of looking, I'd take a picture. It could be anything—carpet, the desk of my dorm room. It wouldn't be about the thing exactly but just trying to mark that time, remember what I was seeing when I was aware of seeing it.

Isn't that what Daniel Dunn did also? Your professor?

Bernie shifted her weight, moving her foot down so it made contact with the sticky floor, and when she did, a splotch of warm red light from one of the chili peppers settled on her left cheek so that it looked like someone very beautiful and glamorous had kissed her there.

I suppose, Bernie said. I suppose that is kind of what he did. Not in the end, but earlier. With his road-trip photos. You really can google, huh? Bernie said.

It's kind of my specialty.

Impressive. Then you probably know he died, too.

I didn't actually, Leah said. I'm sorry. Was he ill?

In a way, Bernie said.

I did read about the sexual assault, or, harassment stuff, though, Leah said. I'm sorry if that, um, affected you. I guess how could it not.

It didn't really, Bernie said. I guess I was lucky in that way. I feel bad, like I got the best of him, and other people got the worst.

But you still got it, Leah said. It was all in there. He was the same guy with you that he was with the ones he, you know, hurt.

Obviously, Bernie said.

They both drank their beers.

Try me, Bernie said.

What?

Try me on why writing is complicated for you.

Leah shook her head. I'm all mixed up, going in too many directions. I like too many things, and big things. I spend hours reading about how artists are given government funding in France or how there are children who were convicted of crimes in Pennsylvania and sentenced to life in prison. I just can't seem to find my subject, what I'm meant to write about. I'm a generalist, I guess.

Not a bad thing to be, Bernie said.

Isn't it? I had a professor in college once who gave me back a paper I wrote. On it, he had written, *This is exhaustive and exhausting*.

Asshole, Bernie said.

Yeah, Leah said. He was. And I never forgot that. Whenever I write something that's bad, I hear in my head: *exhaustive and exhausting*.

Bernie nodded, sipped her beer. I know what you mean, she said.

I did get a grant though, Leah said. From my program, for the summer. Pretty much carte blanche. I've been thinking it over a lot. And I'm actually glad you wanted to come tonight because I've been meaning to talk to you.

Oh? Bernie said.

It feels like words by themselves are no longer working for me, Leah said. I think I need images too, photography, but I don't know how to do it. I don't know how to take pictures in a way that means anything beyond just pointing my iPhone at something. But you do. Is there any way you would consider coming with me? I want to drive out of Philly and into Pennsylvania. I don't know where yet. I have some ideas.

I just want to drive around and look at things and I'd write things down and you'd photograph them. I'd pay for everything out of the grant—gas, film for you, whatever you need within reason. But I would need you to drive. I can't, as you know.

Hmm, Bernie said, in a tone that was impossible to read.

Why don't you go with Alex? Bernie said. She could get a camera from her job.

Impossible, Leah said. Alex would never go on a loose fishing expedition like that and she'd drive me crazy with her planning. Plus it's not about taking pictures to illustrate what I'm writing. I have a hunch that I don't have all the elements to do the thing I want to do. I only have half. I need a collaborator.

And you think that could be me?

I think so, yeah.

Bernie took a long drink of the last of her beer, tipping her head way back. Then she put the glass down on the bar and turned to Leah.

Why didn't you ever learn to drive?

New York City, Leah said. No need.

I guess, Bernie said. But plenty of city kids drive. Lucy Vincent drives.

I guess I never had any place I wanted to go before that required me to drive to it.

Bernie made a sound with her mouth then, a kind of snort.

Sounds snobby doesn't it? Leah said.

Bernie nodded. I don't know, Bernie said after a moment. I don't think I can do it. I'm sorry. I haven't been able to take a picture in a long time. I wouldn't want to get out there and freeze up again, waste your time, waste your money.

That's OK, Leah said. I understand.

In the car back to the house, Bernie didn't fidget at all. At the first red light, a cavalcade of dirt bikes and motorcycles roared by, and Bernie rolled her window down, turning her face away from Leah so she could watch them better.

VII.

THERE WAS TO BE A PARTY AT THE HOUSE THE NEXT NIGHT FOR Leah's birthday; she was turning twenty-five. Bernie had stayed up late numbing out her confusing jaunt with Leah and then waiting up for Violet who had never texted back. When she woke, a long housemates email chain was already clogging her inbox: questions of guests and what was a reasonable amount of alcohol to expect them to bring, quandaries of modern-day hospitality and manners.

When Bernie descended into the kitchen, the first floor was bustling with the energy of preparation. Alex was at the kitchen island sink washing dishes, Leah was vacuuming the dining room, and Meena was organizing the pantry. Violet was at the stove making eggs with their back turned, so Bernie lingered a little until Alex pulled the trash from its bin and went to take it outside.

Hey, Bernie said, to Violet's back.

Oh hey, Violet said after a while, turning and taking out their white wireless earbuds. They held a small dish; two orange yolks stared up at Bernie from it like large nipples.

I'm listening to this podcast about octopi and how they

can escape from captivity, Violet continued. Even down holes as tiny as drainpipes.

Cool, Bernie said.

Yeah, Violet said. They came around the kitchen island to where Bernie sat, and took one of the other stools. If I die, I'd like to come back as an octopus, they said. Oh, and sorry I never got back to you last night. I was out with my crew and Angela is going through a really tough thing with Patty so I stayed to keep her company. Hope you didn't wait up.

Nope, Bernie said. A lie. She had waited and waited.

Good, Violet said. They broke the yolk with their fork. Because Lucy Vincent and I talked and we're getting back together, they said. So the thing the other night.

Bernie pressed her palms together in her lap.

I just think it's best, Violet said. If we stay—friends?

Friends, Bernie said.

Great, Violet said. That's great.

They took a bite of eggs and chewed thoughtfully.

You want some? Violet asked, pointing at their plate.

Thanks, Bernie said. But no.

You sure? They're so fresh. The freshest. From the farmer's market.

I'm good, Bernie said.

Suit yourself, Violet said, and put their earbuds back in.

Leah was still vacuuming when Bernie walked through the dining room. They made eye contact and Leah stood up straight like she meant to turn off the vacuum and speak, but Bernie kept on walking. The house was a minefield it seemed; anywhere she stepped might activate something.

In Jaffa all afternoon, Bernie read a mystery about a detective looking for his long-lost brother and nursed a single drink.

Her phone rang several more times with more spam so she silenced it, and didn't return to the house until dark. There was no excuse for feeling hurt by Violet, she had known what would happen all along, and the one time they'd hooked up and the three times they'd hung out here at this very bar and then made out in the bathroom did not a promise make. But something had rolled over in Bernie to make room for Violet. No matter, it could roll back.

Bernie heard the party as soon as she turned onto their street. People of ambiguous gender in black jeans and puffy jackets that came only to their belt buckles, beanie hats and outdoorsy brown ankle boots stood on the sidewalk in front of the house in groups of twos and threes sipping from peeling tomato sauce jars and wiping their mouths with bandanas withdrawn from pants pockets. A tangle of bikes lined the iron railing all the way up the stairs.

On the porch, T-shirts cut off at the armhole revealed tattoos of bare-breasted ladies and tubes of lipstick. There was an unstable, shifting pile of bodies on the porch couch, mostly man bodies, judging by the length of the torsos and the size of the feet in sets of black lace-up boots. If this was true, it would be the most men Bernie had ever seen in or near the house at one time. The whole house and all the people in it, this neighborhood, suddenly seemed preposterous. Bernie wanted to laugh.

Inside the foyer, Bernie paused to take off her jacket. There were their five little metal mailboxes neatly stacked and labeled. Bernie touched her finger to the third one in the stack which was labeled with her name. It gave her a warm, grounded feeling, as if she were an upright citizen of this world.

People sat on or near the overstuffed couches in chairs

taken from the dining room table or they sat cross-legged on the floor. Fades and faux-hawks and baseball caps and trucker hats. A green streak and a rattail, a chin beard on a body with big breasts. The temperature was steamy, literally, the windows had condensed with steam. Some people had stripped down—flat chests and short shorts, cutoff T-shirts over sports bras revealing side boob and armpit hair. Bike helmets and panniers and black jean jackets were stuffed into the spaces between couch and radiator, chair and wall.

Bernie wore a white collared shirt buttoned to the clavicle (stains of blueberries on hem, stains of tea on sleeves), flat chest, no bra, silver ring on right hand, white sneakers. The world out there didn't particularly respond to this look, it was clear, and neither did the world in here. She moved, invisibly, through the crowd; no one turned to look after her. Was she more or less comfortable among queers than she was among everyone else? About the same, came the answer. But if she really listened, really paused, there was another answer, which was: less. The style. The discordance, the mismatching, the pride, the attracting of attention and the comfort in that attention, the physicality to dance, to fuck, to march. The physical in Bernie felt meant for other uses.

Bernie moved toward the kitchen, where she took up a handle of whiskey and poured it into one of the recycled glass jars drying in the rack. Meena stood at the island talking to a group of other buff queers about CrossFit but interrupted herself to introduce Bernie.

Hi, everyone said politely, then resumed talking about the combined effects on muscle mass of taking testosterone and working out multiple times a week. Their athleisure looked thick as butter.

Bernie turned and opened the freezer, extracted a few bulbous, misshapen cubes and clinked them into her glass.

Oh, said a very beautiful woman with long wavy black hair, that's where the ice has been hiding.

Bernie handed the tray to her and she whacked it a few times against the counter, then twisted the plastic to free the remaining cubes.

So you're the new housemate, she said.

Yup, Bernie said, refilling the ice tray, a virtuous thing she never did in normal life.

I'm Anya. Leah speaks so highly of you. She says you're a genius basically. An amazing photographer.

That's nice of her, Bernie said.

Well Leah's a snob, Anya said. So if she thinks so, it's probably true. I'm being mean now. Leah is a snob, but she's also not wrong. She's basically the only one in our cohort I listen to, and the smartest, and everyone knows it. She's the only one of us who was approved for summer research, I'm so mad. Where's my ten grand?

What are you saying about me? Leah said, coming into the room then. She was wearing a mint-green cowboy shirt with white pearl snap-up buttons, tucked into black jeans in a way that only reemphasized the charming bigness of her belly. Her hair looked freshly combed and her face looked extra pink.

Which direction is the hoedown? Anya said. Is there a rodeo in a town I don't know about?

Oh shush, Leah said. The shirt is a classic. And to Bernie: Anya is in my program at Penn.

Regrettably, yes, Anya said. Oh fuck, there's Clarence. I was never here.

Anya handed her glass to Leah and darted into the backyard.

Having fun at your party? Bernie asked.

Yes, Leah said. Took a sip of Anya's drink.

You?

Sure, Bernie said.

Someone called Leah's name from across the room, and it was Alex from a circle of couch sitters by the front window.

What? Leah hollered back.

Alex motioned Leah over vigorously, explaining that she needed Leah to come settle an argument.

Sorry, Leah said to Bernie, then made her way across the room to Alex. Bernie followed. Alex took Leah's arm and turned to a short, squat trans guy in a snapback.

Here, she said. Stop. Leah knows so much more about the two-state solution than you do.

Bernie leaned against a wall in the dining room for a while until a tall boy in delicate, perfectly round glasses looking at his phone squeezed by her and gave her a sharp look. She moved closer to where Leah and Alex were still talking with a group around the couches. Bernie watched them. Leah stood and Alex sat, nodding her head and her foot, as Leah talked. Every so often, Leah would create an opening in the conversation for Alex to elaborate on something she had said and Alex would slide into it.

A toast, someone said, when Leah had finally finished. The friend raised their tomato sauce jar and everyone else who could hear did too. To Leah, and her Alex and this wonderful community they have built here in this house.

Her Alex? Alex said, but she laughed and looked at Leah

and they clinked glasses and everyone cheered. And then Meena emerged from the kitchen with a cake and the music was cut and they all sang happy birthday. Meena cut the cake—gluten free—and served it on sugarcane compostable plates with bamboo utensils.

In the kitchen, Bernie poured herself another drink. The door to the back staircase was open and Jigger was sitting there on the stairs, perfectly upright with her two small front paws pressed against each other. She opened her eyes at Bernie then closed them again.

Hi Jigger, Bernie said, reaching to pet her. But Jigger turned and skittered up the stairs, her low pouch swaying to and fro. She paused outside Bernie's bedroom door, looking at Bernie, then turned and entered it.

In her room, sitting on her bed and petting Jigger's white belly, Bernie took out her phone. She had two notifications, a missed call and a voicemail from a 718 number. She sat on her bed and finished her drink, tilting the glass so far back that the ice cubes and watered-down whiskey fell on her nose and wet her shirt. More stains.

She played the voicemail.

Hi good evening, a man's voice said. *I apologize for the late hour of this call, but I've been trying many times to reach you with no success and it's become somewhat urgent that we speak. My name is Benjamin Pogden, I'm an attorney with the Jack Bowles Gallery in New York. I have some important business to discuss with you about the estate of the late Mr. Daniel Dunn. Please call—*

Thirty-seven minutes ago. Bernie pressed the CALLBACK button and the phone rang.

There was static on the line. A fire truck blared around the corner.

What? Bernie said. I can't hear you. Can you hear me?

Yes, the man said. I hear you quite clearly. I'll get right to it. Mr. Dunn left his archive of prints and negatives to you. Cameras also. His photographic estate.

What do you mean left?

In his will. He willed them to you.

What about his wife?

Ex-wife. No. Mr. Dunn's will was very specific. The photographs including back catalogue and negatives to Miss Bernie Abbott of Philadelphia.

Are you sure?

Quite.

Why me?

That I can't tell you. Generally people leave their archives to people they think will care, take care of them, that is. I know Daniel thought very highly of you. It's not uncommon for an artist to leave their estate to another artist. But in this case, considering everything that has happened to Daniel, the public scrutiny and so on. . . . Plus, as you know, he had no survivors, no children I mean. But I can't say exactly. We only read the will and carry it out, we don't—

OK. His negatives.

Yes, and his cameras. They are in the cabin where he was living. You'll need a vehicle.

I don't have a vehicle.

A pause. Alright. There are some options we can recommend. I can consult with my colleague about whether we can have them shipped, but that would trigger a whole other process, re shipping insurance and honestly I can't really recommend that option due to what I've heard about the state and organization of the materials. I'm told someone really must come in person and sort it out. Are you insured?

Her body was not even insured. No, Bernie said.

I see.

Also, what if I don't want them?

Come again?

What if I don't want to come, do that, don't want any of it. Can't you keep it?

Well, Benjamin sighed, paused. That is certainly your right. But the gallery, no. We decided some months ago that it was in the best interests of everyone involved to sever the relationship with Daniel's work. Given the reputational hit he's taken in recent months, and perhaps more importantly, the losses we have already suffered financially where his work is concerned. In these cases, we've found that it's best for someone who is willing to put in the time, to wait out the public storm, a true long-term steward, if you will. It is entirely possible that Daniel's work will retain some of its value and/or rise in value again, eventually, if his name could be remade somehow.

Is that what he wanted me to do? Bernie asked. Remake his name?

Again, I can't say, said Benjamin Pogden. But there is every reason to think that his work will stand the test of time, once all this ugliness has passed. But, if you are not interested in stewarding the materials, in that case, someone else would have to be found.

Like who?

Well, I can't say at this time. Again, the will specifies that you be the steward. But in the case that you can't or won't, the work would be at the disposition of whoever takes possession of the Pennsylvania cabin.

And who would that be?

That would be um, Benjamin Pogden paused. The Mifflin County Commissioners, he read, to be sold and the profits used for arts education in the county.

Oh, Bernie said.

Disposed of, Benjamin Pogden said. Most likely.

DOWNSTAIRS, THE PARTY HAD TAKEN a turn. In the kitchen, people were drunker, leaning farther over each other and letting their heads loll back and rest against the brick wall. Someone knocked over a green Stella Artois bottle perilously close to where Jigger had been sitting on the counter, and she jumped onto the floor in displeasure.

Bernie put a handful of ice in a new glass and tipped the handle of whiskey upside down.

Whoa, said a large boy in a very tiny hat. Save some for me.

What's it to you? Bernie said. What do you care?

Jeez, the boy said, holding up both of his palms.

The living room was dark now except for the string lights that were draped around the window casings and pulsing, the light seemingly thrown from one bulb to the next. The music had been turned up, a low electronic beat. A few people were dancing, their ponytails bobbing and thigh tattoos winking. Violet was there, and Lucy Vincent, and they were dancing together, close. Meena and Alex were dancing, though Alex was looking over her shoulder, perhaps for Leah, who was not there.

The music changed to a dancy anthem, a song that seemed to skip like a strobe light. *Somebody said you got a new friend, does she love you better than I can.* My jam, my jam, several voices said, standing up from the couches and lifting their faces to the ceiling and pumping their arms, and then most people in the room were dancing, weed smoke hanging thick in the air despite the draft coming in through the now-open front window.

Violet and Lucy Vincent made out as they danced, a difficult feat considering the height difference. Violet had their head turned all the way down and Lucy Vincent had hers turned all the way up and Violet was gripping Lucy Vincent's head with a hand on each of her small pink cheeks. Even Lucy Vincent's lips were reaching up for Violet, extended like a duck's. Then Lucy Vincent pulled away and wiped the sweat from her forehead with the edge of her gray pleated skirt and laughed. Violet looked at her, watched her. Didn't laugh.

Bernie danced too then, what else was there to do. She danced mostly from her elbows, jutting them out into the space, then extending her arms all the way and wiggling her fingertips as she twirled. At first people laughed and gave her room, but when she started to twist her body with great energy, letting her arms thwap against her body and then against a crowd of femmes with golden barrettes in their dark hair one of whose glass of red wine got spilled, the crowd changed. The people moved away from Bernie and clustered elsewhere, turning their heads over their shoulders to whisper.

There was always a moment, Bernie thought, when they turned away from you. But if you could stay still, right where you were, much could be revealed. What was revealed was that her teacher was dead and his poisoned work was hers now, though it had always been hers actually, his poison had entered her and was living there; Leah had said as much. Could Daniel Dunn still take photographs where he was now, in that other place? Doubtful, Bernie thought. She took her phone out of her pocket to take a picture, but it was useless—too dark; only the multicolored string lights gave any contrast.

The music was changing, had changed. Bops from the early aughts, then again to sadder, slower ballads. Eventually, Bernie sat down on the dance floor, then lay down on it, first on her back but then on her side, moving her hand along the grooves in the hardwood floor. She found one of the girls' gold barrettes and a quarter and put these things in her shirt pocket. It felt good to have her cheek on the floor. It felt good to feel the vibrations of other people's feet in her face.

Hey hey, a voice said, a hand shaking her shoulder gently. Leah shook her again. Let's go get you some air.

No, Bernie said. I'm good here.

But there was Leah's hand. Small nails, rounded pudgy fingers with little pockets of luxurious fat stuffed under the skin between the joints. Bernie took it. They were through the foyer and onto the porch and people were looking as they went and then they were sitting on the porch couch. Bernie rubbed her eyes with her fingers, making them burn. She looked down at her hands and saw that they carried dirt and lint and bits of Jigger's fur.

Leah sat far away from Bernie, all the way at the other end of the couch.

I'm good, Bernie said. I'm fine.

You're not, Leah said. You're crying. She had one leg up on the couch at an angle and the other on the ground. She took off her glasses and then her little dark eyes were looking at Bernie.

I'm not, Bernie said.

You are.

It's just my eyes, Bernie said. They sting.

Bernie was aware that their porch was exposed, visible to anyone standing on a porch in either direction, left or right. Bernie looked both ways, but no one was out or if they were, it was too dark to see them. Then, somewhere down the porch line, someone stepped out. They turned on a bright light and a fan whirred on too. Bernie closed her eyes which relieved the burn. Bernie covered her eyes with her hands.

I'll go, Bernie said.

What? Leah said.

I'll go with you on your trip. I'll drive you.

You're drunk, Leah said.

Correct, Bernie said. But even so. I'll go. And I'll try to take some pictures. I'll bring the camera and all my shit. But on two conditions.

Go ahead, Leah said.

First, I would need you to cover my portion of the rent for next month. I'm already tight for this month.

Done.

OK, thanks. Second, I need to stop at Daniel Dunn's house. I don't know for how long. A day or maybe two.

She told Leah of Benjamin Pogden's call and what was now possibly required of her.

Maybe this is just what you need, Leah said.

I doubt that very much, Bernie said.

He's dead, Leah went on. The slate is wiped blank. The slate belongs to you, now. Literally.

Where do you want to go? Bernie asked.

I don't know, Leah said. We could decide. We could go get

breakfast tomorrow at the coffee shop and look at the map and decide.

If this were a different kind of story, I might tell you that there is only a certain amount of time a living person can remain asleep and/or suffering before they wake up and change their life, and that for Bernie if it hadn't been Leah wanting to be driven out of Philadelphia it would have been some other thing that knocked against Dunn's death to produce action. People roll toward happiness, eventually, goes the theory.

But if you want to know how long I really think a person can stay asleep, the answer is: a whole life. People do it all the time. I believe it was Leah who changed everything for Bernie in this moment. I believe in what happens on the smallest possible human scale, in the specific atoms that flow between two specific people and produce a particularly juicy—even lifesaving—force field. Leah knew this, I think, even as she pretended not to know it.

Bernie opened her eyes.

Leah's face. Leah's soft round nose, her plump throat, her shirt that was open for three buttons and then closed the rest of the way down. Leah who was waiting for Bernie's reply.

OK, Bernie thought. Why not me? Was there a reason Bernie should not get the things other people seemed to get all the time, without even trying—basic things like a car to drive and someone to sit in the passenger seat? Why not why not why not? Bernie thought. She could think of no reason.

PART 2

I.

I REMEMBER THE SPRING OF 2018 WHEN BERNIE AND LEAH drove out of Philadelphia in Alex's car as simmering, the season in which the grenade had landed, smoking and strange, but had not yet exploded. At that time, I could see some cracks but I thought they were delicate, spidery fissures, moving slowly enough to be contained. I did not yet know that the grenade had exploded a long, long time ago and that it was already causing deep, wide chasms into which big chunks of rock were falling. The water was already boiling. I just wasn't in the pot yet.

Bernie and Leah left in May, on the same day as Meghan's royal wedding to Harry and they saw America as it was after *Minnesota Police Stop Ends in Black Man's Death; Aftermath Is Live-Streamed* and after *He's Hired, Trump Reverses Predictions, Is Elected President* and after *Far-Right Groups Surge into National View in Charlottesville; 1 Dead as Car Charges into Crowds* and after *From Aggressive Overtures to Sexual Assault: Harvey Weinstein's Accusers Tell Their Stories* and after *The Family That Built an Empire of Pain: The Sackler Dynasty's Ruthless Marketing of Painkillers Has Generated Billions of*

Dollars—and Millions of Addicts and after *Fox News Host Apologizes for Mocking Florida School Shooting Survivor as Uproar Grows* and after, just for some relief, *The Ubiquitous Lettuce That Could Kill You, Romaine Is a "No-Go"* Consumer Reports *Says*.

But put Bernie and Leah on the road and bring them back just before *Trump Administration Opens Tent City Near El Paso to House Separated Immigrant Children,* before *"Indelible in the Hippocampus Is the Laughter": Kavanaugh Confirmed to Supreme Court Despite Credible Blasey Ford Testimony* and before *"They Showed His Photo, and My Stomach Just Dropped": Neighbors Recall Antisemitic Synagogue Shooter Who Massacred 11 as Loner* and before *At Least 9 Dead in California Wildfires as Tens of Thousands Flee Homes* and before *We Are Past "The Point of No Return" When It Comes to Climate Change* and before *Senators Demand CEO Mark Zuckerberg Answer Questions After Whistleblower's Revelations at Hearing* and before *New Coronavirus Can Cause Pneumonia-Like Infection and Sicken Otherwise Healthy People, Studies Show* and before *From "I Want to Touch the World" to "I Can't Breathe": George Floyd's Death in Police Custody Sets Off Protests of Tens of Thousands in Minneapolis, New York, Los Angeles, Philadelphia, Atlanta, Chicago and Others* and before *The End of the Line for Trumpland Is a Landscaping Shop in North Philly* (also for relief) and before *All Eyes on Crucial Swing State Pennsylvania as Volunteers Count Votes Inside Philadelphia Convention Center Despite Trump Threats* and before *In 6-to-3 Ruling, Supreme Court Ends Nearly 50 Years of Abortion Rights* and before so many other things that I did not know we would no longer need to imagine. In other words, they went right in the middle.

It's impossible to say now with any certainty if I know what I know about Bernie and Leah from those early moments of leaping inside their house or from all the articles and press that would be written about them later, or from some combination of the two. I suppose this is a thing that happens more and more often now that so much is written and freely available about people who are not even that famous. A person can do any little thing these days and it will be written about, whereas I remember when The Housemate's third book was published, she could not get anyone to write about it for love or money. To be fair, it was an odd book, composed of transcriptions of the interviews she did for the small-town carnival project. It was *good* though—first-rate even. I have seen, by contrast, so many tenth-rate artists get rich and famous who never had what she had, but that is another story.

THE PLAN, MORE OR LESS, which Bernie and Leah worked out at the anarchist coffee shop over black bean burritos on the day I first saw them: They would go to Daniel Dunn's house a few hours away and collect what needed collecting—Bernie said she guessed it would be mostly his cameras, and whatever negatives, contact sheets, prints, and other materials were in good enough shape to move. Then they would drive as far south and west as they could before having to turn around and come back north and east. It would be a sort of loop, the size and exact destinations unknown and to be determined, taking as many small roads as possible (more to see) and staying in cheap motels whenever they got tired.

After the coffee shop, Leah returned to the house to find Alex, whose car, and possibly feelings, were an important piece of the puzzle. Standing in the third-floor hallway, Leah could tell that it was Alex in the shower because of the way the water ran—hard—and the amount of steam escaping from under the bathroom door—so much.

Leah lay down on Alex's bed—neatly made of course, with its ugly but comfortable quilt. Jigger joined too, letting out a powerful chirp as she leapt onto the bed and another as she trotted up to the pillow and headbutted Leah in the eye.

Purr purr purr, Jigger said, flopping onto her side, then raising her head to make sure Leah was paying attention. As Leah massaged the sweet skin of Jigger's primordial pouch, she looked around Alex's room, at Alex's white plastic lamp and Alex's desk with its line of folders and binders. Who even used those anymore? Alex did. Also at the mantel of the boarded-up fireplace where Alex kept her collection of little owls—plastic, glass, stone.

It hurt a little, this room. Always had. Alex had once tried to break up with Leah in this room, a year ago or so now, when Leah had first moved in.

Is there someone else? Leah had asked then.

In a way, Alex said.

Who?

My work. It is my primary relationship. I'm not sure I'm good at romantic relationships. I always thought I'd be on my own forever, and maybe I was right.

Who *is* good at romantic relationships? Leah said.

Maybe, Alex said. Then, when pressed, she'd taken the breakup back, saying she'd just gotten scared because of the newness of cohabitation. It was good they were living with other people instead of just the two of them, Alex said, as she had seen dyadic living destroy so many couples.

HI JIGGER, ALEX SAID WHEN she came in now, in small cotton shorts and a loose black T-shirt that was stretched out around the neck. Her hair was wet and dark and hung to her exposed clavicles. Alex was the girl, would always be the girl to Leah, the girl who knocked on Leah's door one night when they were only twenty years old, in their second decade of life but having racked up no years within it yet, asking if Leah was alright, saying that she had heard Leah crying through the wall and was everything OK? The girl who showed Leah documentaries and sent her articles. On the occasion of their first sex—Leah was a virgin whereas Alex had had sex with her high school girlfriend—Alex had made Leah get dressed up and take a picture under a cherry blossom tree before going to an Italian restaurant off campus. Petals had fallen in their hair and on their faces.

Leah kept that picture in the drawer of the nightstand in her room downstairs, her and Alex with their eyes closed, Leah's arm wrapped around Alex's waist, the petals streaming down their skin like ridiculous, clownish tears.

At Alex's voice, Jigger opened her eyes and hopped off the bed, rubbing her raised back against Alex's still-wet legs.

You greet the cat but you don't greet me? Leah said.

Hi to you too, Alex said.

Leah told Alex the plan with Bernie. If that's OK with you, Leah said. I'll pay you for mileage.

OK, Alex said. You can take the car. Have fun.

That's it?

What do you want me to say? I know you've been unhappy. I didn't know if it was school or the paper or something else. I think this will be good for you. Productive. A change of scenery. I know you and Bernie get energy from each other, you're interested in her work. I think it's great.

She's interested in my work too, Leah said. And what will you do while I'm gone?

Oh I've got plenty on my plate, Alex said. That series on the teachers' union is taking forever and the piece on the concession workers' strike at the stadium has issues and Tara wants me to find a second source who will speak on the record which no one wants to do. I'm swamped actually, it's good timing.

Leah felt that stab that came when someone said something that was good, quite close to being enough, but not quite enough.

But won't you miss me? Leah said.

Oh Leah, Alex said, sitting on the edge of the bed and taking one of Leah's hands in between hers.

Leah began to cry and Alex held her. Leah felt the tops of Alex's rounded shoulders and then the curve of her waist and stomach through her T-shirt. Leah felt. Leah felt every inch of her own wide, wide body. More body, more problems. More body, more nerves, more surface area, more square footage, more receptors, more follicles, more folds, more places to get caught and to get expressed.

Leah liked, in sex, to be kissed on the neck and along the tops of her breasts, but no farther down—no suckling was appreciated. If she had top surgery the tops of her breasts would remain the same, retain the same skin. It was this top skin that Leah felt connected to but not the rest. She had pondered top surgery several times and it was pleasurable to ponder but she'd always decided that for her, it was not absolutely necessary. Yet it would have been nice, even very nice, to go to a beach or a lake and wear synthetic fabrics on only the bottom half of her body, while she felt the air on the skin of her whole top half.

Leah lay down and Alex curled around her back, hand submerged platonically just below the waistband of Leah's sweatpants. Platonic—Leah had been reading about the word lately. Apparently it did not mean what Leah had thought (feared) it meant—chaste, the absence of passion—but rather came from the actual guy, Plato himself. She was too lazy to fetch her college copy of the *Symposium* from the box in the basement—molded, almost certainly—but the internet had given a thousand muddled interpretations. "Platonic love," offered Wikipedia, "concerns rising through levels of closeness to wisdom and true beauty, from carnal attraction to individual bodies to attraction to souls, and eventually, union with the truth.[clarification needed]" In essence, it seemed that platonic love was a different kind of love than sexual and/or romantic love, but not necessarily worse or lesser than. Possibly even better. Or higher.

Alex was soon asleep. Leah's phone vibrated with an email, from her cohort mate, Anya.

Hi friend, Wanted to drop you a quick note to say how excited I am about your summer research, which I heard you're calling "Changing Pennsylvania." Anyway, be safe. Keep your ears open. Have a good trip. Like Jack Kerouac says, "Nothing behind me, everything ahead of me, as is ever so on the road."

Jack Kerouac! What a throwback. Like so many sensitive and pretentious children before her, Leah had once had a poster of this white man on her bedroom wall, with his face and a long quote about how the only people for him were the mad ones. What had become of that poster? What had become of Kerouac? Leah googled it. "In 1969, at age 47, Kerouac died from an abdominal hemorrhage caused by a lifetime of heavy drinking." His estate had gone to his mother.

BERNIE AND LEAH LEFT THE house on a Saturday. The interior of Alex's station wagon was dirty, the back seat carpet stained with cola or coffee though it had been vacuumed smooth of crumbs and crud. The whole car felt heavy and sunken and so close to the ground.

Leaning into the trunk, Leah picked up Bernie's big green duffel bag, stuffed to the point of hardness, turned it horizontally, and pushed it back to make room for a sleeping bag and camping stove.

Aren't we staying in motels? Bernie asked, turning around in the driver's seat.

Is she making you take everything and the kitchen sink? Alex asked Bernie through the open passenger-side window. All the housemates had come to see them off.

She does this to me every time we go anywhere, Alex said. She came and gave Leah a hug and a kiss.

Aw, Violet said. I feel like we're women on the prairie bidding our menfolk goodbye as they go off to hunt bison or something.

Where did that come from? Meena asked.

I don't know, Violet said. *Oregon Trail,* I guess. Lucy Vincent has been playing a new version of it and has been sending me screenshots.

At the mention of Lucy Vincent, Leah saw Bernie look down at her hands and crack her knuckles.

Violet leaned into the car then, resting their forearms on the passenger window ledge.

Well Bernie, they said. I hope you find what you're looking for. At that guy's house.

I don't know what I'm looking for, Bernie said. I have no idea what's there.

Even better, Violet said, stepping back to make room for Leah.

Leah opened the car door and got in, and Alex crossed her thin arms over her chest, hugging herself against the wind.

I love you, Alex said, which was good of her to say. She could go months without saying it and Leah sometimes had to remind her.

I love you too, Leah said.

Oh go on already, Violet said, pointing down the street.

IT WAS ONLY A FEW minutes until they were outside city limits which was one of Leah's favorite things about Philadelphia—how easy it was to leave it.

Bernie drove the way she lived: completely distracted and completely attentive at the same time. She sat slouched back, her skinny left knee folded up like a cricket's by the door's plastic pocket and her right leg free and extended. Her left hand stayed wrapped tightly around the thin leather steering wheel but her right hand could go anywhere—to her forehead to scratch at a small pimple at her hairline or to the console where she had stashed a can of Sprite—even when she was changing lanes to pass. She wore a faded black T-shirt with the outline of a yellow Ferris wheel on it. Her hair was parted on the side closest to Leah, and her short blunt bangs kept getting blown back toward the corners of her forehead.

The road was divided by a grassy median and bordered on both sides by low beige storefronts grouped together into small shopping plazas—THE OLD VILLAGE SHOPPES in fake stone—or standalone buildings with names full of initials—H & K FLOORING, B & I ROOFING. Developments with names in gold script—THE CHESTERFIELD, OAK GROVE. Political signs dotted every bit of grass—blue, red, red, blue, blue, red. It was not clear if the red signs were gloating about the catastrophic election of two years ago or gearing up for the midterms, about which Leah, if she was being honest, was only vaguely informed.

They had discussed their potential soundtrack and concluded that neither Bernie nor Leah cared enough to take on the task of curating one for the trip. Leah pressed one of the old stereo's round buttons and the radio came on, a pop station that said it was the number one destination for everything hot. Leah was just about to make a snide comment about the size of this claim when Janelle Monáe's "Make Me Feel" came on. There was something legitimately hot about the clicking of those tongues.

The wind felt warm and good on Leah's face and on her body as the song played. Winter was over; it was really spring now. She breathed in deeply and felt that her body could hold more breath than it had been able to in a long time. She breathed and breathed.

It was forty-five minutes before they saw their first horse and buggy, but after that they saw one every few miles. The roadside became full of signs offering AMISH GOODS, THE REAL

AMISH EXPERIENCE. A Mennonite woman in a white mesh hair covering stood by the side of the road waiting for a bus, a trash bag slung over her shoulder.

As they approached a buggy to pass, it slowed and veered off onto the right shoulder and Leah took out her phone to take a picture.

Don't, Bernie said, just as Leah pressed the button, capturing a man in a black suit and long beard driving the buggy and a woman sitting next to him in a gray dress. The woman was turning her face away and covering it with her hand.

They don't like having their picture taken, Bernie said.

Sorry, Leah said. But why did she cover her face? It's like a sin or something?

Second commandment baby, Bernie said. Thou shalt not turn thyself into a graven image. They think that being photographed promotes pride, is dangerous to the community. We had lots of Amish kids in my town.

I guess it does, Leah said. Promote pride, I mean. In the sense that it makes you aware of what you look like? But isn't it also just showing you what you look like? It's not like the camera invents it, the camera just shows what's already there. Seems like there's plenty of ways to have pride without photographs. Mirrors, for example.

Sometimes the camera invents, Bernie said. A lot of them don't have mirrors either.

They entered Paradise. Paradise Grocery. Paradise Sneaker Emporium. They drove through a four-way stop and Leah saw someone standing there, far away down the straight road. It was an Amish boy, wearing the big black hat and the black suspenders but in miniature, and he had his thumb stuck out.

Look, Bernie said. Let's stop for him.

No way, Leah said.

It's alright, Bernie said. This is what you do in the country. I used to do it all the time growing up.

Haven't you ever watched a road movie? Leah said. The hitchhiker always kills the driver.

I thought it was the driver who killed the hitchhiker.

There are those movies too.

So if the hitchhiker is afraid of us and we're afraid of the hitchhiker, Bernie said, shouldn't everyone's fear just cancel each other's out?

It should, Leah said, but it doesn't. If the hitchhiker is a woman and the driver is a man, the driver kills the hitchhiker. If the driver is a woman and the hitchhiker is a man, then the hitchhiker kills the driver.

What if the driver is nonbinary? Bernie asked, already easing the car onto the shoulder.

It was not so much physical safety Leah was worried about but something else. Contact. Exposure. They had left the bubble of the neighborhood and gone somewhere else.

Leah watched in the side mirror as the boy hitched up his pants and started to run.

Bernie rolled down Leah's window. He was going to Lancaster, which was on their way, and added no time. Leah could see this plainly for herself on the map on her phone.

You guys making a movie? The boy asked when he was settled into the seat behind Bernie.

No, Bernie said. Why?

Because of that, the boy said. He pointed to Bernie's tripod and big camera bag which sat on the seat and in the footwell behind Leah. We get a lot of people coming through to make movies about us.

We were just talking about this, Bernie said. I was saying that your community does not like that.

Yes and no, the boy said. There was a man on my street who spoke to a guy from Europe who came here to make a movie about us last year and they shunned him for months and made him sit separately in church. But that was because he showed his face and spoke directly to the camera so there was no way for him to deny it. Also he told the camera secrets people were keeping, like what the bishops were getting up to with the unmarried girls in early morning bible study. But there are many ways to do it and deny it. If you don't show your face for example. Or if you turn your face away but nonetheless give the camera your best angles, like my friend Polly did when she got on the cover of a magazine last year when she was on vacation in Florida. She got a husband out of that and even briefly appeared on *Ellen,* sitting behind a screen of course.

Leah looked over at Bernie, but Bernie had one eye on the two-lane road in front of her and one on the boy behind her.

What do you think makes people so interested in you? Bernie asked.

Oh plenty, said the boy. It's Saturday. So people did their errands and now they're heading to the Smorgasbord. You can eat and smoke and hang out there. That's where I'm going, if you would be so kind.

Certainly, Bernie said. You're allowed to smoke?

Well, you say you're going to the bathroom but instead you go outside through the parking lot and stand behind the pillars. Oh and there's a kid who stands at the back entrance to the Smorgasbord selling black T-shirts from packs he buys at Walmart. You buy one, put it on over your clothes so it absorbs the smell, do your stuff, toss the shirt in the trash can on your way back in.

Leah was interested now, despite herself. She felt her riled-up meter ease down from a nine to a six.

What else happens there? Leah asked.

Well you eat there, obviously, the boy said. And I have a girlfriend who works there, in the kitchen. She's English, like you all. So I go to see her. I don't take part in the other shenanigans anymore, the action that other boys will do behind the pillars. But not me. My heart belongs to Alisha.

How old are you? Leah asked.

Thirteen. But I'll be fourteen in August.

Will you go on Rumspringa soon?

That's not really a thing, the boy said. We don't get Rumspringa. Everything counts, there's no time off. You just decide.

And what will you decide?

Oh to stay, obviously.

Why?

My parents are pretty cool. They don't care if I go to the Smorgasbord for example, or they wouldn't, if they knew. I just tell them I'm going to town to do the shopping and they get it. They think I walk though, that is the only lie I tell. Sometimes my sister and her husband will take me in their buggy to Lancaster, but today my sister is sick. She's having another kid, even though she doesn't want to, so she's not feeling well. But anyway, one time she and her husband took me to the small mall near Lancaster, we'll pass it here in a minute, and I got to talking to this kid, about my age, English, who was there for sneakers too, but by himself. He couldn't decide which sneakers to get, he had a black sneaker on his left foot and a white sneaker on his right foot and had no one to ask which one looked better so he asked me. I said the black one. And my sister came over then and said, Hi and who is your friend? And he said his name and asked her which sneaker she liked better and she said the black one just like I said and she smiled at me and touched the top of my head like she does when she loves me and it kind of hit me then how lonely it would be out there. His mom had just given him money and said, go.

Leah turned around to look at the boy. He wasn't wearing his seatbelt and one of his shirttails had come untucked from his pants.

Is everyone white? Leah asked.

White top? No.

No, white like race. Do you have to be white to be in your community?

Yeah pretty much, the boy said. Alisha is Black though.

Is that rare? Interracial dating? Even being friends?

No, not really. We wouldn't talk about it at church, or I guess with my grandparents, but everywhere else.

Why not?

My grandparents live in a different world from me, from my parents even.

What world do your parents live in?

The boy thought for a minute.

There's like three worlds, he said at last. The one that's in the books about us, that makes people want to make movies about us. That's the one my grandparents live in. Then there's the one that is our actual lives now, where me and my sister and her husband and my parents live. And then there is the one that is out there where you all live.

Which two are closer together? Bernie asked then. Your life and your grandparents' lives or your life and our lives?

It was a good question and Leah wished she had been the one to ask it. She waited for the boy's answer.

I don't know, the boy said. Maybe they are the same distance away.

The boy gave directions then rolled down his window at the turn off the divided highway. The Smorgasbord turned out to be a whole complex of many stores—grocery store, feed store, holy book store—all linked by parking lots.

Well thanks a lot, the boy said, when he was out of the car and standing by Bernie's open window, the red-awninged entrance behind him.

Hey, he said. You wanna take my picture?

That's OK, Bernie said. We're on our way somewhere else—

Come on, the boy said. I'd like it if you did. I'll turn away so I can deny it. But no one ever has before.

Bernie rubbed her eyes with the tips of her fingers and Leah watched the way the skin under her eyes stretched and purpled with the movements of her hands.

OK, Bernie said. Why not.

WHERE DOES A MEMORY COME from and who does it belong to? The Housemate used to say she was convinced that a memory isn't so much a recollection of a thing that has already happened so much as a dream of what has yet to come. I never believed her until this moment, until I was with Leah as she watched Bernie unzip the big camera bag, secure the camera to the tripod, and point its big face toward the Amish boy's back as he posed in front of the wide Smorgasbord complex, his hip popped out at a jaunty angle. As Leah watched Bernie, she felt something, knew something brand-new. It was Bernie's, unmistakably, and it was as sudden and clear as if Bernie had handed it to her.

On that cold night when Daniel Dunn had thrown the rock through Bernie's dorm window, he had taken Bernie back to his house on campus. He'd walked Bernie down his dark tree-lined street, up his steep driveway, and around the back of his house to the garage. Unzipped the familiar bag, hoisted the camera out from its soft center compartment.

This camera is called an Arca-Swiss Discovery, he said, his earlier drunkenness seemingly evaporated. Everything that the camera you've been using does automatically, must now, with this camera, be done by hand or by eye. This is the lens and the lens board, he said, reaching around and pointing to the front of the camera. This is the bellows, he said, pointing to the accordionlike folds. This is how you change the angle of the camera up or down, he said, indicating first one set of knobs then another. This is how you move it forward along the rail or backward, to get closer or farther away. You'll need a light meter to know the exposure speed and a loupe to get the focus right.

He pointed to the gridded square of glass inches from his chest. This is the ground glass, he said. You look through it to see what you are photographing. It will look upside down and backward, he said, because it is. You'll get used to it. Soon you won't be able to work any other way. In return, this camera will give you better pictures than any you've ever known.

Around sunrise, Daniel Dunn and Bernie drove out of town, across the wide valley floor and up a mountain. They parked in a wide turnout and walked, equipment in tow, through a yellowed, trampled grassy field. Above them, fat power lines bounced and swayed. The sun felt immense, thick, rippling across the underbrush and outcroppings of rock that barely pushed through the surface, like new teeth trying to be born. When they came to the edge of a sheer cliff, Bernie knew where they were: the Highlands, an outcropping of rocks created by the Juniata River. This river, Bernie knew from high school, had been what once separated the settlements of the Scotch Irish from Native American land. Thousands of people, mostly Indigenous, had died here. Below the rocks where they stood was a sharp drop-off that led down to the river and the train tracks below and back to town. Behind them, to the west, were the ridges of mountains that ran all the way through Pennsylvania and on into Ohio.

Daniel Dunn stopped, put the camera bag down. He had Bernie set up the camera on her own, calling corrections and pointing at knobs and holding out his hand periodically for the cloth and the loupe to go under and check her work. What she saw was luminous, green, upside down. She could make no sense of it. Each time she could sort of grasp what the picture looked like on the ground glass and got the focus down well enough to ask for the film holder, she messed it up, knocking into the camera with her shoulder when reaching for a knob or nudging her knee against the tripod when cocking the shutter.

Calm down, Daniel Dunn said. Or you'll make more mistakes.

She did. She made every possible mistake, ruined nearly every piece of film. But she did take one picture successfully—

a tight frame of a rock, sliced by a mark of pink graffiti, the wide valley floor slightly blurred behind it.

Dunn came over, picked up the camera and tripod, and moved it back a few feet.

Why? Bernie said.

It's figuring out which height makes the photo more active, not so boring, he said. Never mind, he said. You'll just have to wait.

For what? Bernie asked.

For the light to change, for it to be not just that bright white behind the mound, that's dull. It needs to get more delineated, less flat. When there's no clouds like this, it's almost impossible.

Bernie sat down on a rock.

A good photograph with this kind of camera is not about capturing a moment, Daniel Dunn said. It's about making one.

So it's not objective?

Fuck, Bernie, Daniel Dunn said. No photography is objective but this kind really is not. You're making all these little decisions. You have so much control with a camera like this, so much range, the ground glass offers even more than the human eye can see. And with everything upside down, you're off-balance, seeing everything in a new way. You're creating a world that is not the one you see.

I thought you said the goal was for it to look exactly like life? Bernie said, from her rock.

I take it back, Daniel Dunn said. The goal is to make a new world that is more like life than life is.

AT THE SOUND OF THE shutter's tiny click that day in Amish country, Bernie stood up and, Leah felt, saw her for the first time. To be seen, really seen, by Bernie Abbott felt forceful and overwhelming, like being witnessed by a whole crowd, a whole audience yelling *Yeah!* and *Atta girl!* and *Brava!* Leah returned Bernie's look, trying to communicate all that she had remembered of Bernie's life and something more: It was no longer then. It was now.

II.

I SHOULD SAY AT THIS POINT THAT THERE WILL BE GAPS IN MY story of Bernie and Leah, times when they fell off the map and I lost them. I think these gaps are only natural when you are telling a story that is not about you. The Housemate used to say that when she was writing and she got stuck, she would pick from among her favorites: food scenes, sex scenes, party scenes. Trust the body, she was always telling me.

Trust it to do what? I would ask.

What she may have meant is that there is no way to understand Leah's obsession with knowing without also understanding her family's obsession with her body. The two things are knotted together like a sweater knit simultaneously with two different colors of yarn—every stitch touches both threads.

In the apartment where Leah grew up, what they lacked in air-conditioning—for gentiles!—they made up for in knowledge which, according to Leah's father, would protect you. From what? From a second Shoah, from the pogroms, from poverty, from difference, from weakness, from loneliness, and definitely from fatness.

In her parents' bedroom on the surface of his dark wooden

mission-style desk, Leah's father kept a photograph of himself as a little boy in short pants as a reminder to himself to never be that fat and dispossessed again. When he turned thirteen, his mother had begun taking him to a doctor on Grand Army Plaza to get injections of speed, but one summer day the doctor's office was unexpectedly closed and so she took him to the big library instead. The little branch he usually went to in Brighton Beach had just a few books, almost all in Yiddish. But here, at the big library, the books were in English, and they had the Johns—Dos Passos and Cheever—displayed out on a table for the Fourth of July; Hemingway too.

It was here that Leah's father learned what books could do to your mind and also to your life. He saw on the flaps of these books that their writing had won these men awards, prestige, money, love, respect, women. These writers had all gone to elite private high schools or boarding schools where they had played tennis or water polo and all had wives with names like Mary and Martha and Pauline.

It took Leah's father more years than he would have liked to complete the journey from Brighton Beach to Manhattan, from shtetl Jew to bagel Jew, from his given name of Mandelbaum to his chosen name of McCausland, from plastic beach chairs to wooden Adirondack chairs, from the ocean to the swimming pool, and from punchball to tennis, but he made it eventually, even marrying a Mary and having two children—a boy and a girl—and so he felt that in offering these achievements to his offspring as their starting point in life, as a parent, he had already succeeded.

You're from New York, Leah's father would say to her and her older brother, Evan. So you know.

Know what? Leah would ask.

Everything.

But, it seemed, simply living in Manhattan was not enough for Leah's father; he wanted to achieve more than location. An estate lawyer, he was constantly angling for the better office, the better view. In his last and longest book-filled office in midtown which Leah visited exactly once per year on Take Your Daughter to Work Day, he had a shelf that held two ceramic tiles. TRUST NO SYSTEM OF THOUGHT was etched on one; on the other, just the word RIGOR.

When Leah entered high school, he insisted, as he had done with Evan, that she switch from her laissez-faire downtown public school to an Upper East Side prep school. The motto of this new school was "Go forth unafraid," and she had to take three trains each morning to get there. Every morning and afternoon, a line of black town cars would form in front of the school's double doors, snaking down the block and around the corner, waiting for their tiny child or adolescent passengers. All the girls had rectangles of shiny blown-out hair, zippered Kate Spade pencil cases, two-toned bags which were rumored to have originated in Paris, and fur-lined boots that plumped a girl's ankles into bear paws even in summer. A brief visual: give Leah a tight ponytail made tighter by hair clips inserted behind each ear which she believed had a slimming effect on her face, a green JanSport backpack, and a lot of polar fleece.

For gym, Leah's school bussed the students to an island that also held a prison, the only place nearby where a child could run an uninterrupted mile. As Leah huffed and puffed, she could see the incarcerated people off in the distance, also running. Once, in a relay race, Leah was on a team with the other kids who had not been at the school since kindergarten—

the Asian girls, the Black girls, the other weird white girls—and when her team lost, the other team sang them a little song: *That's alright, that's OK, you're gonna pump our gas someday*. The song was from a movie that had come out a few years before, but nonetheless, their meaning was clear.

The school had two English teachers—Ms. R who taught creative writing and had published a novel and had two daughters, girls half her height but twice her width whom she was parenting alone and who sometimes shared the table in the English teachers' lounge with Leah in the afternoons after school, and Ms. L who taught American literature and drama and wore ankle-length dark green velvet dresses trimmed with lace at the cuffs and neck. Her laugh—Leah loved when another teacher said something funny so she could hear it—caused her face to contract cheerfully around her nose, and she lisped slightly, heavy on the Ts and Hs. She was dry, sarcastic, rolled her eyes, employed straight-fingered air quotes, and used the word *quality* a lot, as in *a shiny quality* or *a quality of the terrible*.

From the vantage point of the table in the English teachers' lounge, Leah watched Ms. L and Ms. R type on their computers, underline and make notes in books, debate the meaning of words and the meaning of news, arrive in the morning with cups of purchased coffee, and leave in the afternoon to pick up daughters and groceries and daffodils wrapped in brown paper.

Leah's writing always returned from Ms. R covered in critical comments in light pencil. Then one time a piece came back clean except for a single endnote: *Good. Keep going*. Rereading her own words, Leah despaired: she couldn't keep going. That was all she had; she had given Ms. R everything, and still Ms. R wanted more. Ms. L sometimes used words like *soar* and *transcend* to talk about how the books she was teaching Leah in class made her feel. Leah had some of the best teachers that her parents' money could buy, but, it seemed, they could not teach her how to do that.

I too have often pondered the question of whether the ability to bridge the gap between OK art and great art can be taught. When asked if money could buy happiness, Van Halen musician David Lee Roth said no, "but it can buy you a yacht big enough to pull up right alongside it." Still, this response implies, the leap between your boat and the other must be made, and money can't make it for you. And it seemed that Leah could not leap.

It makes sense to me why not. To communicate in Leah's family was to sit around the dinner table and argue, the purpose of which was to demonstrate how much or how little you knew. You ate your food and you picked a position and you put on your armor, and you prepared to defend yourself to the death, which was what losing meant.

At dinner, if Leah's father or mother used a particularly juicy word, Leah's father would ask Evan and Leah if they knew what it meant. If they said they did, he would ask them to define it. If they said they didn't or defined it incorrectly, he sent one of them to the big dictionary, spread across a wooden stand on a table in the living room.

Louder, Leah's father would call at Leah if she was reading the definition. Louder!

Leah mostly did not communicate at all during these dinners, but Evan did. Evan was fat and he wanted God, two things that Leah's father could not tolerate. Evan wanted to go to synagogue, Evan wanted to be bar mitzvahed.

You want brainwashing, their father said. You want someone else to tell you how to think!

Maybe I do, Evan replied. And would that be so bad?

Leah's father stood up then, threw his napkin down on the seat of his chair, and instead of looking at his family—people he called son, daughter, wife—he put his hands on his hips and stared at the kitchen floor, breathing hard, as if no one in the world, no man or woman or child or beast, had ever been so stunningly stupid.

What Leah's father did not understand, and perhaps what no parent ever understands, is that whatever you hate and fear in yourself will come back around and take vengeance upon you in the form of your child. *Children will listen.*

And so it did, in Evan's and Leah's physical forms. Evan was fat from birth, basically, a clear kind of fat that drew comments from strangers and was used by their parents as justification for weight-loss summer camps and yearlong after-school diet programs. Leah's fatness was more gradual, appearing to the untrained eye around puberty and accelerating rapidly through high school.

After the speed injections stopped, it had taken Leah's father years of not eating food to become thin, but once he had, it was very easy to maintain: all he had to do was stay hungry for the rest of his life. However, his ear cartilage and lobes remained fleshier than average, the thing which, Leah and Evan believed, allowed him his superhuman ability to hear the consumption of any food in any room of the apartment. Even if Leah used her tiny dexterous child fingers to unseal the refrigerator door from itself with the tiniest sound, her father heard and demanded to know what she was eating.

What was she eating? Leah was eating one kind of food in public and an entirely other kind in private. At the dinner table, she was eating fat-free cottage cheese, skim milk, bran cereal, pineapple, chicken breasts with broccoli, snow peas in sauce. But in her room, she was smuggling in cookie dough without eggs, pints of mint chocolate ice cream, crunchy clumps of sesame chicken with white rice.

In her own room at the far end of the apartment facing the street with the door closed, Leah could hear her parents' arguments with Evan reaching a rageful, almost transcendent pitch. Both of Leah's parents, for different reasons and despite the fact that Leah's mother was a therapist, behaved in those moments like raccoons caught in a trash bag. There was nothing—no secret, no insult, no wounding, no weapon, no lie—they would not say in order to get free. You're lazy, they would tell Evan, you're selfish, you have no willpower, you say you want to lose weight but then you do the opposite. Fat people die young, they would say; the world will beat you down, no one will hire you, no one will love you, no girl will fuck you. In response, Even behaved only like what he was: a child whose refusal to comply was the only power he had. Their words ping-ponged back and forth across the apartment—*yes you will, no I won't*.

In her room by herself as all this was going on, Leah communed with Baba Yaga, with Peach Boy, with Scheherazade, with Aimee Mann, and Pink Floyd and Sylvia Plath and Michelle Kwan and her drawings of the taxidermied wild animals at the Museum of Natural History. Leah's mother had given her fairy tales; also books about twins with purple hair, one girl and one boy, who switched gender presentations so that the girl could train to be a knight and the boy could train to be a witch.

Yet she could not stay there forever. In order to eat or shit, it was necessary for Leah to cross the great space of hardwood floor in the middle of the apartment watched over by Leah's father from his perch at the white pine dining room table. The table would be stacked high on one end with the detritus of intellectual, liberal life—pins they'd all gotten upon completion of the AIDS Walk, Leah's mother's Eileen Fisher catalogues with their voluminous linen pants in appealing shades of burnt orange and taupe, and her father's unread back issues of *The New Yorker* with its write-ups of the newest shows of iconoclastic art in galleries not three blocks away from that apartment. Many people think that these objects and what they signify will save your life. But they will not.

Nothing protected Leah from the inevitable moment when her body, crossing that space, would be appraised by her father's eyes, his head turning to follow her as she moved, his disgust and disappointment palpable in his silence or sometimes in his remarks: *Have you ever considered exercising more? If you wore your hair up, your face would look more attractive. Don't wear those pants, they're unseemly*. There were some times, even when starving or stewing in gastrointestinal juices, that she could not cross it, thinking *I'll die out there*. Once or twice, she'd considered pooping in a plastic bag in her room, but realized that she'd need to find a way to get the bag across the space too, which would only attract more attention.

Their apartment was in a building that had once been a car factory so in order to cross the space, Leah would sometimes pretend. *I'm a car, I'm a car,* Leah would think as she hurried over the hardwood floor and then over the black-speckled linoleum kitchen tiles which were losing their top layer, to the broom closet where her father could no longer see her. *Vroom vroom.*

When Leah became eligible to take driver's ed through her high school, she signed up. By then she was properly fat, able to fit into some seats in movie theaters and airplanes and not others. She worried about if she would fit into the car, knew it depended on the make and model, on how much space there was between the driver's seat and the steering wheel, between the end of the driver's side door and the beginning of the gear shift console. Some cars had bulky driver's side door pocket compartments which only compounded the problem. The seatbelt was another thing. She hated the way it cut between her boobs, accentuating them, and also cut into her stomach, sometimes so sharply that it left a deep mark.

The driver's ed teacher, a white man whose mustache smelled like cigarettes, was fat himself, which should have made things easier but somehow didn't. He pulled up to their school with the smallest car in all the land, into which he stuffed the four teenagers, Leah the only girl. When Leah wasn't in the driver's seat, she sat in the back, the whole right side of her body pressed into the body of a boy with red hair she knew from math class who was clearly and extraordinarily high. *Gimme gimme,* he said to the other boys, one white, one Black. He kept reaching out for their Doritos, their Swedish Fish, their sodas or their change, and then withdrawing his arm, tight with its prize, right into Leah's gut with painful micro jabs.

Fatness changed her gender somehow, made her into not

a girl to these boys, maybe into not a human being, something she had turned over in her mind when she started identifying as nonbinary in college and that she was turning over still. After that first session, Leah stopped going to driver's ed. She lied to her parents about it and used the time to sprawl in the grass of Central Park, eating and reading.

Instead, she walked. On the street between school and home and on the subway, Leah always knew which men would pass comment on her body. They were the same ones who stood in line eating their lunches under the scaffolding of the trade school or squatted outside the donut shop on the corner where Leah caught the express train. She could feel their interest before they felt it—in her breasts and her belly and her thighs. It was the same way—staring, appraising, objectifying, rejecting—that her father looked at her body and that Evan now looked at it too.

It is a strange feeling to know that there is no man in this world to whom your body is sacred.

III.

CONGRATULATIONS, MS. JEAN WOOTEN—THE BIG 85! BLINKED an electronic bank marquee before the letters scuttled away. A fire station advertised a chicken and waffles dinner. They'd eaten sandwiches in Lancaster after photographing the boy but the words spoke to Leah's second, more pleasure-oriented stomach. Outside a school, girls played lacrosse against a huge white sky, standing far away from each other, their ponytails waiting.

We're getting close now, Bernie said, the first thing she'd said in many miles.

They'd crossed the Susquehanna a while back, which required a substantial bridge over fast rushing water. The river that their two-lane was following now was the Juniata, according to the map on Leah's phone, a thing that Leah had prepared for. Back in her room in Philadelphia, Leah had read Galway Kinnell's poem, "Dear Stranger Extant in Memory by the Blue Juniata," a strange and hard-to-follow poem that was apparently based on real letters Kinnell had exchanged with a mystic named Virginia who lived on the banks of this river.

At dusk by the blue Juniata—went the poem, *"a rural*

America," the magazine said, / "now vanished, but extant in memory, / a primal garden lost forever . . ." / ("You see," I told Mama, "we just think *we're here . . .")*

Look it up, look it up, Leah heard her father's voice in her head, so she'd looked up *extant* and found it meant: still in existence, surviving. Currently or actually existing. *What an odd word to need,* Leah had thought then, and thought again now, as they drove along the Juniata River. What an odd thing to be asked to prove you still existed, that you had not been lost, over and over and over again. Kinnell had written those words in 1971.

Even odder to be told that you didn't exist *and* that you were responsible for the catastrophe. Leah had read all the internet think pieces like everyone else—*Rural People Whose Way of Life Has Vanished Fueled His Victory; Empty Landscapes of Social Decay: The Rural Voter's Revenge; Their America Is Gone but He Tricked Them into Believing It Could Be Revived*—but even to a city kid like her, they'd never quite added up. If their America was gone, why were we all now living in it?

Leah looked over at Bernie, who had her window down and her arm lining the opening. She was from here too, a thing that Leah sometimes forgot.

It's beautiful here, Leah said.

Yeah, Bernie said, after a pause. It is.

You get back here much?

It's hard without a car, Bernie said, but that's not really an excuse.

And your mom?

Moved back to Baltimore a couple years ago. My brother's a little hard to get on the phone and I'm not real tight with people from high school.

Same, Leah said.

It's not people I like to see so much as the land, Bernie said. It feels good to be here.

Are you gonna be OK when we get there? I mean, to Dunn's house.

Yeah, Bernie said. I'll be OK. I just want to get in and get out. Find a motel for the night.

The houses of the last town they went through sat right up against the road as if they wanted to be seen. The day opened up, the flatness of the white sky breaking up into clouds both fat and thin that moved swiftly across the landscape. Leah's phone was giving directions in tenths of a mile now, and after turning off the blacktop onto a lane that pitched steeply uphill and wound around a switchback, they were on Daniel Dunn's road.

It was gravel and straight, just ranch houses and two-story clapboards until they turned in to the driveway, which was dirt and badly rutted. They passed a small pond lined by a curtain of reeds and a hoop house covered in torn opaque plastic, and then around the bend sat a two-story white board-and-batten farmhouse.

The placement of the trees along the edge of the back field gave the impression of a wide audience of natural eyes as Leah and Bernie stood at the screen door and Bernie inserted one of the two silver keys into the light and new-looking metal door.

At first, Benjamin Pogden had insisted that he or one of his colleagues from the gallery would meet them here, but when trouble arose with their newest installation—a set of self-portrait collages by a young Black woman from Mississippi who turned out to be a young white Jewish woman from Queens—Pogden eventually caved and just mailed Bernie the keys with a note: *Please let me know when it's been completed.*

The door opened with a whoosh, as if the air in the house had been trying to get out.

I can't take you inside Daniel Dunn's house. I can't show you around its low ceilings and wood-paneled walls or open its kitchen cabinets with their black hinges. I can't tell you about the incredible firmness of the floral couch and its two matching armchairs or the impressive layers of dust on the sliding glass doors. Let Leah and Bernie go inside. I'll stay here.

I met Daniel Dunn once at a party in Los Angeles given by a museum celebrating a show we were both in, though he was in it much more than I and his name was printed much larger on the poster. He struck me as a fine guy, maybe even a little bit boring. Wore a tie. Kept turning around to look for his wife.

Have you seen my wife? he asked me.

I hadn't. That is one thing that we get wrong about these guys, I think—how obsessed they are with their wives and how, more often than not, it is the wives who leave them rather than the other way around.

He was one of those men who asked no questions, who just talked. He talked *at* me rather than *to* me, as if I could have been anyone, which it seemed I was. This was not necessarily an uncommon experience for me when it came to men of Dunn's demographics. There is a thing that happens when either you are a lesbian, or you become more comfortable with yourself in your late thirties and early forties, or both, and men start to pick up on the fact that you are no longer sexually available to them. So they ignore you, treat you as a nondescript piece of furniture. You are no longer dressing for their eye and they know it, and so they do not rest their eye upon you.

But something about Dunn was different than this. It was more that he seemed unable to spend even one moment alone with his own thoughts. When I was talking but paused to look at the waiter, coming around with his tray of pre-poured white wine, Dunn began talking again. He seemed to be trying to stop a festival in his mind and the more words said out loud and in a straight line, the more reliably he would be able to corral the festival's attendees. He told me that he had gotten very into cooking lately. Specifically Italian food. Specifically risotto.

The trick is in the broth, he said. *People think it's the rice, or the stirring, or the parmesan garnish, but it's not. It's the quality of the broth which must absolutely—this is nonnegotiable—be homemade.*

Oh, I said. *Is that so.*

Oh yes, he said. *And turkey broth is even better than chicken actually. It's the best thing about Thanksgiving—the risotto that comes after.*

LEAH AND BERNIE CAME OUT of that house with seven cameras and eight bankers boxes. Someone had cleaned up the downstairs, Bernie would later say in an interview, but the upstairs had been mostly actual trash (liquor bottles, pizza boxes covered in grease, strips of white contact sheet paper too small to save) except for the cameras which had been well cared for, each in its own padded case, and the boxes which had been neatly organized with dividers by project. When they had put these in the back of the station wagon, Leah lifted the lid from the nearest box.

I still can't get over how big the negatives are, she said,

taking out a contact sheet. The sheet itself was as big as a piece of computer paper, and translucent, but it held four negatives, each four inches by five inches, the size of a postcard. Leah put her hand over one—almost a perfect match.

Why did you think it was called four by five film? Bernie said, but she was smiling.

Leah rearranged the boxes and their luggage a few times, each time asking Bernie if she could still see, and Bernie, sitting in the driver's seat but not looking in any mirror, said she could.

They walked around the house then to the field behind it. The day was warm and the cicadas were buzzing. Leah heard a squirrel or perhaps a bunny hopping through the brush around the shed.

I think that door is open, Leah said, pointing to the shed.

I was in there once, Bernie said. Chipmunks were always running in and out.

But as soon as Leah touched the door, she felt it: the thick presence of something not human, not animal, not vegetable but alive. Leah felt around for a light switch first on one side of the doorway and then the other, then hit it.

The room was no dark woodshed anymore, but a whitewashed and drywalled one, and it was photographs—all four walls, ceiling, and floor. The photographs had been printed big as posters and then lined up end to end to form an enormous grid that continued across every surface to create a kind of cube of images. There were also some rectangles of text, printed and collaged to take up the same space in the pattern as a single photograph.

Fuck you Daniel Dunn was Leah's first thought. The house and its few cameras and boxes had been a decoy. This was what he had really wanted to leave Bernie—a thing that could not be picked up or moved, could not be reproduced or sold. It would have to be swept and tended for years. Possibly forever.

Leah turned and there was Bernie, swinging around the shed's doorjamb. Leah watched as Bernie's face went from bathed in natural light to touched by fluorescent.

Fuck you Daniel Dunn, Bernie said, and then covered her mouth with both hands.

It's everywhere, Leah said. Every inch.

Bernie bent down and touched the floor, so Leah did too. It was not clean but it was clear; the images and text had been printed on high-quality paper to avoid ripping or rippling, then covered with a translucent matte substance like industrial-strength Mod Podge.

Bernie went left, so Leah went right. They moved slowly along their respective walls.

It was Eileen Dunn, the mother, on Leah's wall at eye level. Eileen, looking very fat and well, in long shot profile on the porch couch, rolling a cigarette, a dog at her feet, the grass very green, her neck a mannequin for silver chains. A wide shot of a house interior, perhaps the upstairs of this house, all her clothes and chains laid out on a blue bedspread, Eileen nowhere in the photograph. The same dog, black-and-white and tired on the floor, holding a woman's shoe in its jaws.

What've you got over there? Bernie called.

His mother, Leah said. You?

His wife, Bernie said. Her sculptures. A trip they took to Italy, maybe? But also other women, naked, and some naked men too. Letters from a childhood friend, asking how he had been holding up since the divorce.

Leah made a sound of acknowledgment, but she could not stop looking at her own wall long enough to talk. As Leah walked, the wall of Eileen came into a corner and then became a new wall, the back wall. This wall had Eileen too, but it was Eileen sick, sicker, then Eileen dead. There were other kinds of death too. A letter from the same friend: *I shot a ten-point deer and hung it and am listening to its blood drain as I write this letter to you*. Small-town newspaper articles: a dead girl found in the creek, all her clothes on. *Mrs. Trina J. Mathias, math teacher at Lewistown Middle School for 64 years, has died of ovarian cancer. "She taught school until the day before she died," said George Mathias, son of the deceased. "She was grading tests when I heard her fall."* Photographs of old graveyards, their stones thin and brittle, mossed over and nearly submerged. Photographs of new graveyards, their stones glossy and square, their engravings fresh and their crypts modern and rounded.

In the near center of the wall was a wide shot of a field, just an ordinary field with a large rock in the middle distance and the tops of hundreds of people's heads, people in uniform. Flags. It wasn't an especially good Daniel Dunn photograph, Leah didn't think, but neither was it an especially bad one.

Shanksville, Bernie said, his most famous one. Where the plane went down on 9/11. This was one of his big moneymaking prints, everyone wanted one. It's not far from here actually.

What plane? Leah asked. In Pennsylvania?

Yeah, Bernie said. It's the one that the passengers took down on purpose. They revolted, I guess, took control of the plane back from the hijackers. It looks like a field but it was actually a coal strip mine. He was interested in that—how everyone thought the plane went down in empty land, just open space. But it didn't.

It was then that Leah looked down and saw Bernie, low down on the back wall, nearly on the floor. A photograph of a black sedan's nose and Bernie, sleeping. She was in the passenger seat but facing the camera straight on; Dunn had shot it through the driver's side window. Bernie's legs were folded up to her chest. Her arms were crossed and shoved into the space between her thighs and her stomach. Her head was lolled back, resting against the open edge of the passenger window. Her mouth was wide open and dark. Her mouth! Throat so small and white. Nostrils so big and gaping. With the incredible resolution of large format, Leah could even see Bernie's fleshy septum and the slight fuzz of her nose hairs.

Look, Leah said, pointing to it.

Oh, Bernie said. Oh wow. I never knew he took that.

It made Leah want to roar with pain and wanting. She had never, not once, seen Bernie that unguarded, that odd, that open and soft to the world.

How was it possible that men whose blood and energy could pool in such dark places, who could touch and drink and talk with such disregard and impunity, who said things that could fester in the mind for a whole life, could also make things that were so blindingly beautiful and true? Did their ability to make these things stem from the same source as their ability to ruin? Were these things connected? Were they opposed? Unrelated?

Do you want it? Leah said, gesturing to the photograph of Bernie.

But Leah did not wait. She bent down, took out her keys,

and opened the pocketknife she kept on the ring. She looked at Bernie then—one last chance—but Bernie just stood there, watching her. Leah plunged the knife into the wall. It went in hard but right, and Leah began to cut around the photograph's edges.

It took several minutes because of Daniel Dunn's commitment to adhesive, but ultimately the edges of the photograph were free, and Leah could stuff three fingers of her hand behind the photograph's backing and peel Bernie off the wall. It didn't come off perfectly, some bits were left behind, but it came off. She held the picture out to Bernie.

Bernie took it in her hands. She looked down at it a long time, and then she held it up at arm's length and looked at it some more. Leah looked then too, moving her eyes back and forth between Bernie's real face and her face in the photo.

I have looked at this photograph, studied its angles, even tried to re-create it myself with my own car and a doll, one of those torsos they use to teach CPR, and also at many other photographs of Bernie's face to try to understand this moment, the moment I believe, though I have no evidence of this, that Leah started loving Bernie. She had loved Bernie before, sure, when I first saw them, but that was only the potential for love, the pre-love that is more about the lover than the beloved. This love was about Leah yes, as the vessel of the love, but it was about Bernie too, the actual her that Daniel Dunn had captured in this photograph. Leah felt huge then, enormous, and weightless; full of so much love.

Bernie let her arm with the photograph fall and looked at Leah. And Bernie told Leah then. The way Daniel Dunn had singled her out. The days he'd taken her out shooting and their talks. The night into morning when he'd first taught her to use the big camera. The way she'd used him for knowledge and money, money he didn't have, as it turned out.

I don't blame you, Leah said. No one blames you.

I blame me, Bernie said. What if it's in me?

Leah blinked at Bernie, waiting for more. She was learning that Bernie usually only said half of what she was thinking at first and then the rest came moments later.

How he thought, I mean, Bernie said. What he did.

How can it be in you?

Women can be terrible too.

Of course.

He taught me. He taught me how to see.

No he didn't.

Yes he did.

Alright. He did and he didn't. You don't have to do anything with this place. Just because he gave it to you, doesn't mean you have to take it.

Easy for you to say, Bernie said.

Outside the shed, a bird cried. Screamed, really.

Why do you cry in the night? Bernie asked. In your bedroom, at home.

You can hear that?

Of course, Bernie said.

Not much though, Leah said. Only every once in a while.

No, Bernie said. Often.

Oh, Leah said. It's hard to explain.

Try, Bernie said.

I'm not a good person.

I am the mayor of that town, Bernie said.

I pretend to believe in things that I don't believe in.

Me too.

I pretend to care about things, to feel for people I don't feel for.

I do it too.

I don't like my friends.

I don't have any friends.

Alright, Leah said after a while.

Alright, Bernie said.

THEY STOOD THERE IN THE shed a long time, way longer than Leah was expecting, way longer than anything that was normal. They looked at each other. Then Bernie looked away from Leah and began walking around the room. She walked one way, then walked the other way. She didn't speak. Leah watched.

What happened next was that Bernie asked Leah to help her move everything they'd put into the car here, into this shed.

Also the trash from upstairs, Bernie said.

Cameras too? Leah asked.

Yes, Bernie said, except one, and except the film. Film I'll use.

It took them several hours. After they moved the boxes and cameras from the car, all except a little 35mm camera—a Canon AE-1 like the first one Bernie had ever used—Leah found some contractors' trash bags and then they used those, stuffing in his magazines, his bills from the water company, his hunting catalogues and clothing catalogues and mass letters made to look like personal letters in fake computer-generated script. They smooshed in Daniel Dunn's cans of oil, his crushed Poland Spring bottles, his Monsters, his Red

Bulls, his USB cables and defunct tangled phone cords, his handkerchiefs crusted in dried snot. In the shed, Bernie directed Leah to empty them out again, to pour them onto the floor.

When they were done, there was a great pile in the middle of the shed. The boxes were more or less at the bottom of the pile but gravity had done the rest of the organizing, the rags and empty cans up near the top and the water bottles—half-full—near the bottom.

What now? Leah asked.

I'm going to photograph it, Bernie said, already halfway out of the shed. It was dusk—a good time to take a picture, not that it mattered since they were working under the fluorescent lights of the shed. But Leah watched Bernie's back as she ran away toward the car in that good light, and then her front as she came back with the tripod and the big camera.

A couple hours later, at the house's front door, standing on the porch, Bernie would turn the bolt to its locked position, put the keys Benjamin Pogden had FedExed her on the small table by the entryway so she couldn't change her mind, and pull the door closed.

But when she stepped back into the shed now she was out of breath, panting with anticipation.

It's like he always said, Bernie said as she began setting up the camera. You don't capture a moment in a photograph. You make one.

IV.

THE GIRL BEHIND THE MOTEL COUNTER WAS SHOULDER DANCING to Britney Spears's "Piece of Me." She was young and wore a white velvet headband in her hair.

Good song, Leah said.

Oh I know, the girl said. Through a doorway, Leah glimpsed a back office where an older Indian American couple sat, each at their own computer, the girl's parents.

But now I feel bad, the girl said, filling out Leah's forms. You know they say Britney is unfree? Made to sing against her will, by her dad?

I've heard that, Leah said, and handed the girl her credit card. But is it that her dad is making her sing or that he is making her tour and taking her money? Like would she sing without him, on her own terms?

Hmm, the girl said, of that I am not very sure. But I think, if I am being serious, yes. Yes she would.

She leaned forward over the counter and lowered her voice. I saw Britney once, in concert, in Pittsburgh. She sang and sang and never stopped singing. Even when the audience had stopped applauding and some people were turning to go she kept singing.

The door clanged and Bernie walked into the small lobby then, and so did the girl's mother, rising from her office chair and coming behind the girl to push some buttons on the computer.

Hi, Bernie said to the girl, and the girl smiled back.

Number sixteen, the girl said to her mother.

Number sixteen, the mother said to Leah. Round the back. Queen bed deluxe room.

Oh, Leah said. I'm sorry but no, we'll need two beds.

The mother narrowed her eyes and looked from Bernie to Leah to her daughter back to her computer and then back up at Leah.

Ah, I see, she said. Brother and sister!

LEAH SWIPED THE KEY, PUSHED the door open, and stood back. Bernie plopped her bag on the bed closest to the door then went to investigate.

Sorry, Bernie said at the mirror. That OK?

I prefer it, Leah said. I always take the window seat on planes.

Bernie moved her shoulders in a fake shudder. So trapped! What if something happened?

Exactly. In the aisle, people will trample you to get out. At the window, you're safe.

Bernie vanished into the bathroom.

You hungry? Leah called. I'm starving.

Not really, Bernie called back. But I could drink beer.

Leah walked to a gas station she could see illuminated down the divided highway. It was fully dark now and the moon was coming up behind a brown hill. Somewhere far away, a motorcycle was revving up, but otherwise it was quiet. There were no sidewalks here in this place made only for cars, so Leah bounded quickly across the wide road.

Where are you? came a text from Alex.

Leah could imagine where Alex was: in her office at the paper, eating a falafel sandwich from the cart outside.

Leah stopped in the empty illuminated parking lot of a furniture store to text Alex back.

A motel near Harrisburg, Leah wrote. *You?*

The office working late, came Alex's reply. *Falafel for dinner.*

Leah knew then what she had not wanted to know, that she loved Alex but she did not love the possibility of Alex. She did not feel excitement to find out who Alex would become five, ten, twenty years from now. She already knew who Alex would become because she knew who Alex was now and Alex would not change. There were people who were constantly changing (Bernie, Violet, Evan) and there were people who were constantly remaining the same (her parents, Alex). Meena did not fall into either category, Leah realized, which was interesting. There was nothing wrong with either path, but it was easier to love someone on your same track, whichever one you were on.

The gas station was not a chain but an actual store called Mountaineer Mart and as Leah touched things—a purple rabbit's foot dangling from a cheap silver chain, a newspaper with the headline *Local Painter Makes Mural in Tribute to Lost Dog*—she knew that no one in her life—not Alex or Violet or

Meena or her parents or Evan—knew where she was or could imagine it. She was here with Bernie, she had watched Bernie do something extraordinary—cast off a ghost. For the first time in her life, possibly, she was exactly where she was supposed to be.

And what luck! A decent-looking pizza spun underneath inviting orange lights.

The boy behind the counter spatula-ed up two pieces of pepperoni and put each into its own snug little triangular box.

You walk here? The boy asked Leah. He had long dreadlocks held back by a red headband and a bag of ice wrapped around his knee as if recovering from some strenuous sports-based activity.

Yeah, Leah said. I don't drive.

I feel you, the boy said. My test should have been last year. But my mom won't let me take it. She says if you don't drive, they can't kill you.

Smart mom, Leah said. What do you think?

I think, the boy said, they'll kill you either way.

Leah nodded. She went to the sliding glass fridges and picked out a green six-pack.

Where would you go? If you got your license? she asked.

Go? the boy said. Nowhere special. Just drive around. Leave when I want. Come back when I want.

That sounds nice, Leah said. I'd like that too. What happened to your leg?

Hurt it in practice. Coach is trying to teach me some new crossovers.

Meaning?

It's just bouncing the ball from one hand to the other to fake out your defender so you can score. But Coach wants me to sell it. He says it doesn't matter how fancy your footwork or other moves are, if you're not making the other guy believe it with your feet and your shoulders and your eyes.

Eyes?

Oh yes, your eyes are the most important part. Look at this.

The kid took out his phone and pulled up a video of a basketball game where half the guys were in white jerseys and the other half in blue.

Watch this guy, the kid said, pointing to a skinny man with braids. Leah watched as the man dribbled, paused, then turned his head.

See that? the kid said. You think he's going to go right.

For sure, Leah said.

In the video, the man bounced the ball to his other hand and planted his foot hard right. His defender leapt then and the man switched his weight to the other direction, wide open for a beautiful jump shot, which he took. The net swished.

Holy shit, Leah said.

I know, the boy said.

BACK AT THE MOTEL, LEAH stood at the door, a plastic bag in each of her hands, one bulging and weighty, the other slack and light. When Bernie opened it, a gladness rose in Leah just to see Bernie there, in the doorway.

You're back, Bernie said.

I'm back, Leah said.

The motel's walls were green and textured like expensive wrapping paper. Nothing in the room—not the desk or the chest of drawers with the TV on top or the white mini fridge—

touched anything else; a few feet of space separated each item from the others. Leah rested on the mattress's edge eating the slices of pepperoni out of their cardboard houses, her legs stretching into the space between the two beds.

You sure you don't want any? Leah asked.

I'm good, Bernie said. She had two beers on her side of their shared nightstand, Leah had one, and the other three lay on their sides in the mini fridge. Leah watched as Bernie rolled over on her bed holding one of the beers and the remote, and lay down on her stomach, her head at the foot of the bed. Murder shows on every channel.

Oh, Leah said, when Bernie paused on one. This is the one with the skateboard and the uncle.

No, Bernie said. This is the one with the handcuffs and the radiator and the dad in Staten Island.

Oh you're right.

Leah was impressed. She opened her second pizza box, took the slice up in her hand, folded it in half and scooched back on the bed to lean against the wall as she ate it. Bernie finished the first beer and started in on the second. The episode ended and another different but related show came on, this one primarily about rape instead of primarily about murder, though rapes and murders happened in both shows.

Bernie seemed not to want to talk about what had transpired that day. Another thing Leah was learning about Bernie: once a moment had passed, it had passed. There was no way to reach back and bring it into the now.

Bernie turned away and put her feet down on the floor by the room's door. Rummaged around in her bag until she produced a red hoodie. Took off her shirt in one movement so Leah could see the little naked blades of her shoulders moving around fast beneath her pale skin. Lifted her tiny ass and pulled her jeans off too. Leaned over, showing the slightest inch of ass crack. Pulled on soft black shorts.

Bernie's body seemed frail somehow, a marked contrast to her emotional firepower, and disconnected from its soul, as if the very Bernie-ness of her did not reside in her physical form but somewhere else. When she flopped back on the bed again, she closed her eyes.

Leah took her clothes with her into the bathroom, a habit left over from being a fat child in a locker room. For all of Leah's wonkiness about her body, her Leah-ness did live there, inside it. After her shirt and binder were off, there was the smell again, sweet and pungent like bread dough left to rise. There was a big mirror over the sink so Leah grasped her breasts, one in each hand, and turned their nippled ends to face each other so they made a kind of boob croissant. They were so big and loose that Leah could make all sorts of shapes with them. When she saw topless women on TV or in porn with their small, pert breasts, or even large shapely firm ones with browned nipples that swooped up toward the sky, they seemed like such alien body parts that they were almost unrecognizable. Also, extremely hot. Leah had spent more than one hour of her life googling "Emily Ratajkowski breasts" and masturbating to the results. Even thinking about that now was dangerous, with Bernie in the next room.

Lifting up her own breasts to her chin, Leah saw that their undersides were angry again, the line where the tissue met her torso was colored bright red in two horizontal commas. Intertrigo, the internet called it—what happens when folds of skin stay folded. Not enough air gets in, moisture breeds bacteria, and things go wrong. Alex had seen all this eventually, though she liked to turn off all the lights except her desk lamp and touch Leah only on the surface of her skin.

When Leah emerged from the bathroom, Bernie was already in bed with her light off, body facing the door. Leah got under the covers. On the nightstand between their beds were two ridged and individually wrapped plastic cups, an empty plastic ice bucket, a pad of paper with the motel's logo on it, and a pen. She picked up the pad and pen and began to write.

Philadelphia, PA, to Dillsburg, PA, she wrote. Since Bernie had photographed him, she wrote about the Amish boy, about his outfit and what he had said. She flipped the page and still the energy to write was not exhausted.

Bernie coughed.

The light bothering you?

A little.

Leah pulled her headlamp out of her backpack, put it on, and turned off the lamp. When she finished writing about Daniel Dunn's shed and the photo of Bernie and the boy at the gas station, she pulled out her nighttime book.

What are you reading? Bernie asked, still turned away.

Fairy Tales from the Brothers Grimm, Leah said. They relax me.

Read me one.

Leah read to Bernie about the couple who longed for a child but could not have one.

Why do all stories start this way? Bernie asked.

With yearning?

For a child.

I don't know.

I do not long for a child, Bernie said. Do you?

No, Leah said.

Leah read about how the man's wife said she would die if she did not get a salad made from the special lettuce called rampion so he climbed down over the wall into the witch's garden.

Wait what? Bernie said. Why would he do that? That witch is going to mess him up.

Well, Leah said. His wife was going to die.

Like actually die? OK. Keep going.

HELLO YES I'D LIKE ORANGE juice, water, pecan waffles, two eggs over medium, bacon, hash browns smothered, and cinnamon toast, Bernie said, once they were seated side by side on spinning stools at the counter of the Waffle House across from their motel.

Good, said their waitress, a white woman in her early forties with nice bushy blond eyebrows.

Leah did not know what she wanted and seeing Bernie want so much only confused her further.

And for you sir?

It was not that Leah deeply minded being taken for a man, it was just that each time it happened she was reminded that her body was bizarre, didn't make sense, didn't compute. Back in the neighborhood, it was sometimes, for very brief moments, possible to forget this.

Leah ordered eggs and the waitress puttered away.

This is how my body is, Bernie said. It runs on low for several days and then it cranks way up high.

Don't you get hungry in between?

Sure. But it's like, delayed or something. Things take me a

long time to process. It's like my body is sleeping or in hibernation and then it wakes up.

What wakes it up?

Feelings can do it sometimes, Bernie said. Anger. Excitement. Surprise.

Were you angry before?

I don't know, Bernie said. Maybe I should have been or I should be now. I feel like he wanted to trap me. He wanted me to come and see what he had made and love him again and feel sorry for him.

Yeah, Leah said. He did. But you didn't do it. You didn't fall for it.

I guess, Bernie said.

And you took two photographs yesterday. That's huge.

I did. They didn't feel right. But I did take them.

Leah watched a young white woman in a black suit jacket with a beautiful brown leather briefcase come in, sit at the far end of the counter, and order coffee. Leah wondered where she was going, and if she was happy or sad. Leah would have liked that briefcase for herself, imagined her hand closing around its pleasing, neatly stitched handle. A white man with a healthy case of rosacea and wearing an orange reflective vest that said PA STATE across the back ordered chocolate chip waffles. There was the sound of their waitress asking follow-up questions and the sound of shredded potatoes being extracted from a moist ziplock bag and placed onto the hot grill, scraped once, twice, many times, then flipped by a short Latino man in clean white tennis shoes. The waitress put her hand on his shoulder as she passed. He said to be careful of the rubber mats which were still a little wet and she said thanks.

Their food came, and Leah broke her egg yolk and watched it run in thick luxurious rivulets.

I like to eat, Bernie said. But so many things get in the way.

Such as?

Look at that woman, Bernie said, indicating the business-woman at the counter. Is she coming or going? Happy or sad?

I know, Leah said. I do the exact same thing. But when there's food around, all that gets quieter for a while. I think that's one of the reasons I like eating so much.

Lucky, Bernie said.

I guess. And also not.

Not how?

I'm still working on figuring out eating.

What's there to figure out?

Well, people say, listen to your body. Listen to your hunger. Eat, they say, when you are hungry. Then stop when you are full. The body sends you signals, they say. But I don't know, I think my signals are broken.

Why?

How much time do you have?

A lot, Bernie said. Three weeks.

Leah smiled. Bernie's body was so small, small like Violet's and Meena's and Alex's and most all the queers in their neighborhood. No way to make her understand.

I hate that shit, Bernie said then. Listen to the body, listen to the body. It's like, why? What does the body know? Driving does that for me though, I think. Focuses me. Things get quieter. We're going to teach you how to drive before this trip is done.

Don't count on it, Leah said.

I am, Bernie said. Counting on it.

Anything else I can get you ladies? The waitress asked. She had sensed her earlier mistake and was now going hard the other way. OK, well girls, just holler if there is. I'm exhausted so I'm going to sit down for a while but I'll be right over here if you need anything.

How come? Leah said.

How come I'm so tired? The woman's body was caught mid-motion, not following the impulse to go but not turning to stay either.

Leah nodded.

Well, the woman said, I've been here since six A.M. for starters and Marielle who was supposed to take over for me at two has to go to court for her son tomorrow so she won't be coming in. I'll be here till eight, a double and a bit. So there's that. Also some kids decided to throw a party in the parking lot last night. They go buy pills and then they come here and party in the parking lot and sleep till they're hungry. So there's that to clean up when I have the extra time which I don't. My car's making a weird sound also.

What kind of sound? Leah asked, as the question train had left the station and there was nothing to do now but follow it.

Like a squealing or a shrieking when I press the brake. Only when I press the brake and only sometimes. I took it to the car place and they drove it around some and came back and said that there was nothing wrong with it. But did you hear that sound? I said. What sound? they said.

The car was gaslighting you, Leah said.

Gaslighting?

The woman looked from Leah to Bernie back to Leah.

It's like when you know something to be true but then

someone else tells you it isn't true, Leah said. They deny it. They deny your reality.

Why didn't you just say that then? the woman said. Why does there need to be a new word for every little thing?

I don't know, Leah said. I guess people think it's quicker.

It's not though, the woman said. Look how much longer it just took for you to explain it.

You're right, Leah said. I'm sorry.

No, I'm sorry, the woman said. I'm just tired. Marielle's son. He's always getting arrested in Harrisburg and needing to be bailed out. He uses words like that all the time and then looks at me like I'm stupid if I don't know what they mean. It's annoying is what it is. So fucking annoying.

THE WOMAN HADN'T LIED. IN the lot were perhaps ten cars parked too closely together and outside the lines.

Bernie walked closer, and Leah followed. On the ground were: an empty pack of Marlboro reds, a small plastic gooseneck lamp, one emerald-green high-top sneaker, three crushed black-and-green energy drink cans, a school photograph of a small boy in a blue cardigan, an empty bag of Doritos (original nacho cheese flavor), a Kit Kat wrapper, an open jar of dill pickles on its side (mostly juice), some nickels and pennies, a single pink wireless earbud, and a small book (possibly for children) on how to identify trees.

Must have been some party, Leah said.

I've done it, Bernie said. Not in a Waffle House parking lot, but I've gotten fucked up drinking and then slept in my car. Plenty of times, in the woods. Mostly if it rained, or snowed, but I should have done it many more times. It's dangerous to drive. I bet you never have.

Have what?

Partied, then slept in your car.

You're right. I haven't.

There was a time when I would drink anything, Bernie said. But I never took OxyContin. I'll barely take aspirin. If you met my brother you'd understand.

He's an addict, then? Leah touched her toe against the pickle jar and it rolled on a ways.

Yeah. He's a lot of things, Bernie said. But addict is one of them. Not the tragic kind though where he's going to kill himself. Small doses, just enough to survive. He's going to live forever.

Sorry, Leah said.

It's OK, Bernie said. She gestured to the scene with her arm. Write this down though.

Why don't you photograph it? Leah said.

No, Bernie said. Write it down.

They went back to the car and Leah got her notepad—the one from the motel, no longer blank—and they sat on a bench outside the Waffle House as Leah wrote.

The passenger-side door of a maroon lowrider opened then and a man stuck his leg out. Leah waited. But there was no more movement, perhaps he had fallen back asleep. Leah was about to start writing again when he did move. He pushed the car door open with his hand and stepped out into the morning. When he was upright, he looked right at Leah. Lifted his hand. He had a very pale head covered in very light hair, so blond it looked almost white. Bernie lifted her hand back to him.

You know him? Leah asked.

No, Bernie said. It's just what you do here.

The man ran his hand back and forth over his head as he stood, taking in the sun.

Why though? Leah asked then. Why don't you want to take this picture?

Because a photograph of this is too—Bernie wrinkled her nose.

Too what? Leah asked.

It would show just one thing, Bernie said. One side, like, oh look how messed up these people are, or oh how sad. You'll get to put that in, how the man waved to us. With words, you can go wider, you can talk about your conversation with the waitress. You have more space, time passing. I don't want my pictures to stand in for any bigger idea, like drug addiction or poor country people. I just want them to be what they are.

But you'll have my words too, Leah said. To go with whatever you make. It won't be your image alone. That's part of the point of all this.

I forgot about that, Bernie said. She looked at Leah a long time, squinting into the light of the day. Leah went back to writing, but after a few more minutes Bernie rose, went over to the Volvo, and took out her equipment.

Leah finished her sentence then followed. Once they had crossed the whole parking lot and were almost to the access road for the highway, Bernie looked back. Leah tried to imagine it. The shot would be not just of the cars but of the whole lot, Waffle House restaurant and sky behind.

I still need to get farther away, Bernie said.

Alright, Leah said. What about over there? She pointed to

a strip of grass that separated the Waffle House from the Burger King next door.

Better? Leah asked, when they were standing in it.

Yes, Bernie said.

Why?

I'm not sure.

Try, would you?

I guess because the parking lot, the asphalt, is most of the picture now. It feels more open, more free, more spacious. More like their party would have felt, maybe.

Leah did not understand this, but she wrote it down.

Bernie extended the tripod's legs, then set the camera on top. She went to the camera's front and opened the shutter all the way, letting in the most possible light. Then she unzipped the top of the camera bag, pulled out the dark cloth, wrapped it around her shoulders like a cape, and pulled the cloth forward so that it covered both her and the camera's ground glass.

Leah had watched YouTube videos, taken notes on documentaries, downloaded e-textbooks and highlighted them, but nothing had prepared her for the extraordinary slowness, the silence of the day and the silence of Bernie underneath that cloth. Underneath the cloth, the shape of Bernie's head and the shape of the camera looked like the same shape, like two cameras bobbling around. Into Leah's mind came an image of dancers performing the lion dance in Philadelphia's Chinatown that she had gone to with Violet last year, the way the person doing the head and the person doing the butt moved out of synch but in concert, making the swaths of red-and-yellow fabric go taut and then slack.

Bernie emerged from the cloth by taking a step back, lifting the front of the cloth up, and resting it on the body of the camera with her hands. Bernie's hands. Leah was aware of the way each finger moved on its own, all the way from the knuckle down the bones in her fingertips, which were almost visible through her pale skin. She wrapped her right hand around the neck of the tripod, gently, so gently, so that the first joint of each finger got lit up by the sunlight but the rest of the fingers were still hidden in shadow.

Bernie picked up the whole setup, tripod and camera, and moved it a few feet closer to the restaurant. Back under the cloth. She adjusted, she adjusted. The camera's face, tilted a few centimeters up, then down. She retrieved the small loupe, like a single binocular on a necklace, put it around her neck, then went back under the cloth. She was focusing.

Raised her hands again and again the cloth was gone. Walked around the camera and held the light meter up to the sky.

We're lucky there's no clouds, she said. Otherwise we could have been here for hours.

She turned and futzed with the lens of the camera, turned a few dials there. Returned to the ground-glass side, back under went the hands, and back down came the cloth.

Several minutes went by. A fat ant crawled over the cloth, burrowing into its creases, disappearing, then reappearing.

Fuck, Bernie said, from under the cloth.

What?

I forgot to lock this in and I moved it so now I'll have to refocus all over again.

It's OK, Leah said. Take your time.

Leah waited. Ten minutes went by. Fifteen. Twenty. Lost count. The sun was on Leah's face, then on her arms, turning them pink. She pressed the pad of her index finger into the skin there and watched it turn momentarily white.

Finally, finally, Bernie took the film holder from the film bag, a step that meant taking an actual picture was close. Went to the front again. Fiddle fiddle. Closed the shutter. Slid up the lever that cocked the camera's shutter. Fed the film holder into the camera. Withdrew the film slide. Set the shutter speed.

I'm going to do it, Bernie said.

OK, Leah said. Do it.

Bernie pulled again ever so slightly on the lever. The tiniest click.

I did it, she said. She looked so proud.

V.

EVER HAD AN ABORTION? BERNIE ASKED. SUN RUSHED THROUGH the tall grass in the median which was dotted with little yellow and purple flowers. They were headed southwest, Leah having a vague idea about Gettysburg, and Bernie about Hagerstown, even though it was technically in Maryland.

No, Leah said. Never had sex with a man. Fourth grade, I think, I knew I was gay. You had to watch that show about the kids, two boys and two girls, in California. Three of them are rich and the fourth one is a kid from the wrong side of the tracks who joins their world. The little brunette. *That girl,* I would say, *is really pretty. Sure,* my friends would say. *No,* I would say, *she's like really pretty.* I was trying to communicate something. Eventually, I realized we did not mean the same thing when we said *pretty.*

Bernie was in the left lane driving them tightly behind a dark blue SUV, rounded and bubbled—an American car, Leah was learning. To their right was a truck bearing the insignia of the everything website, white with smears of red clay dirt. Where had that dirt come from? Arizona? Wyoming? California? The truck's license plate said MISSOURI.

Strange, no? Leah remarked, that in this year of our lord in the twenty-first century in America, it is still trucks on eighteen wheels that move most of our goods from here to there? Like our scrubby sponges and scrunchies and potted plants and books and peel and stick wallpaper and diapers and four-pronged canes are transported on these trucks driven by human beings?

Not strange to me, Bernie said. How else would you think it would happen?

And then the SUV moved out of the way, cleared into the middle lane in front of the truck and Bernie pulled them forward. The man who was driving the truck was young and wearing enormous headphones and eating a banana. He looked blankly at Leah as their station wagon passed him. Leah wondered what he was listening to.

And then there were no more cars, not a single one. They were so exposed, all of a sudden, alone on this wide, wide road.

Don't you ever wonder about guys though? Bernie asked. If you've never been with one.

That's kind of a fucked-up thing to say.

You're right. One thing you should know about me is that I say kind of fucked-up things sometimes.

So I'm learning, Leah said.

Actually, I do wonder about guys sometimes, Leah said, after a time. There is a very specific type of guy who will hit on people who look like me and one time when I was very drunk right in the beginning of college I made out with one. He is in the theater now, directing plays and starring in them and he has that quality, that theatrical quality that feels kind of shape-shifty—tall and short at the same time, masculine and feminine at the same time. I would have had sex with him that night if I hadn't been on my period. But then afterward, the next day, I freaked out. I had like, a really bad anxiety attack and threw up.

Like your brain was down but your body was saying no?

I think. Or maybe the reverse—my body would have been down for it in that moment, but all my thoughts and feelings, once they came back to me, were saying no.

Hmm, Bernie said. I had an abortion once.

When?

In high school, she told Leah. Her boyfriend was a football player but only technically, as he never played. He had no grand ambition to excel at football, was content to be part of the team, to use words like *we* and *us* and to cheer the loudest for the fastest boys. He was starstruck by the idea of a community, by the idea of belonging, by the relief of no longer being judged on his individual merits. On his own he was fine, had asked Bernie if he could kiss her and then if he could take off her shirt. But as a member of a group he was excellent, always buying extra sandwiches and drinks for his teammates and suggesting plays that the coach often liked and even implemented. He had gotten the money from his parents and driven her to the appointment in Harrisburg, and paid for the motel room the night before where they had watched TV and ordered pizza and not had sex or fought. Then he had waited in the waiting room and driven her the hour home, stopping for gas and chicken sandwiches.

He sounds nice, Leah said.

Yeah, Bernie said. He was OK, in the end.

Their car was in the middle lane now and two cars passed

them at the same time, one on either side, like twin rocket ships blasting off without you.

LEAH KEPT PUSHING FOR SMALLER roads, so they got off and found a two-lane headed south. Leah looked at things—a red truck parked in a driveway with stickers that said NO FARMS NO FOOD and the word FRACKING in an oval with a line through it. She smelled the grass and the trees on her side of the car where things were darker and no sun fell.

When they went through the Tuscarora Mountain Tunnel, a tube bored through the side of a mountain that was over a mile long, the radio turned to static, just searching and searching, and when they came out the other side, it had begun to rain. At first just light commas of sun shower, then the blue sky went away altogether and the rain became pipe cleaners thwacking against the windshield, then handfuls splatting, like someone was cracking great eggs full of water and finally, harder still—bucketfuls of water being thrown across the windshield in a horizontal motion.

Should we stop? Leah asked.

Where? Bernie said. The shoulder was closed, and tight guardrails on both sides.

Up ahead, Leah could barely make it out, a cluster of cars had stopped in the middle of the road, honking at each other. After a few minutes, it became clear that a big puddle was obstructing any traffic; the road was washed out. Some were pulling off into a parking lot or pulling illegal U-turns.

On the left, a small country route with a slender green sign indicated the MICHAUX STATE FOREST.

I'm going to turn there, Bernie said. See where it goes.

The park name sounded familiar so Leah googled and, despite slow reception, learned again what she vaguely remembered: two lesbians had been murdered in this park in the 1980s. Actually, scratch that, one lesbian was murdered there and the other one was shot but survived. According to the surviving lesbian's memoir, which Leah was just barely able to pull up on Google Books before she lost the signal, they were shot in the middle of sex.

The one who lived put her beloved's shoes on her beloved's feet and put her own shoes on her own feet, but it quickly became clear that her beloved was wounded much worse than she, and could not walk. She had to decide: stay with her beloved and die, or walk by herself and maybe live. She felt, she wrote, her beloved's spirit telling her to go. "Something in me said 'Walk,'" she wrote. She walked four miles before she was picked up by a passing car; her beloved bled out. The man who did it had a face like a starving person and was homeless at the time, living in a wooded ditch behind his aunt's house. The road was littered, it seemed to Leah then, with the bodies of dead lesbians.

Out there, men were doing things—scratching their balls and flopping their dicks in women's faces and taking off condoms, secretly, halfway through sex. They were peeing letters in the dirt and shaking drops of their urine onto toilet seats and they were coming on women's faces and tits. All of these things were happening, Leah knew. She knew it from living and from articles she had fact-checked about love and movies and rape and from the few friends she still had from childhood, straight women who included her in their group text called "Ladies" which she hadn't had the heart to object to. Let them have this one thing, she had thought. For better or worse, but she suspected for better, Leah had made a life in which men did not figure prominently and she never—not ever—saw their naked bodies.

Bernie turned the car down a wide one-lane with no oncoming traffic and the water was easier to take at the slower speed that this new road allowed. Through the rain, Leah saw log cabins and wooden houses set back from the road, shielded by great trees with red-brown bark. Confederate flags. Tibetan peace flags. Lifted pickup trucks. VW buses. What was this place, Pennsylvania, that had two hearts?

The rain slowed after a while and it got a little misty, then very, very misty as they went up a hill. They were going straight into the mist.

Can you see? Leah asked.

Not much, Bernie said.

Every time they crested a hill, Leah braced for impact. Beyond the hill was more road, presumably, but who could be sure. Leah had no trust. In the driver's seat, Bernie was calm. She leaned back but her hands were firm on the wheel.

Whose story was this anyway? Was Leah a character in Bernie's story or was Bernie a character in Leah's? Leah suspected then that she might be a character in Bernie's story, a thing that made her feel anxious. But not necessarily bad. Go forward, Leah thought. Find out.

They passed a "gentlemen's club" with its sign, a silhouette of a sexy woman with long hair that ended in a sharp point and huge breasts with no nipples. Then there were horses. Horses in a pack, horses running, splitting up and then coming back together. There was a tiny brick post office with the name of a town printed on its side.

No reception, Leah said, checking. No map.

And then they were in the apple trees. It was unmistakable, such huge fruit growing on such small trees. On both sides were rows and rows of the little trees, their bright fruit shining and red.

What is happening? Leah asked.

I don't know, Bernie said. It's spring. Shouldn't be seeing apples for months yet.

Down a hill they went, around a curve, and the mist was even thicker here and so were the apples.

Now it was Bernie who was asking, What is happening? And Leah who was saying, I don't know.

The road widened with gravel shoulder on both sides to accommodate the apple crates that now appeared there, old wood-slatted cubes and new white plastic ones, stacked in great piles. An apple facility of some kind, huge and low, with no one in the parking lot. HIRING, a marquee sign said, FOR THE THIRD SHIFT. The road straightened out and up ahead was a great piece of machinery, a gray-and-black crane sitting atop a flatbed, parked in a turnoff.

I'm going to stop, Bernie said forcefully, surprising Leah. Bernie was leaning far over the steering wheel now and her face looked pained, like she could cry. I'm going to stop, Bernie said again.

OK, Leah said. So stop.

Bernie pulled the car into the turnoff, and they dipped slightly, tilting toward Leah's side. Leah looked at the trees just out her window which were very green and very red and very white, and at the sky which was white and thick with fog and moisture. She looked at the piece of machinery; how wide it was, and how much space it took up. One apple hung down from a nearby branch, touching the crane. It was red but only part red, like it had been blushed, or painted with a dry brush. It was so wet. Huge droplets of water clung to its waxy surface.

Have you ever in your life seen something like this? Bernie asked.

Leah looked at Bernie and thought: I love you driving. I love being driven by you. But instead she said, No. Are you going to photograph it?

Yes, Bernie said. I've got to. But not until the rain stops.

So we'll wait.

Bernie turned the key and the only sounds were the rain and the tick tick tick of the car's engine cooling. Leah's body felt aerated and jangled. Bernie had her left leg crossed over her right, left ankle to right knee, a thing that Leah could not fathom—taking up that little space. Also, Bernie was still wearing the loupe, the little magnifier she used to focus the shot under the dark cloth. It was funny to see this necklace on her, as Bernie sported no other adornments—no rings, no earrings, no barrettes, no nail polish. Nothing.

Leah's phone buzzed with one bar of service. A text from Alex.

Big breakthrough on the story, call me later so I can tell you about it? See I'm trying to be more communicative. Hi to Bernie. I love you.

Alex, Leah said. She says hi to you.

Hi Alex, Bernie said.

A beat.

Do you love her? Bernie asked Leah then.

Alex? Yes of course, Leah said, putting the phone down. Why?

You seem so different, Bernie said.

They say opposites attract, Leah said.

They do say that. But you're not opposites either.

We have all the same values, fundamentally, the same politics, the same hopes for the future. We just go about them in different ways.

Hmm, Bernie said. Do you think Alex wants to be happy?

Doesn't everyone?

Bernie shook her head.

Oh. Well I think Alex does. Simple things make her happy. Jigger for instance. We found Jigger together, when we were still in college and volunteering for this arts nonprofit in North Philly on Saturdays. We were walking down the street when we heard this panicked meowing, the saddest meow you've ever heard. It was Alex who insisted we stop and figure out the source of the meow and there was this cardboard box set out on a curb and inside the box was a plastic Tupperware with a kitten inside, meowing her head off. No air holes. They just left her there to die. She would have, in a few more hours, maybe even just a few more minutes. It was Alex who insisted we take her back to our campus apartment and Alex who cleaned her up and fed her for days from an eye dropper.

I can see that, Bernie said.

Yeah, Leah said. She's happy when she can help. She's happy when she's being productive, when she's organized, when she's effective. When something she does causes something else to happen. She's happy when she's useful and when people tell her she is doing a good job. She's happy when she makes goals and then achieves them.

Does she always achieve them?

Always. Oh except for this one time she wanted to introduce herself to everyone on the block, our side and the side across the street. She read something about how working for racial justice means nothing if you are gentrifying a neighborhood and you don't know your neighbors personally. So she started knocking on doors. She set a goal to learn everyone's names and learn one single thing about them—didn't matter what it was, if it was their job or if they had a hobby or their favorite color or whatever. And she almost did it, she talked to everyone on both sides of the street. It took a long time, months actually, this was back before you moved in, everyone, that is, except for one house, that one directly next to us. The main floor and the second floor are a group house like us, but there's a guy who lives in the basement apartment. Young guy, handsome, Black, maybe late twenties. He must work nights because he was never home whenever Alex tried—evening hours and on weekends.

One time, Leah continued, in the summer I couldn't sleep so I went out into the backyard and I saw him smoking weed on his steps at around four or five in the morning. I went back to bed and told Alex and she whipped the covers off and put on her sneakers and charged down there. Apparently he just sat there, smoking and not answering any of her questions. He didn't say a word, wouldn't even tell her his name. She got madder and madder but still he didn't cave, nothing. It was a blow, the only thing I've ever seen her fail at. She spent the whole next day in bed.

Impressive, Bernie said. That's commitment.

Her, Leah said, or him?

Both, Bernie said. Come on, or we'll lose the light.

LEAH KNELT IN THE GRASS, her back to the apple orchard that lined the curve in the road. She dug her pen from her hoodie pocket and braced the motel notepad against her thigh. The storm had passed and the afternoon was still.

Bernie stood behind the camera and turned the knobs that moved the camera's lens plate.

I'm adjusting the tilt, Bernie said. I'm adjusting the swing. In short, I'm focusing. Now I will go back and look at the ground glass.

And what do you think?

It's not good, Bernie said.

Why?

It's not what I want. I want what I saw when I was just looking normally, with my eyes, without the camera. This will make a picture that looks like a picture not a picture that looks like life. I need to fix that.

How do you fix that?

You change everything. You change the placement of the camera. You change the structure of the picture, the way things are arranged.

You mean the composition?

No, Daniel Dunn always said structure. He said composition was for painters, but structure was for photographers. Painters start with nothing, photographers start with life.

Meaning?

Bernie pointed. I've got that apple crane in the distance, see? And I've got our car there. And the road close up. And then all the apple trees on the left. I'm selecting things and figuring out where to put them, in a way that makes sense and will feel right later. I'm not conjuring them up. I can't move them.

Like journalism, Leah said. Or all nonfiction. Any writing that's true true.

I guess, Bernie said. That's your department.

It seems like you know where to put the things, Leah said. You have an instinct for that.

I don't know, Bernie said. I still know how to do all the technical moves, but they don't feel right. I remember, when it was good, there used to be a little something—a glimmer maybe. Or that's not the right word.

Shimmer?

Yes, exactly. Shimmer. Bernie moved the tripod to the right once again.

There was a little wind then, which blew the edges of Bernie's dark cloth around. The back of Bernie's T-shirt was riding up and the top of her pants was riding down, exposing a slice of flesh—knobs and pale back.

Leah noticed that the quality of her own eyes, the quality of her seeing, had changed even in just the two days she had been watching Bernie photograph, waiting for Bernie to photograph, trying to look and predict what Bernie would photograph. Things seemed sharper now, slower, more pronounced, more contrasted, less flat. She wrote this down.

Bernie released the shutter, taking the picture.

Shimmer?

No.

Ah well.

Leah heard gravel and fast feet then; a tall white man and a dog were walking up the road. The dog was red, the reddest dog Leah had ever seen, and he took off running toward them.

Oh hello, Bernie said, crouching down to rub the dog's head.

That's Pepper, the man called. He's friendly.

Pepper was sitting on Bernie's foot now, looking at Bernie with enormous love in his eyes. Bernie was stroking Pepper's nose. His long silky fur turned caramel when the light hit it.

He likes you, the man said, drawing closer. His body was tanned and the same thickness all the way down, radiating easy energy, easy potential. When Leah coveted masculinity, she coveted masculinity like this.

What the fuck is that? the man said, pointing.

A camera, Bernie said.

That? the man said. That's a fucking gun, for sniping. Sniper, sniper, you a sniper?

Leah understood what he meant. The camera did look odd, even aggressive.

Are you? Leah said. In the military?

No, the man said. Oh no no no. You couldn't PAY me to do that. Not with all the stolen tea in China. Not with all the blood diamonds in Africa. I read about Baghdad. I read about Kabul. I read the news. I read the blogs. I listen to the podcasts. I read it all, all morning and sometimes all afternoon. The only time I don't read it is at night.

I know what you mean, Leah said. Sometimes I start reading the news and I lose hours, an afternoon, a whole day.

Exactly, the man said. It's scary is what it is, no sir. Are you a sir?

No, Leah said.

Didn't think so. But it never hurts to ask.

It doesn't, Leah said. Not at all.

Pepper left Bernie and started running along the edge of the apple orchard, smelling the apples that had fallen. He picked one up in his mouth and brought it to the man, who removed it and threw it back into the orchard. Pepper looked from the man to Leah, bereft.

They talked about war, war on people, war on the environment. The man ran a website tracking the progression of fracking in this area, including a map. People could write in with the locations of fracking wells and the man would put them into his map so people could go protest or cut the lines in sabotage. They talked about complicity, about impunity, about a book the man had just read about the Kennedys and Chappaquiddick.

Out of the corner of her eye, Leah saw that Bernie was at the camera again, back under the cloth. Pepper came to sit by Leah, so Leah sat down too. She held his supple, scratchy paw.

Do you want to hear something that will blow your mind? the man asked Leah.

Definitely.

I was there, he said. On Chappaquiddick Island that day. For a party, my old buddy from when I worked on Wall Street, before I retired and came back here. I was standing around waiting for the teeny tiny ferry to take me back over to the main part of Martha's Vineyard, you know. And this man was at the pay phone and he slammed the phone down and came over to me. I had a cellphone then before other people because I was working this fancy corporate job—shitty, awful, Jesus it was so bad—anyway, I was talking on it. It was huge this cellphone, as they were then, you know, a behemoth, big as a quart of milk with an antenna that you had to pull on and a part that needed to be flipped down, the whole deal. So this guy comes over to me and says, give me your cellphone and I'll give you a thousand dollars. He takes out a thousand dollars in cash, ten one hundred dollar bills, counts them in front of me and puts them in my hand. So I give him my phone and right away he extends the antenna and starts dialing. That was one of Kennedy's lawyers, one of the fixers they called in that day,

I learned later. She, Mary Jo you know, she might even have been still alive in that moment we were standing there having that conversation. She was trying to breathe they say, there was some air left in the car they say, she lived for hours they say, following that air pocket around from this part of the ceiling to that part, which was in actuality the car's floor. I just stood there and watched him dial one number after the next, dial, dial, dial, talk talk talk.

Wow, Leah said. So why did you come back?

Here? Not sure. Well maybe I am. Humans are like animals. We have habitats. Places we feel good and places where we feel bad. I feel good here.

Leah nodded. Pepper rose and took off running again.

I'm Dennis, the man said. Where are you all headed?

Leah said her name as she stood up. Not sure, she said. We'd talked about Hagerstown.

Oh, Dennis said, eyes perking. Go to Rock Candy. Tell them I sent you. It's a bar. You'll like it. Go now. Go today.

From behind her left ear, Leah heard it—the click of Bernie releasing the shutter again.

Fuck, Bernie said.

Leah turned to look.

The dog, Bernie said. I set it all up, with the crane in view just there and the apple trees just there, and at the last second, he bolted across the road and into the shot. He'll be all blurry.

That's Pepper, Dennis said.

But he wasn't blurry. Mistake or miracle, when this particular photograph would come back from being processed and scanned, the red dog was sharp and clear. Perhaps Bernie had released the shutter a moment before she thought she had, or a moment after, or perhaps she'd messed up the shutter speed, but the resulting image was arresting; it arrested me, small on my computer where I first viewed it, and then even more so later when I saw it blown up the size of a picture window. There *was* something about its structure, to use Bernie's word, that wouldn't have worked without the dog there. It was the dog that made me finally understand this picture, and many of Bernie's photographs that came after. There, the machinery of harvest. There, the trees of fruit. There the road and the crates and the car. And there, in the lower left corner, a small creature of delight, crouching, back legs straight and front legs bent, caught in the moment just before the leaping.

VI.

EVERY ROAD TRIP MAKES ITS OWN LANGUAGE SO WHY SHOULD this one be any different? Leah read the signs aloud—BOOT EMPORIUM, FRESH BAIT, WOOD 4 SALE, LAND 4 SALE 27 ACRES, REAL WOMEN DRIVE TRUCKS, DRAIN THE SWAMP, SWEET POTATO PIE, SAPLINGS FOR CHEAP, VOTE YES, VOTE NO, EVERYTHING MUST GO, YOU ARE ALWAYS LOVED BECAUSE THE LORD LOVES YOU, SEXUALLY PROMISCUOUS? FREE TESTING FOR ALL, I CAN'T BREATHE, FRIDAY'S 1/2 PRICE WINGS, COLD BEER ALL DAY, WHEN WILL THIS END?, FOR SALE GOOD TRUCK TIRES NEW. Any sign at all would do. Leah wrote them down in her notepad where she was also keeping track of miles driven, stops made, and each photograph Bernie took.

At a Sunoco station off a two-lane byway, an inflatable hot dog man into which air was being continuously blown flung his head skyward, then fell over, again and again, all the while waving his Gumby arms.

Can you fill while I change my film? Bernie asked Leah.

I've never done it, Leah confessed.

You'll figure it out, Bernie said.

Bernie opened the driver's side door, took the changing

tent, which resembled a loose black garment bag, from the back seat and took it to a small metal table on a nearby patch of grass. Bernie had only two film holders, she'd explained, which each took two sheets of four by five film, so after every four pictures she had to put the used film, two orange Kodak boxes—one empty, one full—and her arms into the lighttight changing tent where she'd reload the film holders with new film by feel.

At the gas pump screen, Leah inserted her credit card and the machine beeped, directing her to select fuel type. Each of the three options—regular, extra, and supreme—flashed green, beckoning her to pick them.

Hey, Leah called. Which one?

I can't believe you've never pumped gas before, Bernie said, once they had both finished and were back inside the car.

Alex always does it, Leah said, smiling from awareness of how ridiculous and coddled she sounded.

Alex always does it! Bernie cackled, peeling out of the station.

Sunoco not Mobil, no, BP not Sunoco. Which was the one that was run by a climate change denier? Which was the one run by a Holocaust denier? Which was the one that sent guns to Israel? Chick-fil-A, Popeyes, Wendy's. Which was the one that contributed money to bomb abortion clinics? Which was the one that funded the Proud Boys? Gay chicken, homophobic chicken, misogynist chicken, racist chicken.

Don't know, Bernie said.

But you could look it up, Leah said. And then you would know.

Just leads to more questions, Bernie said. The universe is this big, she said, making her arms into a circle in front of her around the steering wheel. Then she made her hands into a globe and set it in the middle of where the bigger circle had been. This is how much humans can understand.

That little you think? Leah asked.

Yeah I do. Maybe even less.

Words from Leah's fairy tales—*Rapunzel, rampion, greens, straw, gold, cloak, giving up of the firstborn.* These words reoccurred, were uttered again and again in different contexts. Words from Leah's history lessons, Wikipedia, her endless googling, her word of the day app: *slake* (thirst), *dyke* (trough; a dam). There was the sound of Leah's fingernails scratching her scalp for treasures—bits of dandruff, pockets of sebum, scabs—and the sound of her teeth scraping against her nails to extract what had been collected there. There was the sound of Bernie picking her lip and then rolling down the car window to release the skin into the wind. They listened to whatever was on the radio. It was almost a rule. They didn't change the station, no matter what came on. Even when *Delilah* came on, a radio talk show hosted by a very white Christian-lite lady that seemed somehow to be on all the time on every station. People called in with their problems and Delilah asked them questions and played a song relevant to their struggle. But after several days of listening, Leah realized that Delilah only had about five songs in her roster that she offered up for wildly different situations. For example, she played the *Golden Girls* theme "Thank You for Being a Friend" for an estranged mother and daughter, a girl whose best friend was moving to Kansas, and a man who wanted his wife, who had cheated on him, back. She seemed fine, the guy said, but then one day I came home and she was just gone. Leah began to cry a little bit then. What Delilah did was stupidly simple but shockingly effective. It wasn't complicated but it worked, god damn did it work.

People liked it and were grateful. It helped them, changed their mood. It had changed her mood.

This is what I want to do, Leah said then.

Be Delilah?

Something like that, Leah said.

They listened and listened to the same radio station until it went totally static. Then they pressed SEEK, and the whole process began all over again.

Favorite pleasure? Leah asked, as the sun was going down and Hagerstown was drawing near.

Bacon, Bernie said.

That was quick.

It's true. Thick cut, the fat crystalizing and dissolving.

Yes, Leah said. For me, it's swimming.

Swimming is good, Bernie said. Yes. And driving.

My hair up in a ponytail, I miss that sometimes. That was a nice feeling.

It's whatever, Bernie said. Braiding other people's hair. Now, that's nice.

Pants, Leah said. Really good pants, when they feel loose but button just right with a metal button.

Elastic pants, Bernie said. A front-facing baseball cap in a bright color. Well-worn.

Yes.

Ironwork, Bernie said. Iron fences and security doors and old street sewer openings. White houses with dark blue shutters. Lilacs. Peonies.

Sunflowers, Leah said. Cucumbers with salt. Yellow peppers. Orange peppers. Red peppers.

Not green?

Nope. Too bitter.

I like the bitterness, Bernie said.

Basil, Leah said. And cilantro and mint and lime.

Ice, Bernie said.

Ice cream, Leah said.

Ponds. I miss the pond we had behind my house as a kid. Orange lizards. Electric blue crawdads.

Cows, Leah said. Petting horses between their eyes. Those things you can buy that are designed to scratch your whole scalp. You push down on them and the little beads at the end of the wires go everywhere on your head.

I can't take those! Too much stimulation. They make me shudder.

Really? Leah said. I find them very calming. That, or a human hand doing the same thing.

Picking my nose, Bernie said.

Yes, when it's dry.

Yes. I like to approach my nostril in a parallel manner and slide out a full sheet of booger.

Yes, Leah said. A thin layer.

Exactly.

LEAH AND BERNIE STOOD IN an unlit courtyard bordered on two sides by a redbrick building and on the other two by low wrought iron fences overgrown with weeds. According to the internet, this was Rock Candy. They did three full laps around the outside of the building before they finally just waited and listened for music.

There, Bernie said, pointing at a gray metal door being held open by a single cinder block, and then they were inside.

A thin Black woman in a strapless yellow dress stood at

what might have been a speaking lectern. Behind her, a red velvet curtain.

Welcome welcome, the woman said. She checked their IDs, took Leah's money, and asked where they were coming from.

Just passing through, Leah said. Dennis sent us.

Dennis! the woman said, clasping her hands together. We love him. Though we do worry about him, all by himself out there in the boonies, running that website. You know people call his house on the regular threatening to bomb him, kill him, kill his dog because of it? But he just keeps right on doing it. Anyway, she said. Welcome, wayward travelers. And, enjoy. She ripped off two little arcade tickets. For the raffle, she said.

The room was lighter than Leah had expected in a bar, with blond parquet floors. Where the wainscotting ended halfway up the walls, grand windows took over. They were closed, keeping out the night.

The music was sharp and woozy, emanating from a single enormous speaker propped up on little legs by a stage. The whole scene seemed like a wedding, created temporarily with the intent to be packed up later. Clusters of people sat around small round wooden folding tables or stood at a bar which was so dark and ornately carved that it might have been plucked from a historical house of entertainment.

She was standing, the bartender told Leah, on the original floor of the old Hagerstown Palace Theatre. Taylor, the woman who greeted them at the door, had lobbied the city to allow them to operate a gay bar here on the weekends. During the week it belonged to the church choir and the Paperbag Players—a lot of Sondheim. But who knew how long this could all go on, she said, setting down two frosted lowballs of frothing liquid, vaguely yellow and smelling strongly of citrus and ginger.

Leah slurped hers appreciatively, while Bernie tossed hers down like a great shot.

Meaning? Leah asked.

Oh they're trying to shut us down, the bartender said. The zealots. But also the universe. Look. She pointed behind Leah. That whole wall has been declared unstable, soon to come falling down. The bathroom pipes leak rust water. Taylor used her motherly wiles to round up a bunch of handy queers to try and fix it, but it's no use.

The skin of Leah's back could now sense when Bernie was nearby. Leah turned to look at her, then at where she was looking. This was the effect Bernie had started to have on Leah—directing her attention outward, making it bigger.

Plump butches, the fronts of their hair gelled, sat at the tables or danced with each other and with femmes in tight dresses and fishnets. There were tomboys wearing short-sleeved shirts over long-sleeved shirts who leaned on bars and on the corners of tables. There was a bachelorette party of straight women in sashes dancing in a circle and a tangle of gay men in cowboy boots by the mirrors rehearsing what might have been a line dance. One person in a bow tie was fat, possibly fatter than Leah, their substantial belly tucked snugly into a black button-down shirt and draped over the top of their belt. Ah to be one of several, or many, fat people in a room! Leah smiled at this person but they did not smile back. Leah hated this, how sometimes masculine queers would ice her out, like men did to each other.

Kind of sad, isn't it? Bernie said, slurping her last slurp.

It's like we traveled twenty years back in time. I wish I could photograph this, but it would never come out. Can we come back tomorrow?

Sure, Leah said. But I don't know. Everyone seems so happy.

Leah filled out one raffle ticket with her name and phone number and handed the other to Bernie who rolled her eyes but took it.

Need another? the bartender asked, and Leah watched her as she poured. She had the Justin Bieber lesbian swoop and Leah watched the way her hair fell into her eyes as she shook their drinks. The glasses were beautifully cold.

When Leah gave the new drink to Bernie, there was a petite girl with a long ponytail in a button-through lavender dress looking their way. Looking Bernie's way.

That girl is checking you out, Leah said, in a teasing voice.

Bernie downed her second drink in lieu of replying, but it was not ten minutes before the girl came up to Bernie and asked her to dance. It was so loud that Leah couldn't hear what was said, only that the girl stood in front of Bernie expectantly and Bernie leaned her ear down, and then Bernie was looking back at Leah as she moved to the dance floor.

When she was gone, she was gone, she didn't look Leah's way again. Bernie lifted her hands up a lot as she danced and moved them a lot from the wrists. When the girl put out her hands and Bernie took them, Leah had a slightly ill feeling.

Before long, Taylor hiked up the hem of her yellow dress with her thin muscled arms, climbed the stairs to the stage, and tapped a wireless mic. Someone cut the music. Bernie and the girl stopped dancing along with everyone else, but Bernie was leaning her head down again, her hair moving across her neck as the girl said something. Bernie nodded quickly, and looked at Leah. There was clapping.

I want to thank you all for coming out tonight, Taylor said, her Adam's apple bobbing gracefully, to our benefit raffle for Sarah Blakemore, a longtime friend and sister here at Rock Candy. People cheered. A tall redhead wearing jeans and sensible slingbacks came up on the stage. Waved. Got a little teary.

You want to talk? Taylor said, but the second woman waved the microphone away for a few seconds. Then took it.

I just want to say I am very touched. I am grateful to you all for trying to help me to get this surgery. And to this place, whatever becomes of it. We've had these years. I'll remember them.

More applause and someone shouted, We love you Sarah!

No no, Taylor said to someone on the floor in front of the stage. Aw fuck, really? OK. OK. Sorry y'all, Taylor said, speaking into the mic again. But we'll have to use the port-o-johns again tonight.

A collective groan.

I know, I know. But do not despair. It is time for the raffle winners! If I may please have my lovely assistant come up here. Lovely assistant where are you?

The fat butch in the bow tie appeared with a large glass fishbowl full of tickets.

Here he is. Is he not lovely? Yes. Give him a round of applause. Now here we go, I swear there is no favoritism, I will close my eyes. OK people, check your ticket stubs.

The prize was a romantic stay for two at a Gettysburg bed-and-breakfast, a top-of-the-line vibrator that looked like a modern art sculpture, and a set of nipple clamps. The crowd hooted.

OK, Taylor said. She stuck her hand into the bowl, cast about in it for a while, and then pulled out a ticket. She read off a long string of numbers.

Woo hoo, someone cried, and one of the beautiful femmes in fishnets came galloping up to claim her prize.

And now the runner-up, Taylor said, and again closed her eyes and chose from the bowl. She read the number. Silence.

Read it again! someone called, so she did. Still no one rose to claim it.

People, she said. Check your tickets people.

Bernie pulled hers from her pocket and looked at it a long time.

Oh! she said and raised her hand. It's me.

The crowd applauded.

Ahhh we have a winner, Taylor said. Our out-of-town friend—what's your name?—and for you Bernie we have two tickets to The Caverns and a nice pocket-sized vibrator! It's small, but it's mighty!

On the stage, Bernie put one arm in front and one in back, bowed, and accepted the brightly decorated prize bag. She reached her hand in and pulled out the thickly packaged vibrator, showing its little silver egg and big white plastic controller to the crowd.

ALL THE WAY BACK TO their motel, Leah teased Bernie about the girl and the toy. No sidewalk so they walked in the dark, warm street. People had gardened, they had created flowers. There were sheds and redbrick alleys and piles of trash in open areas.

Bernie, Leah said, my little gay bar queen.

That's me, Bernie said. She was breathing loud and smiling and swinging her arms. At one point, Leah even caught her doing a little skip.

I know you and Violet hooked up, Leah said. Sorry, thin walls.

Not your fault, Bernie said. I blame the person who put a door between our rooms and the housemate before me, what was her name? Who would put a piece of insulation *outside* a wall and expect it to block out sound?

Kate, Leah said. I know. But you and Violet?

Over, Bernie said. Kaput. They're back with Lucy Vincent I guess.

Nightmare, Leah said. I give it a month like last time. Any other prospects?

Not a one.

But love. Dating. A relationship or several. Do you want it?

Bernie took a long time before answering. She began to kick a rock ahead of her as she walked.

I don't know, she said, having lost the rock. I want parts of it?

Which parts?

I don't know. Maybe the parts where you talk, do things together.

No comfort? No sex?

Yeah, Bernie said. Those parts too. But not the parts where you can't separate, where you meld together, where you feel smothered, where you're fighting for who's in charge.

Definitely not, Leah said.

But how to avoid that? Doesn't it always become that, eventually?

Separate apartments maybe, Leah said. But on the same

floor. Or in the same building? Like Susan Sontag and Annie Leibovitz. Though from what I've heard, that's no model. Sontag was always bullying Leibovitz, telling her like, You're so dumb.

Really?

Yeah. I watched this documentary about it. Sontag's son was like, Mom, you either need to be nicer to Annie or you need to break up with her.

Yikes, Bernie said.

I know, Leah said. But the rest of it.

Bernie found a new rock, a smaller one, and kicked that for a while. Yeah, Bernie said. It could work.

IN THE MORNING, IN LIGHT that Bernie deemed good enough, they returned to the Rock Candy parking lot and Bernie photographed the building. She only took one picture, but Leah talked to five people in that time who wandered by and wanted to understand the camera. It was fascinating, how people flocked to this camera when they would flee an iPhone. Put an iPhone in a stranger's face and watch them recoil. But this camera? It attracted. Each person wanted also to tell Leah, as she ran interference for Bernie, about another place they should photograph. The church over on Laurel which will not be there much longer. The quarry outside Millersville that's been filled in with water. The diner on 15, with its original sign. Leah wrote all these down dutifully in her notebook.

They did go to that diner, a busy one with a menu as big as a book. Leah was decisive this time, ordering exactly what she felt—pancakes and potatoes and coffee and chocolate milk, and Bernie was still doing a lot of smiling. They were still carrying a little glitter from the night before on their skin. The waitress had a beautiful purple satin bow in her hair which Leah liked to watch as it moved around the room, now folded over, now pulled taut with gravity.

As they ate, they were joking and—was it possible—flirting? Bernie had been asking for stories of young Leah, of Leah before Alex.

I used to go on a lot of dates, Leah said. If you can believe it. I was so horny in college, since high school had been such a wasteland. I would ask out anyone I thought might say yes.

I believe it, Bernie said.

Leah cocked her mouth to respond, then felt herself sway. Everything tilted then, slowly then very fast, and she caught herself hard with her right hand just before her head hit the floor. She was nearly lying on her side. The edges of her sneakers' rubber soles squeaked along the linoleum floor as she moved her legs to a sitting position. Her glass of chocolate milk had spilled and was dripping off the table onto the floor. The chair she had been sitting on had fallen into the aisle behind her; a shard of its leg was splintered at an odd angle and the rest had broken clean off. Leah looked around for the missing piece of wood.

I don't know where the leg went, Leah said to Bernie, who was crouching down next to her.

Are you alright? Bernie asked.

I broke the chair, Leah said. I'm sorry.

Don't be, Bernie said.

Rising up on her knees, Bernie grabbed a handful of brown paper napkins and began laying them out over the brown milk.

It happens sometimes, Leah said. I'm really sorry, she said again.

Why are you apologizing? It's their shitty chair. Bernie stood and offered her hand but Leah could not take it. She had to use her own knees and her own hand to push off and get to her feet. People were looking. The waitress with the purple bow was looking. A fat straight couple seated at a booth were looking but in a way that meant solidarity or scorn? Leah didn't know.

Bernie pointed to an open booth. Let's move there, she said.

Leah felt dazed, dehydrated, like all the blood had fled her brain.

Reinstalled, Leah held her plate with both hands and looked down at it. It held a pile of brown potatoes, red with ketchup, and two pancakes wet with butter.

What were we talking about? Bernie asked.

Leah's chest felt tight and shallow and it was difficult to get the breath through and over the dam there. She breathed and breathed. Drank some water. I'm not sure, Leah said.

Here, the waitress with the purple bow said, bringing over some new silverware. It was impossible to tell if she was annoyed at Leah, though Leah touched every note of her voice to find out.

We were talking about you, Bernie said to Leah. What a fuckboy you once were.

Leah's eyes detected the flying thing too late to move her face out of the way. It collided softly with her cheek, leaving a sweet, doughy smell.

Bernie cried out and turned her head around the room. A chunk of hot dog bun lay on the table next to Leah's water glass. Then a snort came from a table that held a foursome of white tween girls, who all erupted into apoplectic laughter, and squinched down in their booth. One girl with shiny brown hair pushed back in a large blue headband said something Leah couldn't hear and the others shushed her and pushed on her arms.

Bernie was on her feet and then she was at the edge of the girls' booth, squatting again, spreading her elbows out on the edge of their table and resting her chin on top of her overlapping hands.

Hi, Leah heard Bernie say.

Hi, one of the girls said.

I'm talking to you, Bernie said to the girl with the blue headband, who had taken out a phone and was busying herself with it. So you better pay attention.

Bernie made her voice too low for Leah to hear. She spoke to the girls for several minutes. Their faces became more and more stunned and then grave and then ashen until Bernie stood and walked back to Leah. She took some cash out of her ass pocket and dropped it on the table.

Let's go, she said. She took Leah's arm and lifted Leah to a standing position. Leah let herself be walked out of the restaurant.

Get some new chairs, Bernie said to the waitress with the purple bow, as they passed her, and she stared back at them openly, mid–pad scribble.

What did you say to those girls? Leah asked when they hit the parking lot.

Not much, Bernie said. I just quietly explained to them how their bodies were about to change. How first their necks and thighs would start to bulge and then they would get these things everyone calls breasts but are really just sacks of fat. And I explained to them how when they got these sacks of fat, their bodies would suddenly become fair game for boys and old men to say things about, from cars as they drove by, and in school and at parties. And that their bodies would suddenly become fair game for girls and women to say things about, across kitchen tables and doctors' desks. And I told them that these comments might lead them, if they did not have the words of some other powerful perspective, to change the way they lived forever in a way that was irreversible and that would haunt them for the rest of their lives. And that if they didn't want to be like any of those people, they should shut the fuck up and never do what they did to you ever again.

But how do you know? Leah asked simply then. You're thin.

I have eyes, don't I? Bernie said. It's obvious how that made you feel.

Back in the car Leah felt righteous, and also, shamed. Why did people feel so many feelings about other people's bodies? It made no sense. But other people's shitty comments and actions were not the whole problem, Leah knew, maybe not even the main thing. If she could just rewire the hardware that told her brain what she was seeing and what it meant, she would be in business. Because the worst part was not even what other people did to her but what she did to herself. She didn't have to look down at her body to know how she felt about it. *Disgust* was the best word for it she supposed, though she didn't have to name it anymore, it was automatically understood, the groove so worn that she felt the word rather than thought it.

The main thing could also be her own eyes, if you considered the eyes as only physical, as only instruments of sight, impartial conveyers of information. Though how did Leah know they were impartial? Maybe her eyes themselves distorted. It was possible, though the internet did not know. Leah had googled this before, but come to no conclusion.

Do you think it's people's eyes or their brain that makes them hate fat people? Leah asked then.

Bernie was turning them onto the ramp to Interstate 81.

Brain, Bernie said. There's nothing wrong with our eyes.

VII.

ALL THE WAY DOWN THE LONG DIRT ROAD TO THE CAVERNS, SAD giraffes shoved their small heads through bent chain-link fencing. Bernie parked the station wagon in a sparsely occupied lot by a yellow house with scrolled white columns that resembled a grand mansion shrunk down in miniature. LUXURY HISTORIC HOTEL, a sign read. CLOSED FOR PRIVATE EVENT, PHUNG & LEWIS WEDDING.

Leah followed Bernie down a path marked by mossy stones to the entrance/gift shop, a small building shaded on all sides by the branches of a towering maple tree, as if the forest were slowly reclaiming it. By the entrance, a monumental piece of rock cut into a shape as tall and phallic as the Chrysler Building sat atop a limestone pedestal.

Inside, they were selling "authentic" pieces of the caverns that had been polished and cut in half, ranging in price from $15.99 to $309.99 depending on their size and luster. There were picture postcards for two or four or twelve dollars, their fronts offering up floodlit photographs of The Caverns' insides in all their textural, colorful glory. Stalagmites? Tites? Who can remember.

Not I. I too have been to The Caverns; The Housemate and I took our friend's kid here for his fourth birthday. Back then—this was the year 2000, I think—it was pristinely cared for and packed, cars idling along the driveway, with waits as long as an hour or two to get in. After the boat tour, we took the "Safari Tour" to look at all the animals they used to have—wolves and cheetahs and bison—and our temporary child had a ball running around and taking pictures of the animals with my Canon AE-1. The Housemate and I sat in the grass with our charge and had a picnic, though we were careful not to touch knees or press shoulders. There was no way around looking gay for The Housemate, but I might have passed for the kid's harried single mother.

BERNIE AND LEAH'S BOAT TOUR guide, a petite Black woman with firm, muscular legs and a beige vest, held out her hand first to Bernie, who hopped easily onto the boat and took a seat on an open piece of metal that spanned the small vessel's width.

Easy does it, the guide said, holding out her hand to Leah now.

Leah took it and stepped slowly onto the floor of the boat, which rocked a little but not too much. Bernie scooted over, making room for Leah. They sat close, their knees and shoulders touching. The other people on the boat, several white families, a Black family, and a young Chinese couple with two old women—possibly their mothers or aunts—tittered and adjusted their backpacks and cameras.

The guide did something then and a sound warned of wireless audio, like a one-sided walkie-talkie. The guy onshore unhooked the boat's tether and passed it to the guide. The boat began to move, and the air became colder as they approached the darkness of the cavern's entrance and then passed into it. The light disappeared, and with it, the warmth of the day. Leah hugged herself and moved her hands along her arms for the friction. There was a squeaking sound that might have been bats, and quiet murmurs from the boat's passengers. The young couple said nothing but they clutched each other's hands, interlacing their fingers, as if it was the easiest thing in the world to be so attached. The two older women reached in their bags, each for their own camera.

Once upon a time, Leah heard the guide say, in the beginning, there was a massive single supercontinent surrounded by ocean, and Pennsylvania was at its near exact center. Things happened, time passed, slowly in reality, but quick for our purposes. Pennsylvania was a lush tropical rainforest, then covered with water. When dead plants are submerged and then sediment falls on top of them and applies pressure for a very, very long time, you get coal. When the same pressure is applied to mud at the bottom of the ocean, you get limestone.

Plates kept crashing into each other and creating folds, then separating, their edges stretching out like taffy. A glacier came, covering much of North America with ice a thousand feet thick. When the glacier melted, acidic groundwater filled the crevices of the limestone and then drained out, again and again, dissolving the soft rock and widening holes into caverns like this one. Water dripped and dripped for thirty million years. When stalactites, dribbling downward from the ceiling, meet stalagmites, building up from the floor, you get columns and pillars. Here's one that looks like the Statue of Liberty! Here's one that looks like a roaring bear!

This cavern was first discovered by the Seneca, the largest nation in the Iroquois Confederacy and the one that gave us voting and democracy. But in a series of bloody battles with white settlers, the land that became The Caverns was taken from them. Some people say that when this happened, some of the Indigenous peoples threw themselves down into these waters rather than give up their home. That their ghosts are still here, calling out in the night. Spooky huh?

Look, cried a little blond girl, pointing to where a motion-sensor light was illuminating the side of a rock face adorned with smudged black drawings of figures—deer, and horses maybe.

Think they're real? Leah asked Bernie.

Who cares, Bernie said. They're beautiful.

The guide was teaching them now about the kinds of rocks that were here and not here, but Leah had stopped listening. She did this sometimes when she reached informational or emotional overload. Nothing more could come in, or out.

Duck, the guide said, and all the boat's passengers did, narrowly missing a low shelf of rock, and then they were in an enormous chamber that was both dark and light at the same time, dark because they were in a cave and light because many powerful floodlights were pointed up along the rock formations, almost to the ceiling.

For a long time, the guide went on, these caves were regular waterways, ways to get from here to there, no more, no less. The only thing we added were the lights. The guide pushed another button and all around them then were deeply mottled formations, lit up with warm amber light, white and gray and camel brown, a marbled effect of muted colors like you might get on dyed paper. The rocks looked as if a storm of golf balls had hurtled into their surface over a long period of time.

Shit, said a teenage boy.

Lord, said a mother.

In the gift shop, the words *Cathedral Room* had been used, and now Leah could see why. The height was the thing, the sheer height of the columns that rose from the water and went to the ceiling, and their intricacy, their colors and shadows, their nubbins and grooves. It was shockingly quiet in the space but for the sound of the boat moving through the water and the rumpled sounds of the other passengers—the breath coming in and out of lungs, the whoosh of fabric against thigh when hand went into pocket.

And then another hand moved and it was Bernie's hand slipping into Leah's. All the air was sucked from Leah's lungs and she was afraid to move even an inch for fear of spooking Bernie.

Excuse me, one of the fathers called. And which chemical compounds produce which rocks?

Leah looked at Bernie but Bernie was watching the guide.

Calcite, the guide said. Gypsum. Calcium carbonate. Flowstone.

The boat floated on. A few minutes later, Bernie took her hand back.

WHEN THEY EMERGED FROM THE cave, when they climbed the steps, both Leah and Bernie panting a bit; when they stopped to put their hands on their hips and have a sip from Leah's water bottle and look at the families streaming by—here a father not waiting for his children, there a daughter not waiting for her parents—and when they followed the straight backs of a girl's knees all the way to the top step where the cave entrance and the gift shop entrance and the inn entrance made a triangle, Leah saw, standing in front of the inn's double doors, a couple on their wedding day. A white woman in a narrow white dress that showed off her sleeves of tattoos stood with an East Asian man in a dark blue suit being photographed by a capable-looking photographer who wore a flat cap and a fanny pack. The bride wore a flower crown, not a small one that rested on top of her hair but a large voluminous one that encircled her head, loosely, like a ring encircles the pole of a ring toss.

If I were taking their picture, Bernie said, I wouldn't do it there.

I'd like to see what you would do was all Leah said, before Bernie was striding off.

As Leah watched the couple and their photographer, she remembered that she used to have a dream as a child. In the dream, she was walking through Central Park in a wedding dress. She knew she was being led toward the person she would have to marry but she did not know who it was. In a much too on-the-nose metaphor, the wedding dress was ludicrously heavy, beaded perhaps, and even if she could have lifted up the dress and run, there was nowhere to go; her guests were already lined up on either side of her, pointing the way forward. There was nothing to do but march slowly on toward the altar and whoever was standing there. The dream never concluded, it was never satisfying. The marrying person was never revealed. What Leah remembered most was the sense that she was trapped on a literal path of movement, of direction, unable to step off it.

OK, the flat-capped photographer said. That's enough here, let's go around back to the courtyard.

Leah followed, loitering a respectful distance away. From her location in the grass between the courtyard and the gift shop, she might have been looking for a quiet place to pause after being deeply moved by rocks. The courtyard was decorated with multicolor crepe streamers that all began from a point at the top of one of the stone façades.

As Leah watched, the photographer, holding a chunky digital camera, told the couple to do things—now turn to face each other, now kiss—which they mostly did not do. Mostly they just stood there, holding hands and saying things under their breath to each other. It seemed they had made a silent pact to thwart the photographer and she was seeming thwarted, becoming increasingly shrill and agitated as she directed the couple into more and more ludicrous poses.

Bernie appeared with the big camera bag and stood at Leah's elbow, looking on.

The bride turned her head, looked right at Bernie and Leah, and laughed. It was as if she was inviting them in, Leah felt, as if she somehow wanted to bring her life into contact with what Bernie and Leah were doing.

The groom had broken down completely too which only sent the bride into further hysterics.

Alright, said the photographer in the voice of downtrodden mothers everywhere. I give up. I'll be inside, let me know when you're ready to take this seriously.

I'm sorry, the bride said, collecting herself. My mother

was the one who wanted—we shouldn't have wasted your time.

The photographer walked to the inn's back door, opened it, and let it slam behind her.

Hello there, the bride called out to them.

Leah watched Bernie's face. Leah watched the skin of Bernie's face and the corners of her eyes, which twitched slightly, and seemed, though Leah could not be sure, moist. Without a word, and in what seemed to Leah like a great rush, a speed she had never seen Bernie work at before, Bernie set up the camera.

BERNIE MADE ONE PICTURE WITH the couple standing in front of the stairs that led down to the cave, its dark maw behind them. Then she set up another of them outside the gift shop, the camera far away so it could take in the whole scene—bride and groom, squat building, greedy trees overhead, column of rock.

I'm in the way, Leah said, after Bernie asked her to move out of the frame. I'm going to sit down. Her head felt light, her stomach hungry.

Our photographer had a room, the bride said. Her dress gaped at the armpits and her hair was very red, probably dyed. Upstairs, she said. I'll show you.

She led Leah up a narrow set of stone steps to a little second-floor room above the gift shop. Inside, the room was cold and clean with French doors that opened to a balcony that overlooked the courtyard. When the bride opened the doors, the thick textured white curtains billowed into the room. There were open shelves on the walls which displayed many rocks, pieces of the caverns. Their colors were milky and dull and touched by a powdery white substance but they still conveyed the sensation of clarity and of color. They were orange and purple and black. The largest piece had a shelf all to itself and was large as a human head.

Thank you, Leah said, sleepily, sitting on the room's firm bed.

You'll be comfortable here, the bride said. No one will bother you. And then she was gone.

WHEN LEAH OPENED HER EYES, Bernie was standing above her, and then Bernie was crouching down.

What? Leah said.

I got the shimmer, Bernie said.

Bernie's face. Those heavy cheeks. Her open mouth. Leah could see Bernie's little teeth and her tongue.

A song started to play, loud and ungraceful, from outside. It was a pop ballad from the eighties about being lost and looking, time after time.

What's happening? Leah asked.

The wedding, Bernie said.

They went out to the balcony. Chairs had been set up in the courtyard, sturdy white folding chairs that were full of people, and the couple was walking in together. Some people stood, but others, too old or too tired or not quick enough on their feet, did not, which seemed fine. There were no bridesmaids or groomsmen or even parents, just the two people. There was no one standing at the end of their walk to marry them. *Suitcase of memories,* Leah thought she heard. *The drumbeat sound of time.*

We will marry ourselves, the woman said into a cordless microphone.

We don't have much in common, the man said when it was his turn. My parents immigrants to this country, yours here for generations.

Too fucking long! someone yelled from the audience, and everyone laughed.

But weirdly, we have a lot in common, the man continued. Being from this strange shit county. Pennsyltucky. But we're both proud. Look! You can see the house where I grew up, just there. Yeah, the man said, in response to a cry of surprise from the audience. Why else would we choose this place to get married? Sorry no offense to The Caverns, which are awesome. Seriously take the boat tour during cocktail hour and see some fucking beautiful old rocks.

But, he continued, all jokes aside, no one gets all this more than you do. This place that people are always fighting about and fighting over what it means.

When the man stopped speaking, the woman leaned in and kissed him. Then she snatched the microphone, triggering another chorus of laughter.

I don't have much to say, she said. Except for that it's always been hard for me to feel. I don't know. Together with someone. But with you, it's not so hard. I have enough room.

Awww, went the crowd.

What if, Leah thought then, all this time it was not that the wedding dream was a nightmarish prophecy of the prison that was surely coming for her but rather simply a thing designed to show her own failure of imagination. You could trade the dress for a suit or some other outfit. You could pick the person, or people. You could step off the path.

Someone in the front row stood and was holding a large red tissue-paper lantern, and it seemed to Leah for a moment that they were going to light it on fire. Instead they lit a candle, put it inside the tissue-paper lantern, and then slowly let go. The lantern wobbled a little, rose, descended sharply, nearly hitting the bride's shoulder and drawing good-natured gasps from the crowd. Then it began to lift again, rising and rising on a diagonal before snagging on a long rock that jutted out above the balcony next to Leah and Bernie. The lantern did not extinguish, but only sat there patiently, rippling with internal flame.

A man in a chocolate-brown suit was rushing over and Leah felt relief. He would fix it. His body seemed made for physical heroics and also to be looked at while doing them.

But he did not fix it. He scrambled and scrabbled in his dress shoes but he could not reach; there was no way to climb up the wall.

Hello, he called to Leah and to Bernie. Hello up there!

But Bernie just stood there, as if mesmerized by the lantern's color and its precarity.

Leah turned in to the room, looking for anything she could use to hit the lantern. She found a broom hanging on a wall and rushed back out.

Someone cheered.

Aha! someone else cried. Yes! A broom!

The lantern was just out of reach of the broom's handle so Leah leaned far over the balcony's edge on her tiptoes. She hit it, then hit it again but still the lantern did not dislodge.

The only way was to somehow get to the next balcony. The

space between Bernie and Leah's balcony and this second balcony was not that far, perhaps four feet, but if she missed, the drop could mean a broken limb, or worse.

No way, said one voice inside her head.

Try, said a second.

Using the exterior wall of the building to steady herself, Leah climbed up on the railing of their balcony and, before she could change her mind, jumped.

Another cheer went up from below. Yes! Damn!

From this new location, Leah reached with her hands. Her thighs felt strong and her arms powerful, for what else was fat really, besides power? Force, mass, and acceleration. She jumped a little, exploding from her thighs and calves, and easily hit the lantern free. It hesitated for a moment, wobbling, then took off quickly into the sky.

A great round of applause went up. The couple waved and shouted, thank you, thank you! The woman blew Leah a kiss and the man raised his hands over his head to applaud.

You're welcome! Leah called. Flushed. Out of breath.

Well, the woman said, I guess we're married now.

And the crowd went wild, whistling.

Leah looked over at Bernie, separated as they were now by the space between the balconies. Bernie was grinning.

Can you get back here? Bernie asked.

Yes, Leah said. Now that she had done it once, she could leap across that space ten, twenty, a hundred times.

That was something, Bernie said.

It was nothing, Leah said.

Bernie seemed not to know what to do then. She turned away and ducked underneath the dark cloth, for she had set up the camera on the balcony, pointing down into the courtyard. Pushed down the cable release. OK, she said. Then pulled out her phone.

What are you doing? Leah asked.

Setting an alarm, Bernie said. A long exposure will take hours.

Bernie moved back into the nearly dark room, sat down on the bed, and rolled her neck. Leah sat too, but far enough away that another Bernie could have fit between them. The bed was dense and soft at the same time, possibly a futon.

That was something, Bernie said.

You said that already, Leah said.

Oh, I did, didn't I. She laughed. I wish we had something to drink.

We could go get something from the party.

But neither of them moved. And then, ever so slightly, Bernie turned her body and leaned slowly toward Leah, so incredibly slowly. Leah didn't know if Bernie wanted to go the whole distance on her own or be met halfway.

What a fool Leah was! She waited so long.

When Bernie's cheek made contact with Leah's shoulder, Leah felt the full weight of Bernie's head and smelled her shampoo. Only then did Leah move, allowing her head to loll on top of Bernie's. Several more minutes passed. Then, at last, Bernie turned her face in to Leah's upper arm. She rolled her face, her pointy nose, back and forth against Leah's arm and she opened her mouth and touched Leah's skin with the tip of her tongue.

Salty, she said.

She looked up at Leah with just the very tops of her eyes, and Leah leaned down then. Bernie's face was there, her mouth hot.

There was a way that when she put her mind to it, Leah could get directly to the heart of the matter. Her tongue was in Bernie's mouth and she was also holding Bernie at the back of her skull and the small of her back. Leah felt completely in control and this was fine with her. Bernie was not limp but she was pliable, appreciative, making small sexy noises of good feeling. Bernie's head felt sharp and round at the same time in Leah's hand. Leah could kill Bernie if she wanted to, just crack her head hard against the white, white walls of this room.

Leah was extremely aware now of her cunt which was connected to her stomach which was connected to her mouth and hands and this awareness translated into action. Soon they were lying next to each other on the bed, Bernie naked from the waist down, lovely and open as a book.

Leah's arms felt strong again, thick with potential energy. She used one to prop herself up so she was above Bernie, and the other to touch Bernie lightly all over. She paused in the places where Bernie's breath caught and moved over the silent places. She placed her whole hand on Bernie's stomach causing Bernie to breathe and breathe in quick huffing breaths.

Bernie closed her eyes, then squeezed them tight, then covered her face with her hands.

What's wrong? Leah asked. Did I hurt you?

Bernie shook her head.

What then?

I'm too old, Bernie said. For this feeling.

You're not old, Leah said.

I'm all wrong. Bernie said. It's too late.

You're not, Leah said. It's just the right time.

I HAD WAITED A LONG time for this, for Bernie and Leah to stop squandering their freedom. As I watched them have sex, I felt proud but, if I am honest, angry too. Didn't they know how much easier they had it? Didn't they care? They did not. Everyone lives in their own time, I reminded myself, with no sense of what came before.

I had to go lie down in my own bed. But when I lay down, Bernie and Leah were still there in my mind. I saw them, except now they were out of the story, somewhere else. In my mind's eye, I stood on the edge of a great cliff and below me and all around me was water. It was not Pennsylvania but some other more exciting place, a cove rather than a cave, though the day was white, not blue. I stood with my feet on the edge, and I wore some sort of ruffled nightgown that went all the way down to my ankles.

Below me in the water now were Bernie and Leah. They were not naked or even wearing bathing suits but rather had all their clothes on. Their hair was wet of course, but other than that they looked dry. They were not looking at each other but rather looked up at me.

Come down, Bernie called out.

Yes, Leah called up. Come down and join us.

I shifted my weight to my toes and peered over the edge. The water, with Bernie and Leah in it, seemed very far away.

I began to cry—not in my mind's eye but in my body, there on my bed in Philadelphia. I don't know why exactly. I think it was because I knew that I had to get down into that water and that I would, eventually, but there was nothing in me that knew how to do it. I tried to picture myself leaping, even stepping, off the rock, tried to imagine what it would feel like to fall and hit the water, go under, surface again, breathe. Somehow I knew the water would not be cold, the temperature was not the issue. It was the movement, the stepping off, the leaving of solid ground for air as Leah had done.

I lay there for a while, crying and trying to imagine it. I tried several different techniques. I listened to a guided meditation on my phone. I masturbated and opened my mouth, panting, when I came. This felt nice. But when I returned to the scene in my mind, I was still on the rock's edge and Bernie and Leah were still there, in the water, calling up.

It's time, they called out.

I felt dehydrated, possibly from all the sexy breathing I'd just done.

Just do it, they said.

After a long time—several hours might have passed in my body, or a full day—I had exhausted all the resources it was taking to stay on the rock. And I was able to see it then, I saw myself, not stepping, not leaping but sort of pushing off against my left foot and leading with my right. I felt myself falling and it was alright, fast, but alright. I felt myself hit the water and felt that it was, as I had sensed, a pleasing temperature. I was still in my nightgown, which in this vision was not see-through but a thick enough white cotton to be opaque even when wet.

Hi, Bernie and Leah said to me when I came up above the water's surface. They spoke to me from my eye level now, all three of us in the water, looking at each other.

Hi, I said.

You're here, they said. It's time.

Back in my body, I got up and opened the door to the office closet. I rooted around in The Housemate's things until I found the box of photo albums, the photos I took not for the world but just for me. They had been hard to take—bad light, bad structure—and harder to keep. But The Housemate had insisted.

People had stared at The Housemate when we visited The Caverns all those years ago, and during other travel we did at that time. Little kids would run up to her and ask, What are you? Flipping through the album, I found a picture of The Housemate posing in front of an orange camping tent, from a trip she and I took to a state park near Scranton. In the photograph, The Housemate had her hands on her hips, was wearing absurd pants that zipped off at the knee, and was smiling so wide she showed all her crooked teeth. The tent was an orange so bright it looked incandescent. We spent two nights at that park, and on the second one, I was bitten by a snake. It happened so fast: first the slither, then the sleep. It was that moment you fear: me in a hospital bed, them saying no. No she can't sign. No she can't come in.

Where is your husband? the doctor asked.

No husband, I said.

Oh, he said. A pretty girl like you?

But we have an extra room free for your friend, no extra charge, they would say, it's just there, across the breezeway. Come out with us, they would say, have a drink, just one drink. Let us walk you home, they would say, it's dangerous around here, not safe for girls like you. You better be careful with that haircut, they would say to The Housemate, people will make assumptions, not me but other people. And always, over and over again, they would say: But where are your husbands?

Eventually, we made them up. My husband, Tim, was an insurance salesman from Doylestown and we'd been high school sweethearts. Two children, two girls. But not The Housemate. Her husband was a Philadelphia city boy, through and through. Donald, she named him. An oil painter. A whirlwind romance, she'd say. No children, all we needed was each other. Got divorced and then realized our mistake. We even had a second wedding, with a cake and everything.

SOON, LATER, A LONG TIME after she had made Bernie come, Leah's hand, still inside Bernie, felt Bernie's blood pumping. Felt her walls clenching and unclenching.

Bernie's phone alarm went off. The photograph was ready.

Neither of them moved. The balcony doors were still open and the curtains were billowing again. Some people called this time of day golden hour, Leah knew, or the gloaming. She lay her head down on Bernie's thigh, which was pale and dry and smooth and smelled in a way that was outside of language, and familiar. It was the smell of home, Leah realized. Not a metaphorical place, but a real one. The house in Philadelphia. Bernie smelled like the towels and the bath mat that hung in the bathroom they shared. The hallway between their rooms. The air that came into the house at night.

Downstairs, in the courtyard of the inn, Leah could hear it, people were eating and drinking, clinking knives against glasses and forks against plates, and she would have liked to go down there too, at some point, and eat what they were eating and drink what they were drinking. She imagined cold basil chicken and pesto pasta salad; she imagined champagne. She remembered the lantern, what it had looked like caught, and what it felt like when she hit it free, the way it seemed to hover for a moment, holding still in the air, before it took off and began to rise.

PART 3

I.

AFTER THE SHOWINGS, FIRST IN PINE PARK AND THEN IN OUTdoor venues around the country, and after the viral post and the flurry of coverage and the offers of representation from literary agencies and galleries, it would be the subject of much debate in think pieces and on social media threads and inside living rooms both grand and modest occupied by people who knew or had once known or who would never know Bernie and Leah: Just what was it about what they did that was so special, that struck such a chord?

It was luck, went one sprawling piece for *The Washington Post* written by a boomer white guy novelist who had once been very popular but no longer was. *Pure dumb luck and being in the right place at the right time, like it is for everyone who hits it big. 2016 had us all scratching our heads about rural places, particularly Appalachia, and demanding to know what people in those places wanted. And then Pennsylvania was at the center of the 2020 election in a way that pundits might have predicted but regular people had not understood until it happened. As the pandemic raged and the ballots were counted inside the Philadelphia convention cen-*

ter and the streets outside filled with people dancing in mailbox costumes and threatening bombs alike, Bernie Abbott and Leah McCausland were there, with this trove of striking and significant images and text.

For me it is Bernie Abbott and has been all along, wrote a Gen X white woman museum curator in a column for *The New York Times. Abbott has a kind of prescience that we need to give her, above all, credit for. It is she who is actually from Pennsylvania, who grew up in its hills and hollers, and who knows its diners and rivers and people like the backs of her hands. And it was she who saw that Gen Z was already growing tired of newer and newer technology, newer and newer ways of seeing. I couldn't have predicted that my daughter would be taking pictures now with Polaroid film nor that the point-and-shoot digital camera I used in college would become cool again because of Taylor Swift and Kylie Jenner, but Bernie Abbott could have. She, more than anyone, saw that the only way to capture our ever-shrinking attention spans was to go hard the other way, to pivot all the way back to a way of photographing that has its roots in the earliest uses of light and shadow.*

In a long thread on the text-sharing app, a millennial Black writer who had recently won a prestigious prize for their online criticism wrote: *All those who single out Bernie Abbott, with her aloof attitude and her big camera, are missing the real visionary quality of Changing Pennsylvania and what will make it a culturally significant project for years, possibly decades, to come. Despite the arduous, meticulous and unconventional processes of their making, Abbott's photographs would be just pretty pastoral images without Leah McCausland's playful, elliptical—even strange—overlaid text and profoundly *queer* voice to give it all meaning. By all accounts it was McCausland's idea to go* *on the trip in the first place, it was McCausland's idea to show the pictures not in traditional galleries or photo books but on the big public outdoor screens that made visible the deeply democratic intent of their enterprise, and it is McCausland's commitment to financial accessibility that we see in the nonprofit arm of Changing Pennsylvania, which offers free classes in the kind of photography Abbott practices to women, trans and nonbinary folks as well as native Philadelphians. It is McCausland who runs backend operations for Changing Pennsylvania, including the administrative labor of raising the money that makes the classes possible. Let us not fall into the facile trap of rewarding only the kinds of labor that are shiny, attractive to light. I suspect that everyone rushing in to praise Abbott—a thin, cisgender, largely feminine-presenting white woman—as a genius might not be as willing to extend the same fawning enthusiasm to McCausland—a fat, butch, Jewish dyke.*

"That's super inaccurate," a multiracial Gen Z trans man known for his strong class and labor analysis said to the camera via the video-sharing app's green screen feature that allowed his small head to float against a screenshotted background of the millennial writer's tweets. "If McCausland gets sidelined it's because they—I'm told that's their preferred pronoun now—have simply not traveled as far from where they began. McCausland was born and bred to be an art world darling so to complain about them not getting their due is like saying we aren't clapping loud enough for someone born on third base. Don't forget that while Abbott grew up working class, McCausland went to a ritzy prep school in Manhattan. Poor them, boo hoo. Eat the rich!"

I BEGAN TO KEEP TRACK of every written mention of Bernie and Leah as they expanded outward into the public eye, printing out each relevant article and putting it into a new box I started for just this purpose. The tweets and videos I "bookmarked" or "favorited," aggregating them for later.

By the fall of 2019, I had begun to feel a little better and to visit Bernie and Leah's street corner less frequently. Following their story had made me remember myself, I guess you could say. In the year that followed, I started showering more, and cooking soup again, and occasionally even making sourdough bread, like everyone else during the pandemic. I even called the friend to see what she had been up to, and how her kid was faring in college.

We thought you'd died! she said as she patted my hand, then snatched it away again, remembering the disease. We were sitting on her porch near the avenue, sweating in floral cloth masks.

We all miss The Housemate, she said, though she uttered aloud The Housemate's real name. It wasn't only you who lost her, you know. Though you could have behaved better at the end there, mm?

Upon this friend, I did not call again.

I started curving my walks more consistently eastward, cautiously joining the line to get into the co-op grocery store, and even making it as far as Pine Park where the farmer's market, stalls spaced a safe distance apart, was held each Saturday morning. As I palpated a peach or struggled with the moist friction of putting a head of lettuce into a plastic sack, I ran into all my old people. Their hair was thinner, their children older, or gone, and their speech as rusty and jerky as my own. Though we could not find an appropriate rhythm of conversation, none of us able to figure out when to speak or be silent, it felt good to again be a part of the juicy jagged imperfections of life. The masks, which half obscured everyone's faces, helped me feel at ease, cushioning the full weight of exposure. After my shopping, I'd sit cross-legged on the grass and watch the dogs running, the dueling tarot stalls competing for customers, and the young queers lolling in twos and threes, going over the details of the previous night, hoping that I'd see Bernie and Leah. I never did.

But it was on one of these walks that I saw the flyer, fastened with clear plastic tape to a silver corner pole among the other posters for house concerts and lost cats and play parties.

COME SEE "CHANGING PENNSYLVANIA," A PROJECTED VIDEO SHOW OF PHOTOGRAPHS AND WORDS. OR WATCH AT HOME SCAN THIS CODE. PLUS FREE CAMERA DEMONSTRATION FOR ANYONE BUT CIS DUDES.* FREE. PINE PARK. 9 P.M. **Unless you self-identify as from Philadelphia!*

There were many, many dates listed, and my first thought was that Bernie and Leah should have been more judicious, should have tried to create more of a sense of scarcity and desire.

When I arrived in the dusty portion of Pine Park where dogs and children played, with my teal beach chair and my homemade seltzer, there were Bernie and Leah with one black plastic folding table, one projector, a small projector screen, and Bernie's big camera.

Oh hello, Leah said. Ever the spokesperson. Welcome to *Changing Pennsylvania*.

Thank you, I said, thank you very much indeed. I sounded so old.

Bernie stood up from where she had been crouching, futzing with something under the table.

I know you, she said. You're Ann Baxter.

Leah looked back and forth anxiously between Bernie and me, hating to be out of the know.

That's me, I said.

We looked at your photographs in college, she said. Your series on small-town carnivals? I loved those.

That's nice, I said. No one ever knows that series. I made them with my partner.

Who was your partner? Bernie asked, so I said The Housemate's name.

Never heard of her, Bernie said.

Leah too shook her head.

They told me their names and I made faces of interest as if I didn't already know everything. I chatted with them about the camera and about where they had been on their trips. It was strange to hear them aloud, speaking *to me*, in regular life, when for so long I'd been watching and researching them, unobserved. They sounded and behaved just the same, if slightly more stilted and formal. And then I pointed at the camera. May I? I said.

Of course, Bernie said. Be my guest.

I lifted the tunnel of dark fabric—Bernie had leveled up, having secured a new, tubed cloth to the plate that held the ground glass—and stuck my face inside. It was dark, too dark to see.

I don't shoot large format myself; before I started the Bernie and Leah project I couldn't see why anyone would ever want to in this day and age. It seemed like the domain of fussy macho men with a penchant for making life harder than it has to be and talking snobbishly to each other about the tiniest nuances of equipment. I prefer a smaller film camera where the viewfinder shows you your subject right side up. But I knew enough to move the camera and get it more or less in focus, which I did then, getting Bernie and Leah, upside down at the table on the camera's ground glass. Bernie's body made a strange shape and Leah's made a simpler one and their neutral clothes stood out against the red dirt and I had a thought then. What if this is what it is all about: changing the point of view, making it so that something can be regarded instead of imagined. You take the thing you think is inside you and then you put it outside of you so you can read about it or listen to it or look at it. That's all I had ever tried to do.

NO ONE ELSE CAME TO that first showing. I was the only one.

We are going to get started, Leah said eventually.

I opened my beach chair and sat down in it. All around us, dogs barked and children screamed. I wondered if this had been a great mistake, if I should have left well enough alone. Don't meet your heroes, and all that. Someone walked by with loud music blaring from his phone.

Disaster, I heard Leah say.

No, Bernie said. Perfect. Whatever is around is right. Stop. Relax. Play.

What they played that night and many nights after is difficult to describe. Critics and art writers with much more experience than I in putting the visual into words would also struggle. It's been called a "lecture with images." It's been called an "arthouse social media video" and a "talking photo montage" and "space-specific performance art." It's been compared to the slideshows Nan Goldin did for *The Ballad of Sexual Dependency,* which she set to music and played in bars and at parties and warehouses, and also to "your annoying aunt's vacation pictures."

What happened was this: a photograph was projected on the screen. The photograph was the one of Daniel Dunn's shed—an interior space with all its walls covered in photographs and text, the space looking very small, crammed as it was with so much to look at.

The photo stayed on the screen, still, nothing happening for a very long time. But because it had been taken in large format and had such incredible detail, even when projected shittily onto this screen, it was sort of OK. It made you want to get up and touch the screen, which a young kid who wandered by at that moment did, much to Leah's chagrin and Bernie's delight. At last, words flashed up: *Daniel Dunn's shed,* they said. *May 19, 2018, Mifflin County, Pennsylvania.*

Then the words flashed away and you were just looking at the photograph again. It was kind of annoying, being thwarted in this way, being made to look again at the same thing, unchanged, when you wanted to move on.

Then the voice came in. It was Leah's voice, speaking live, not recorded. She appeared to be speaking into a corded microphone which was connected to a small speaker that also sat under the black plastic table.

Once upon a time, Leah said, or I think she said, since I was indeed missing some words with the kids screaming and the dogs barking. I scooted my beach chair closer.

The photograph changed. It was Daniel Dunn's famous photograph now, the one he had taken of that field where the plane went down.

When I look at this photograph, Leah continued, I feel many feelings. In the photograph there are so many American flags, so many military uniforms, dark navy or black with red patches and gold buttons, and so many people seated, watching. Why do I feel like an interloper here, in this photograph, like if I tried to enter it, I might get caught and turned back, disallowed, with my jean shorts and short hair and my fat belly, from participating? Heroism and bravery and honor and sacrifice. When did we cede everything to these people, the people who made this ceremony and decided which politicians would come? Whose country is this? Is this my country? Am I an American or aren't I? Are you? How does it make you feel?

Leah stopped speaking. Again the photograph stayed a long time. Then, after a while, certain words popped up on the screen and stayed too. Fat belly, was one of the ones I caught. Bravery and honor and sacrifice.

The next photograph was of a large parking lot and an old redbrick building that had once been a factory with a wide river behind it. Very small, ever so tiny, you could make out Leah. She was sitting inside a flat green station wagon, her hands on the wheel.

NOW THAT BERNIE HAD FOUND the shimmer once, she couldn't stop finding it. She found it as they drove west, in lifted signs for fast-food joints and gas stations. Smelled the smell of paper burning and followed it to a paper factory next to a river. Wandered down a path with the camera and Leah and found a vegetable garden there, full of cucumbers growing huge and wild on their sides.

Bernie felt that something else had taken over; her mind felt clear and quiet. The shimmer was not a decision, not consciously, but in another way it sort of was. It was a decision to wait a long time until she felt a sense of deep recognition, almost a déjà vu, as if she'd looked at the scene before. And in a way she had—since she'd looked at it first without the camera. It wasn't exactly the same, not least because it was upside down, but it had the same structure, the same relationship between the things. This process of waiting reminded Bernie of those games, both physical and computer, where you'd have to rotate a cutout shape over and over again until you found the exact right hole where it fit.

Photographed a weird lake, weird in shape and color. Shimmer. Took forever for the light to move, so she and Leah cut slices of bread and slathered them with peanut butter. Leah kissed her and she kissed Leah back, tasting a few nuts and a lot of oil. She told Leah how she had always wanted to learn to play the piano and Leah told her about wanting to get back into playing basketball.

Photographed—accidentally, Leah hadn't even googled it, they just ended up there—the site of a mining disaster where nine miners had been trapped underground for seventy-seven hours in 2002. Camped there for the night, on the very site, just a tiny plaque embedded on a rock to mark it. Leah's headlamp on so she could write. Her writing had gone way past notes, had turned into something more like poetry. Weird line breaks were happening. Sketches of phone screens with images and texts. Sketches of a house, three floors.

Leah laughing, Bernie laughing. Turn it off. I'm not finished. You turn it off!

Photographed a pizza place in Pittsburgh. Shimmer. Photographed the lobby of the little hotel where they stayed which had a pink sofa they both liked. Photographed the Kittanning Public Library with the person working the front desk, a beautiful fat blonde with contoured cheeks and green eyeshadow.

What are your most popular books? Leah wanted to know.

Um, the blonde said. The bonnet rippers, definitely.

She showed them the section. They were Amish romance novels, in which the most scandalous move was the flash of an ankle, and Bernie took another photograph of her there, with the shelf.

Are you having fun? Leah asked then. It looks like you are.

Bernie was squishing the tripod down into its most petite form. Was she? She felt fond of this library now, and this blond woman, and these books. She felt fond of life. Where had that come from? When did it go missing?

Yeah, Bernie said. I am.

When Bernie worked the camera now, Leah would stand a few feet away, taking notes, pages and pages of notes for each shot. What could she possibly be writing? It seemed Leah was writing even more when she was watching Bernie work than she was writing at night now. And asking more questions.

If the ground glass is small and the picture will end up being printed so big, do you ever get surprised?

Oh yes, Bernie said. There's things you'll see in the finished product that you couldn't even see with your naked eye. The camera can see way more than the eye can.

Hmm, Leah said, writing this down.

These parts, fortunately or un, reminded Bernie of her excursions with Daniel Dunn except now Leah was asking the questions and she, Bernie, was giving the answers. When she did not have the answer, she asked herself what Daniel Dunn would say and spoke that. It had been that day at The Caverns that Daniel Dunn first spoke for himself.

Look, he'd said. A bride and groom.

A cliché, Bernie told him.

No, he said. Not necessarily.

Fine, Bernie said.

I'd go higher, Daniel Dunn said. Can you raise the tripod?

No, Bernie said. But I guess I could shoot it from the balcony.

Then do that, he said.

SITTING PARKED IN THE CAR in a town on Pennsylvania's westernmost edge, Bernie watched Leah take another bite of her hamburger as a sauce the color of salmon dripped out one side.

Damn, this is good, Leah said. Wanna try?

The burger, from a small fast-food stand where you walked up to the counter, had a flavor Bernie had never tasted before; the meat was as smooth and melty as butter.

She took another bite.

Hey, Leah said, playing at snatching it back.

It's OK, Bernie said. I'll get my own. Want anything?

Root beer float.

When Bernie returned, she lingered a moment at the driver's side window and watched Leah sitting there. Leah had presence, she filled the car up with it; if she had been on a stage, Bernie would not have been able to look away. In addition to hate, perhaps that was why the girls in the diner had targeted her—impossible to ignore, tempting to touch.

What? Leah asked.

Nothing, Bernie said. You're just hot. That's all.

Thanks, Leah said. She smiled. Now give me my float.

Bernie had never talked so much in her life, never said so many words to a single person in such a small space of time and within such a small space, the leather interior of this low, low wagon. The station wagon was old but nice in the way that things that belong to people who have been rich a long time are old but nice. The steering wheel was thin and hard and the car was lumbering but slow in a way that relaxed Bernie. Nothing could be done too suddenly. She had to prepare long in advance. The bass of the wagon's sound system thumped against her bare left calf and sometimes she used her right foot on the accelerator, big and insensitive, to keep time along with the beat.

Leah had also taken to asking Bernie questions for which Bernie had no answer.

One bed or two? The woman at the counter asked them, that night in a motel just east of Youngstown.

Leah looked at Bernie, but Bernie found she could not speak.

One, Leah said.

Later, in the room: What do you want? Leah asked.

Like sex?

Uh huh.

I'm not sure, Bernie said. It's whatever.

Come on. Tell me what you like.

It's hard to tell someone else.

Leah sat up on her elbow. You still have that vibrator? From the raffle?

Yeah.

No way.

Why not? Have you ever tried?

No.

Well then.

They were staying in an oddly millennial motel, which Bernie had photographed earlier—both interior and exterior—with its sliding barn bathroom door, exposed industrial HVAC, and bedside wall lamps made of elbow-shaped metal pipe. Yet the walls were paper-thin drywall, the bright white paint job was peeling, and the AC was a poorly fitting window unit propped up by a wet red towel that still allowed two inches of outside air. Through the wall behind her head, Bernie could hear a couple next door. Their voices rose to screeches of laughter then fell to whispers. Their television played cartoons—possibly Wile E. Coyote and the Road Runner and Bernie pictured that blue bird with its wheel of feet flying over an abyss as large as the Grand Canyon and then the sharply drawn mammal who followed behind, looked down, and fell. As Leah dug around in Bernie's suitcase, Bernie felt that when it came to what they were doing in this room, Leah was the Road Runner and she the Coyote about to plummet.

Leah tore into the double-edged plastic of the vibrator's packaging with her teeth and pried apart its layers with her fingers. Bernie was afraid then. Of what? Of Leah's face and what Leah would soon do to her, very slowly and with great pleasure. It was the way that Leah was there, in her face, in her throat, in her hands, in her belly. Bernie loved that belly especially, its wideness and its sonorousness; when she slapped it, it made a deep sound like a drum.

It was the excitement with which Leah touched Bernie, the sheer focus and the concentration. Leah kept her eyes open through everything; there was nothing she did not want to see. It was terrifying to be witnessed in this way, as if she, Bernie, were something that could not be missed.

We're in luck, Leah said. They even included batteries.

Leah clicked a button on the little white control tube and the silver egg made a sound. Leah ran it along the top of her own hand.

Wow, Leah said. Small, but powerful.

Bernie didn't say anything. Don't think, don't remember, don't dream.

Here, Leah said, lying down in the bed next to Bernie. Tell me if it's alright.

Leah ran the little egg over the front of Bernie's knee, then around its side and back. It felt cold at first but then it warmed up and felt hot, electric, like the little sparks of pleasure that come with getting a tattoo, a sensation Bernie suspected she liked too much.

It's alright, Bernie said.

Oh, Bernie said a few minutes later. Oh.

An entirely new feeling when she came, not like trying to get somewhere, but like arriving, and spreading out very wide. It was like she had been blown up and pieces of her had fallen all over the top of a mountain and now she had to scurry around, collecting them. Also, no tears.

She told Leah this.

Let the pieces stay where they are, Leah said. We're in no hurry.

But this was true and not true. The library had given Bernie exactly three weeks off when she'd told them her "uncle" had died, but even that had been a stretch, cobbled together across weekends. They hadn't liked it, and with the coffee shop job gone, it was all she had. She was avoiding checking her bank balance.

Stopped for gas in Meadville and the girl behind the counter told her that her small bicep tattoo was beautiful. Bernie thought of Violet's tattoo then, that cabbage, the meaning of which Bernie had not asked after. What was with Violet, anyway? How different being with Leah was from being with Violet or anyone else. With Leah there was no barrier there, no guardrail. Back in the driver's seat, Bernie watched Leah in the side mirror as she filled up the tank, a thing she was still clumsy and overattentive to, holding the nozzle the whole time instead of letting the clip do the work. Leah's big back, no ass, hip popped out as she waited, watching the numbers tick by. That she would be with Leah would have been unimaginable to Bernie at ten, at fifteen, even at twenty.

Photographed a pet shop. Got invited, on the basis of Leah's chatty charms, to a party thrown by the pet store's owner for her friend, an afternoon barbecue in the backyard of a white house in the shadow of a movie theater built on land that had been a strip mine and before that, a mountain. You could see this evolution in the way the movie theater looked—new—and the way the dirt looked—fresh, no tree thicker than a garden hose.

You're overthinking it, Daniel Dunn said to her. *Just look at the glass and follow the shapes.*

But they're not just shapes, Bernie said back to him. *They mean something too.*

Suit yourself, he said.

It was a birthday barbecue and the guests were all young people who had grown up there and were determined to stay. Stay in the county, stay in the region. Not go. Not go to cities,

cities like Philadelphia. Why? Some worked as teachers and some worked at a nearby radio station and some worked at Arby's and some worked at fulfillment centers for the everything website. They have a computer training facility here, one man with a lip piercing told Bernie. They're retraining all the miners. And the rest of us, a tall girl with long hair cut all the same length said. I was never a miner but I can code now. I make six figures from my fucking living room.

Later, there was a music jam with fiddles and banjos and rhythm guitars and blues guitars, all these young people who just knew how to play music well. Some of them not so well actually, as the birthday girl's boyfriend kept messing up the rhythm on his guitar and when it was his turn to call out a song and sing its lyrics, he kept speeding up and then slowing down. On the banjo, the pet store owner with her septum piercing was clearly annoyed, rolling her eyes at these tempo changes, but then later by the food table the two of them hugged and clapped each other on the back.

Did you see that? Leah asked Bernie when they were alone inside their tent, though not alone in the pet store owner's yard; there were many other tents that night, many other headlamps.

The girl's boyfriend was messing up the jam, Leah went on.

I know, Bernie said. But no one cared.

Imagine, Leah said.

It's a good thing you brought this tent, Bernie said, lying back and looking up at the stars through the tent's mesh panel.

I told you so, Leah said. She capped her pen and moved to touch Bernie. Leah had left the rain fly open and Bernie felt drops of water oozing slowly through the mesh. Not new rain but old.

The land changed, then changed again, as they drove north. Less mountains. More space. You could see farther. Alex was texting; Bernie saw the name pop up, since they used Leah's phone for directions. First a little. Then, a lot.

This feels weird, one text from Alex began. A second: *I don't know where you are*. A third: *Please answer me*. Later that day, from Violet: *Hey, so I know it's none of my business but . . .* From Meena: *We're worried is all*.

Photographed a Dairy Queen with a sign that read BLIZZARD IN SUMMER, HOW COME? Leah got a Blizzard with pieces of Heath Bar and cookie dough and the boy behind the counter turned it upside down to demonstrate its texture. Bernie got the Mint Oreo, which she wedged between her thighs and ate with the provided long red spoon as she drove. Cracked the spoon in her teeth. Leah brushed her teeth at a rest stop.

Why? Bernie asked.

Bad teeth run in the family, Leah said, and kissed her, mouth still tasting of ice cream.

Photographed a parking lot outside Erie where a crowd of people had gathered to watch several Black women braid each other's hair while a trio of three other Black women played the banjo, mandolin, and guitar behind them. It's her, someone whispered, when one of the musicians started singing. Two white men in Confederate flag T-shirts were standing at the edge of the crowd looking on. Leah filmed them with her phone, just in case, and the whole crowd seemed uneasy until the men got bored and wandered away. After the show, an old woman and a girl came up to Bernie where she had set up the tripod, and Bernie braced for an explanation.

Look, said the old woman to the girl. This is what taking a picture used to look like.

That night, it was Bernie who crossed the great divide of space between them in the king-sized bed to touch Leah. The vibrator's batteries died but it was no matter. Leah used it in a different way, sliding the cold metal, small as an egg, back and forth until Bernie could not see or hear. It was Bernie who stuffed her hand into the tight crevice Leah's thighs made with each other. As she fucked Leah, Bernie grew tired, distracted; she was not there. But then, when Leah came, Bernie was there again. She touched the backs of Leah's knees, the birthmark on Leah's calf in the shape of some unknown continent. She discovered how Leah liked to be touched and at what pace—very, very slow, then very, very, very fast and for a very long time. She explored every inch of Leah's *flesh*—she said in her mind, but then she thought, no that wasn't right. Leah wasn't flesh. Leah was a body, and perhaps this was what people meant when they said to listen to it.

II.

YOU, BERNIE SAID TO LEAH, ARE GOING TO LEARN TO DRIVE today.

Why do today, Leah said, what you could put off until tomorrow.

They were on the terrace of a terribly hip brewery looking out over Lake Erie to Canada. Women in white miniskirts and heels with ankle straps from which tiny charms and chains dangled sat at picnic tables with men in pink polos, pleated khaki pants, and sunglasses with flip-out lenses. The group yelled and banged their pint glasses on their picnic table, drawing Bernie's eyes.

Sorry, a woman in cutoff jeans and bejeweled flip-flops whisper-yelled. We're celebrating.

Celebrating what? Leah asked, and the woman came over and stood at the end of their picnic table.

We all work at a tech start-up, the woman explained, and we just got acquired.

The company made databases that organized information. The databases were then purchased by other technology companies so that they too could better organize their information. When Bernie looked puzzled, the woman explained that if Bernie shopped on the internet—like, anywhere at all—Bernie was using the technology that she, the woman, and her co-workers sold at this company.

I have so much equity, the woman said. I have equity coming out my vajayjay.

What will you do with it? Leah asked. There was a way in which Leah was not afraid to go right to the center of something by asking the only question that mattered, while she, Bernie, felt compelled to ask around the thing with teasing questions full of implications. Leah's way always took her to interesting conversational places, but it did not always endear her to people.

The woman picked up her piss-colored beer, which had been sitting on Bernie and Leah's table. That's my own personal business, she said. Not yours.

Sorry, Leah said.

I was thinking though, the woman said, after a moment of staring off at Canada. Of starting my own new thing. It would be called Rapunzel Rugs and it would be creating rugs out of like human hair. The hair that people cut off and just gets thrown away at hair salons. That's a renewable resource you know! All that hair. Just wasted.

Aha, Leah said.

Bernie wanted to laugh. *Give me your money,* she wanted to say, *and I promise I'll use it to make something so much more beautiful than a rug.*

Well good luck, Leah said. The woman walked away, still dreaming.

Leah's phone buzzed and she eyed it, then picked it up and slid it into her shirt pocket. Bernie too had things to attend to.

Pogden had been calling and emailing. *Never heard back from you,* he wrote. *Did you go?? Need update* ASAP.

So, Bernie said, sipping her beer. I guess we should turn around, head back east.

Yeah, Leah said. I guess we should.

When we get home, there's Alex, Bernie said.

Yes, Leah said. Alex.

Don't worry, Bernie said. I get it.

You do? Leah said, leaning back. What do you get?

I get that you and her are together. And you and I are—here. But we won't be here much longer. Soon, we'll be back there.

Right, Leah said. She'd begun peeling the label from her empty beer bottle. I don't want to hurt Alex, Leah said.

I know, Bernie said.

Or you either, Leah said.

Bernie turned her head away. The sun was setting and it was getting cold by the water; the company crowd was dispersing with calls of obligation—kids, dinner, husbands, wives.

Leah finished peeling the label and began working on the sticky gunk beneath it with her nails in a dark, focused way. She looked like she might speak again.

That's when Bernie said it. Driving, Bernie said. Today.

Leah protested. The hour, the beers, the light. Bernie fetched her an order of French fries to sober her up.

You're not going to let this go, are you? Leah said, eating them.

Bernie shook her head.

NEXT TO THE BREWERY WAS a parking lot, great and brightly lit and empty, perhaps belonging to some kind of office building. Bernie had parked the station wagon there, on a low curb just beyond the brewery's fence. They were in the car now, nose to Lake Erie.

I'm moving the seat back, Bernie said, still in the driver's seat. The car made a slow grinding sound and the space between Bernie's chest and the steering column expanded.

You can make your own adjustments to the mirrors and the height of the seat. You don't have to wear the seatbelt if you don't want to. We aren't going far or fast.

I don't understand why you're pushing this, Leah said. She was still eating the nubs, the littlest fries that had stuck to the bottom of the waxy brown container.

Because, Bernie said. Because we have hundreds of miles back and I'm tired. Plus what if we do other trips? I can't do all the driving forever.

You think we'll have other trips? Leah looked at Bernie. Her hair was greasy along its part, and more flipped up at its ends than ever.

Maybe.

Leah looked down at her hands.

Don't you want to be able to come back? Bernie asked. Or go somewhere without me?

Leah's eyes filled with tears. Very much, she said.

How could she do that, Bernie marveled. Leah seemed to have these icicles of feeling, feelings that were so clear they stabbed through the noise of living and showed up on her face. It was admirable, Bernie thought, but also terrifying. Bernie paused to listen for any icicles of her own, some jolt of emotion yelling *heart, yearning, fairy tale, wife*. But all was quiet.

I just want you to know, Leah said. That I don't like being told what to do. I wouldn't take this from my parents, or from Violet or Meena, or from Alex.

I know, Bernie said.

OK, Leah said. She unbuckled her seatbelt and got out of the car. She crossed around the back of the station wagon and Bernie crossed around its front.

It was odd to be in the passenger seat. It felt over-warm and creased but Bernie shifted around until she had made a place for herself there. Took her hair out of its ponytail and put the ponytail elastic in the little armrest compartment.

The button's not working, Leah said, pushing the seat adjustment controls.

Try again, Bernie said. It's just there, behind the—

Oh, OK, Leah said. Her knees retreated from the steering wheel and she tilted the seat forward so her arms could reach.

You want your feet to rest comfortably on the pedals but not be too close, Bernie said.

Obviously, Leah said.

And you want your hands at ten o'clock and two o'clock on the steering wheel.

I've watched movies, Leah said. I've seen TV.

OK, Bernie said. Waiting for Leah to move toward each thing, Bernie directed Leah to adjust her mirrors, and then, slowly, to shift the car out of park.

OK, Bernie said. Drive.

The car lurched forward toward the edge of the parking lot and the river beyond.

Fuck, Leah said and slammed on the brake. I can't do this. I don't want to.

It's alright, Bernie said. Go easy. You'll start to figure out the pressure.

Leah was crying again, wiping a tear with the back of her right hand. But she did it. She let her foot off the brake and the car inched forward, slowly, so very slowly.

Oh, Leah said. Its default is movement? Like if I do nothing, it moves?

Yes, Bernie said. Now turn the wheel left. More, more.

The car turned, parallel now with the lot's long edge.

But when I press the gas, Leah said, it's like. She paused. Oh, OK there, she said.

The car moved along. Leah progressed like that for many laps, hardly accelerating at all, just letting the car crawl around and around the lot. It was tremendously boring, and also sweet. Leah was working so hard. Breathing and sighing and leaning so far forward her chest nearly touched the wheel.

They practiced moving between the brake and the accelerator. Then putting the car in reverse and back into drive.

You're doing excellently, Bernie said.

Don't patronize me, Leah said. But she was smiling when she said it.

BERNIE WAS ACUTELY AWARE THAT their time was running out, and so she was stopping them more than ever. In a single day, she made stops at a carpet store that was closing—LIQUIDATION SALE, EVERYTHING MUST GO—a man-made pond up against a factory that made Wi-Fi routers, a long stretch of road where she could see wind turbines in the distance, turning slow, and a Finnish Farmers Club hall with a flapping sign out front—DANCING TONIGHT, 7 P.M.! They pulled into the little grassy parking lot and Bernie photographed the building—white, roof sloped so steeply it resembled an A-frame—alone and then with the hall's caretaker, a white woman in her early sixties who had her hair cut short like Leah's, and sported a thick flannel shirt. They stayed to dance, accompanied by a live band of a clawhammer banjo, a fiddle, and an accordion.

There had been a place like this in the town where Bernie grew up, where mostly old people came to dance in organized ways; Bernie's mom had made her and her brother come on Friday nights sometimes, a fate at the time that Bernie considered worse than death. It was odd to be standing in this hall now, with Leah, as Leah marveled over every detail—oh look at the bake sale, look at the benches, look this hall has been here since 1935, look at the stained glass, look at the school desk where the caretaker sits by the door taking people's money. Leah bumped Bernie's shoulder with her own. Look, she said, and they shared a smirk over the two, three, four, five dances the caretaker gave to a young, stocky woman with a slicked-back ponytail, broad shoulders, and a VOLUNTEER FIREFIGHTER T-shirt. As Bernie and Leah left for the night, the two were still talking. If the road was littered with dead lesbians, as Leah had said once, it was littered with quietly alive ones too.

The next day, Bernie stopped them for an orange house and hours of shooting at a dirt race car track. The entrance fed into an open, grassy area bordered by unpeopled white-and-blue square pop-up tents offering hot dogs, Frito pie, T-shirts bearing the logo of the track, and LuLaRoe leggings. ALL COL-

ORS ALL PATTERNS was written in black Sharpie on flaps of brown cardboard, a sharp contrast with the fuchsia and orange and teal color palette of the leggings, which hung from hangers all around the tents' wired exoskeletons. Advertisements and messages printed on vinyl grommeted signs were tied loosely to the chain link that encircled the racing track: PYLES GARAGE DOORS CALL 1-800-515-DOOR. NO WEAK LINKS. GET WELL SOON POPS JR. LOVE TYLER, ROLAND AND KIRSTEN. THANKS FATMAN FOR 50 YEARS.

The day was too windy; Bernie could feel the air whipping the dark cloth around her shoulders and waist and the image on the ground glass kept wobbling, she couldn't get the focus right.

What do I do? she asked Daniel Dunn.

All the usual things, he said back, in his way.

I've done them. Nothing doing.

What's wrong? Leah asked then, aloud, and when Bernie told her, Can I see?

Don't let her, Daniel Dunn said. *She'll ruin everything.*

Be my guest, Bernie said, and held out the dark cloth.

Leah pulled the cloth up over her head and then slid it forward to cover the camera too.

Here, Leah said after a time, emerging from under the cloth. She picked up Bernie's big rectangular camera bag, took the belt from the loops on her pants, and ran the belt through the bag's top strap and around the center rail of the tripod, weighing it down.

Try now, Leah said, offering the cloth back to Bernie.

Miracle, the tripod barely moved at all. Bernie could see again.

Told you, Bernie said to Daniel Dunn.

What? Leah said.

Thank you, Bernie said.

WHEN BERNIE FOUND ANOTHER PARKING lot, this one attached to an abandoned shopping mall she wanted to photograph, Leah sighed but did not resist. She was less jerky when she circled the mall this time, passing the faded JCPENNEY sign, once, twice, three times, and was even able to pull the station wagon into a spot circumscribed by lines on three sides.

Let's take you out on the road, Bernie said. See how you do.

Isn't that illegal? Leah asked. No license.

Way out in the country, Bernie said, you can do what you like.

Bernie drove them out of town and onto a country route, then pulled over into a gravel turnout where they switched.

I can't believe I'm doing this, Leah said, from the driver's seat.

Why?

I just never thought I would be the kind of person who could. You decide certain things about yourself, and then it's hard to change them.

But this is an easy one to change, Bernie said.

It's not, Leah said. Not for me.

Wait, Bernie said. She got out and opened the door behind where she'd been sitting. On the floor there was Dunn's little camera, the Canon AE-1 that she'd saved and prepped with film. Leah cautiously pulled them back onto the blacktop.

The day was warm, even hot. Leah was driving them along so slowly that every now and again a car would swerve around them to pass. Bernie didn't mind the slowness as now she was able to look out through her open window at the world and photograph with the little, fast, springy camera. When Leah stopped at a four-way intersection near an interesting-looking shed, she could snap it. Leah spoke but Bernie did not hear, so focused was she now on looking.

What? Bernie said again.

Nothing, Leah said. She smiled at Bernie. Just turn the radio on for me, would you?

Bernie did. After many miles, she sat back in her seat and rolled the window up halfway. Without meaning to—she would just close her eyes for a moment—Bernie was soon asleep.

She dreamed that she and Daniel Dunn were going camping. They had made a spreadsheet of everything they would need to bring, but had somehow forgotten everything on the spreadsheet. The only things they had brought were a strap-on dildo, a harness, a can of spiced black beans from Trader Joe's, and a plush toy in the shape of Jigger the cat. They were driving Daniel Dunn's pickup truck, white and two-wheel drive, a vehicle that he had never owned in life but should have. In the woods, Daniel Dunn built the fire and then Bernie burned the plush Jigger. Daniel Dunn began to hit Bernie with the strap-on. This hurt quite a lot so Bernie took out a knife from her pocket and stabbed Daniel Dunn in the eye. She kept stabbing him in many different and nonfatal places—the shin, the upper arm, the shoulder, the pectoral—but eventually the wounds added up to enough blood loss to kill him.

What did you do that for? he asked before he died.

WHEN BERNIE WOKE IT WAS pre-dusk, the car was stopped, and Leah was not in it. Bernie sat up. A sign said SCENIC OVERLOOK and when she slammed her door, Bernie could see Leah a ways off, standing in some tall grass. A lowrider pulled into the turnoff, snapped some pictures out the passenger-side window with a phone, and then drove off.

When Bernie approached, Leah did not turn. In front of them was a valley. They were high and the land in front of them was low, mountains on mountains on sky. The downward slope in front of them blew with cattails.

What's wrong? Bernie asked.

Nothing, Leah said. You fell asleep and at first I reached out to wake you up because I was scared to drive without you. But then it was OK, I just kept going and you just kept sleeping. Then I saw this place to stop. Do you want to photograph it?

Sure, Bernie said.

Then Leah spoke again. I have another idea, she said. Like this trip, but bigger. For you and me.

I'm listening, Bernie said.

We put out what we've made on this trip for free. I don't know exactly how yet. It could be on social media, it could be a website, I'm not sure. All I know is it shouldn't be in a gallery or a fancy book. It should be your photos and my text. Maybe as captions but maybe another way too? Maybe as overlays over the photos, like when you post a story to the photo-sharing app? And also spoken aloud. That way equal attention is given to both formats. The visual element for people who don't read. The language element for people who get meaning that way, and for blind and/or visually impaired folks. We'll have to go out again, we'll have to go out lots more times. We haven't even begun to scratch the surface of what you can do with that camera and what I can do when I'm writing about you with that camera. I don't know all the details yet.

OK, Bernie said. That could work. But what are we doing? What are we trying to say?

It's about the now, Leah said. It's about a record. I have a feeling that a record will be needed. Things are about to change again, I think. Your camera. How you can see with it. It's not a novelty, it's not a gimmick, it's not nostalgia. You're not photographing women in bonnets. It's like a huge fucking eye that can give detail and nuance. Things we're starving for.

I try, Bernie said. But I can never say it. Never say it like that, say what I'm trying to do like you just said it. But it's not just anywhere that I want to photograph. It's here. My— She put her palm out parallel to the ground and moved it everywhere. Her what? What was the word she was looking for?

Pennsylvania, Leah said.

Yeah, Bernie said, like letting air out of a balloon. I guess it's that simple.

The place, Leah said. Where you are from.

Yeah, Bernie said again. But I don't know what I have to say about it. It just is.

Your photographs say a lot, Leah said. And the rest I will say. *Changing Pennsylvania,* Leah said. That's the name I gave for my grant.

I like it, Bernie said.

Good, Leah said. She turned to face the car's nose, then turned back to the view and Bernie.

And another thing, Leah said.

For Leah could never hold back. She could never just quit while she was ahead. She had never, not once in her life, let go when she could have held on.

Leah's head was down somehow, but she cut her eyes up at Bernie.

She's going to give me something, Bernie knew then, something that I can't quite give back. But Bernie just stood there, saying nothing. She made no move to stop Leah.

Oh fuck it, Leah said. I'd end it with Alex, Leah said. If you told me to. If you, wanted me to. If this is, something.

No, Bernie said. Don't.

Oh, Leah said.

Leah did not look pink in the gloaming, there with her hands in her jean pockets and her shirt flapping open in the wind to expose a white tank top underneath. She looked blue.

THEY GOT A ROOM ON the second floor of a motel outside Scranton where the door opened directly onto the night. Leah went inside the lobby while Bernie stayed in the car, then re-emerged, avoiding Bernie's eye and directing her to drive around the back of the motel. Bags over their shoulders and nearly to their room, they passed two young white guys in lawn chairs, leaning against their room's window, smoking.

Evening ladies, one of them said.

Evening, Bernie said.

Once they were inside the room—yellow wallpaper, yellow bedspreads—Leah sat down on the big bed, her back to Bernie. She took off her shoes, one by one.

Peeing, underwear pretzeled at her ankles, Bernie felt

Leah outside the door, heard her breathing. This is what you wanted, went someone in Bernie's mind, as she lathered shampoo through her hair. No it wasn't, went someone else as she rinsed it out.

When she was done, Leah was lying on the bed and there came a knock on the door.

I ordered pizza, Leah said.

But when Bernie answered it, it was the two men.

Hi there, one of them said, his head buzzed, sporty sunglasses perched on top like two extra eyes.

Hi, Bernie said. Didn't smile.

I'm just next door here with my friend—the friend, gelled dark hair and neon-green shirt, raised a hand and waved—and we have a twenty-four pack that we could use some help finishing. We were wondering if you ladies might want to come over and have a beer with us?

No, Bernie said.

Oh? the man said. We're just inviting you for a beer. Nothing, you know, implied. Just the pleasure of your company.

I get it, Bernie said. But no, thank you.

Cool camera, the friend with the gelled hair said, pointing to the Canon that Bernie had instinctively picked up and put around her neck.

Oh, Bernie said. Thanks. She could feel Leah, tense, behind her.

I used to have one like that, the friend said, but I got rid of it.

Mistake, Bernie said.

You a photographer? the friend asked.

No, Bernie said.

Cool, the first man said. Well, I'd be careful here if I were you, he said, gesturing with his arm at the whole of the motel. The two of you girls alone, I mean. We've seen some rough things go down.

Bernie did what she was used to doing then, in moments like these. She neither gave nor received. She made her body flat and hard. Nothing in, nothing out.

The man looked to his friend then back to Bernie. So that's a no on the beers then?

Right.

The friend spoke again then. We're nice guys. And you look like a nice girl. He leaned into the room to look at Leah. And she, I mean it, looks nice too. He swallowed.

Just the same, Bernie said.

The two men spoke nearly at the same time then.

Jeez, you'd think you two were—

Fucking bitch about it—

Bernie slammed the door. Leaned into it and slid the dead bolt. Turned and put her back to the door.

Leah and Bernie looked at each other then. Bernie's stomach was concrete.

Are they gone? Leah whispered.

Bernie opened a crack in the blinds with her thumb and forefinger and saw only walkway, only night air and a single streetlight on in the motel's parking lot.

I think so, she whispered back.

Leah sat on the bed, her back straight. She took several deep breaths. Then she was breathing faster and louder, heaving, then crying and heaving, one hand on each side of her beautiful brain.

Bernie sat down next to her and touched her warm back, but Leah only heaved more.

I can't, Leah inhaled sharply. Get a breath. She inhaled again. The air won't like—

Here, Bernie said, put your head between your knees.

She guided Leah to bend over the edge of the bed. Bernie moved her hand over Leah's back, feeling where Leah's binder ended and each of her shoulders began, and after a while the heaving lessened, though the crying remained.

It's OK, Bernie said. They're gone.

It's not, Leah said. It's not OK. I'm just so. She sat there for a moment. So tired, she went on. I'm not even human to them. I'm not even a person. On this trip, with you, I felt like a person. I felt like—I don't know, hopeful about myself and what we were doing here. And then something like this happens and I'm reminded again of how hopelessly shitty the world is.

Bernie had a flash then, of all the specific acts of violence she would like, if given the chance and opportunity, to commit on the men next door, of all the slow and controlled ways she could make them suffer. She could draw on their dicks, hard, with a ballpoint pen. She could wrap a wire around their balls and pull it tighter and tighter. She could apply a knife or a razor blade to the bottoms of their feet. What would that accomplish? Nothing, Bernie knew. But it would feel good, in the doing.

Watching Leah cry, watching the small streams of water leave her eyes and get wiped away by her palms and dried on her jean shorts, it was all bubbling up in Bernie, it was all cracking through.

Another knock.

If necessary, Bernie felt, she would fight, and she would kill.

This time it really was the pizza, but Bernie put the chain on the door just in case.

They ate dinner in silence, watching TV. Leah didn't even write that night, just turned her light off. Bernie got under the covers, turned out her light too, and lay on her side, watching the balcony walkway outside for any movement. When she couldn't sleep, she rolled onto her back. She looked up at the ceiling. There was a pattern there, a shadow, sharp and tangled. It could be barbed wire, or it could be a tree, Bernie thought, depending on how you looked at it. The feeling that came in the night—that core darkness that told her she was alone, separate, and would never be together with anyone—was still there.

It was then that the music started. It jolted Bernie and shook the wall. It was metal, bass forward, the lyrics dispersing behind background noise so Bernie couldn't pick them out. A grating, enormous guitar solo. A single chord change, back and forth, back and forth.

Bernie clicked on the light. Leah's face was as wide and taut as a plate. Bernie stood on the bed and banged on the wall with her fist three times.

Hey! she yelled. Banged a few more times. Hey! she called again. Turn it down.

The music stopped.

Do you think they're trolling us? Leah asked.

I don't know, Bernie said. Probably just wasted. She turned the light off again.

But after a few minutes the music was back, this time at a higher volume than before, if such a thing was even possible. The song began not at its beginning but in the middle, no opening, no working up to it, just full-on noise, the same paucity of tones, the same hard-to-make-out lyrics, the same voice. Each time the song cut off, Bernie felt relief, but each time the hammering bass and violent tin drum kit returned.

I'm calling the front desk, Leah said.

Don't, Bernie said. That's what they want us to do.

FREE, it sounded like the band was yelling through the wall, *FREE THE PEOPLE.*

What do you suggest then? Leah said. There's no way to sleep.

Let's go, Bernie said. You want to?

Go? Leah said. Go where?

Somewhere else, Bernie said. Anywhere else. We're only a few hours from home.

Leah shook her head. The plan had been to get up in the morning when it was light, make a few more photographs, and use their whole last day before heading home. But she did it, she got ready.

They were outside and almost past the window of the room next door when it occurred to Bernie what she should have said back to those men as they made her stand in the doorway, looking at her body and her camera. She stopped and knocked on the glass. The music, which had started again, stopped. But no faces appeared.

What are you doing? Leah whisper-yelled.

Hey assholes, Bernie called.

Bernie, Leah called.

But the feeling was too strong in Bernie now and she was listening to it. She wanted to break the window and for them to see her face. She wanted them to feel off-balance and afraid, confused and unsure of her intentions, for just a moment. She wanted them to remember her, forever.

We're not girls! she yelled at them. And we're not nice!

Still there was no answer. She banged on the window again, this time with both of her hands, her palms open.

I'm a photographer! she yelled. I go anywhere! She yelled the two phrases again and then Leah took her hand and pulled her back.

THERE IS ONLY ROOM FOR one main character in any story was a thing Bernie's mother had liked to say. She said it so often and as the implied explanation for such a wide range of situations that it became an annoying, empty platitude. When Bernie's friend Gabby's parents had gotten divorced in the fourth grade because her mom fell in love with a lawyer from Cincinnati, her mom had said it. When Bernie's brother had wrecked his car, high for the first time that they knew about, after finding out his high school girlfriend was moving to Oregon, her mother had said it.

And without her having to say it, Bernie knew this was her mother's explanation for everything having to do with her father. Bernie's father was a selfish, selfish man who saw, lit up as real, only his own life. He had no grand talents or ambitions as far as Bernie knew, had worked in a gravel quarry when he'd met Bernie's mom, and hadn't even taken off for more exciting or greener pastures. He still lived in the state, just a few counties away from where Bernie had grown up. But somehow he sucked all the air from whatever room he stood in, Bernie's mom had given Bernie to believe, leaving none left over for others. The more Bernie's mom fought for air, the more he shoved her down in order to find his own freedom. There was only shining or withering, using or being used, loving or being loved. There was no way in the universe of the woman who had made Bernie that two people might work together for their mutual fulfillment, in which one or the other might step forward or backward when needed and on a temporary basis, bobbing up or down so the other one might access oxygen.

This line of thinking came to Bernie again now, prompted by a country song from Bernie's childhood on the station wagon's radio. Bernie turned it up just enough that she could hear it better but not so much that it would wake Leah. She looked over at Leah's face which was closed, turned off in sleep. Leah's mouth made small, endearing smacking noises every few miles.

The song was about two women who were best friends but then one of the women's husbands started hitting her and they murdered him with poisoned beans and wrapped him in a tarp. He became a missing person who nobody missed at all and they opened a roadside stand that sold ham and strawberry jam.

Like the women in the song, Bernie had also been a member of the 4-H club and of the Future Farmers of America. She had always imagined herself as the Mary Ann, the one who went out looking for a bright new world, and not the Wanda who met and married the mediocre, abusive man they would soon be required to kill. The movie *Thelma & Louise,* which Bernie had watched no less than fifty-seven times, also fit into this theme. But if this was so, if she was the Mary Ann and the Louise, that would make Leah the Wanda and the Thelma, which was not right. Neither the song nor the movie had allowed for two Mary Anns or two Louises.

THEY WERE VERY NEARLY THERE, just twenty-two minutes away, when Bernie felt she could not bear to go home. She could not bear to end it here, to return to the house, to Alex and Violet and Meena, to her room and Leah's and the wall between them.

Bernie ignored the exit her phone told her to take, and instead took one that would spit her out near Philadelphia's sprawling Fairmount Park. Off the freeway, the ramp came to a T and Bernie hung a right. The street was dark, the wires between the dim streetlights slack and baggy; trash lined the road's shoulder; flowers too. The scent of jasmine and honeysuckle. Kudzu that grew up every tree and guardrail. Philadelphia.

In the passenger seat, Leah stirred, drank from her water bottle. Asked where they were. Bernie told her.

Just take me home please, Leah said. I'm tired.

I will, Bernie said. Soon.

They passed an illuminated field, and then a dark field attached to a parking lot, empty but for a couple of idling cars. Bernie pulled in.

What are we doing here? Leah said. She sat up and ran a hand over her face.

Behind them, a car rolled down its window and threw a cigarette out, releasing loud blues music into the air.

I don't want to go home yet, Bernie said. I can't.

Leah let out a long breath. I don't understand you, Bernie, Leah said. She was hunched so far over, almost leaning her head on the dashboard. She did lean her head on the dashboard then and closed her eyes again. She was going somewhere then in her mind, Bernie could see, somewhere where she, Bernie, could not follow, traveling fast fast fast.

It was not clear to Bernie then, and it has never been clear to me, if what she couldn't bear to end that night was the love or the work, or if the two were already mashed together like Velcro, the love being the soft, fuzzy side in which lint could get stuck and the work being the hard, clean side. As they sat in the car in Fairmount Park, it might still have been possible to pry the two things apart, with great effort, but after that day, it would no longer be.

Alright, Bernie said. I'd like to, she paused, do it all. I'm telling you, she said, to end it with Alex.

You are? On the dashboard's surface, Leah turned her head and opened her eyes. Her face was dark, smooth. She said it again, not a question this time. You are.

Yes.

What changed your mind?

Maybe there's another way, Bernie said. To be together. Maybe. There's got to be. I don't know how to explain it.

Leah sat up. She put out her arm to touch Bernie's face. She moved the bangs out of Bernie's eyes. In this dark shade-dappled city light, one of Leah's eyes looked blue and the other one looked brown. Bernie moved her focus back and forth between them, trying to take in the whole of Leah's face in one frame, failing every time.

Bernie climbed across the gear shift and into Leah's arms. Leah held her and Bernie turned her head to the side. There was a knot in the fake wood of the console that Bernie watched as Leah touched her. A knot in a tree was what happened when Bernie did not know what. She didn't know what was happening here. It was like everything was knotted and then it was like everything was blown apart. This kept happening. Knotted. Blown apart. Knotted. Blown apart. She couldn't really breathe, it was hard to breathe, which was a thing that happened to her, but now it was also happening with someone else here. Someone else was here now. There was something in the car filling it up and sucking the air out but mostly filling it up. Leah was filling her up now but that was crude, which was not what Bernie was trying to be. What she was trying to be was here. What she was trying to do now was stay.

III.

AT THE HOUSE, IT WAS DARK, EVERYONE ALREADY ASLEEP, BUT the dishwasher was running. In the morning, it would be unloaded and then reloaded with glasses that bore a thin ring of red around their middles. Lucy Vincent had quit smoking but now required great quantities of red wine to survive, and she neglected to rinse her glasses in a timely fashion. Loads of laundry were washed then left in the washing machine to mildew while breakup conversations were had—Alex was not particularly surprised that Leah was breaking up with her, did Leah think she was an idiot?—and grieved. The loads of laundry were washed again to get the mildew smell out before being switched to the dryer, but the smell was hard to vanquish. Meena was the one who switched them, folded them, and brought them up the two flights of stairs to Alex. Seeing Alex's door closed, Meena left them in the strange extra kitchen. Though Alex had seemed un-hurtable, she was not.

The five housemates slept, dreamed, woke, each in their own beds. Bernie and Leah slept separately. Through the wall, Bernie heard Leah groaning when taking off her binder (so tight, the elastic left grooves on her shoulder blades and across her back fat which Bernie missed touching) and Leah talking to Jigger in tongues of love: my sweet plump plumpkin pumpkin pie, there's a good kitty, yes, oh yes, OK, roll, roll, roll, roll over.

For a time, everyone was afraid to open their doors. A great deal of texting.

I miss you, Meena texted her girlfriend, Kate, in Nepal. Whenever it was night in Philadelphia, it was day in Kathmandu. *What are you doing?*

Looking at sneakers online, Kate texted back, a thing so mundane and tender that it nearly broke Meena's heart. Though Meena knew it was not particularly radical, what she wanted most of all was to live in the same city as Kate, maybe even get an apartment with Kate and Kate alone, where she could roast a chicken while Kate sat on the couch scrolling niche sneaker head websites on her phone. Meena could hear Alex and Leah talking in Alex's room again and Meena wished then for one place in this world she could go where the air would be free of anticipation, of someone either having just talked or someone preparing to talk. Though it was late and almost dark, Meena crawled out her window and up to the roof of the house. She stood there for a moment, bending over and poking first one tomato plant's spongy bed of dirt, contained in a white plastic bucket, then another. The soil was too dry, but the plants were alright anyway, even thriving, with yellow cherry tomatoes hanging from thin stalks and blowing gently in the breeze. She popped one in her mouth and let her teeth pierce the skin, the acid juice exploding in her mouth.

In Violet's room, two floors below where Meena stood, their phone vibrated with a call.

Not now Mommy, Violet texted their mother. *I'm busy.*

When are you not ever busy? their mother texted back. *How long will you ignore? If I died in the house it would be days before anyone would find me. Your father is always traveling and you do not care.*

Violet thought a long time about how to reply. Lucy Vincent was there, lying on the bed on her stomach and looking at her phone, slowly withdrawing salt-and-vinegar chip after salt-and-vinegar chip from a small matte-yellow bag and crunching them between her teeth. One day, Violet's mother, if she lived long enough and Lucy Vincent stuck around, would have to move in with them. How would that work? This house had that strange kitchen on the third floor, technically part of the "mother-in-law suite." Where would they find such a setup ever again? Not at Lucy Vincent's house, a trinity of three rooms stacked on top of each other, living room, kitchen, then bedroom on top. What would Lucy Vincent and their mother even talk about? They both loved beautiful things, Violet thought. They could talk about that.

Down the hall, Leah texted Bernie.

I've talked to Alex again.

How did it go?

Bad.

I'm sorry.

It's alright. Did you see what Lucy Vincent did?

The back door again?

No, much worse. She was trying to make dulce de leche, so she put a can of condensed milk into a pot of boiling water and then went upstairs to get high and have sex with Violet and it exploded!

Bernie laughed. Unsure if Leah could hear her through the wall, she also texted Leah the laughing/crying emoji.

Lucy Vincent and Violet spent a full day washing dried

burnt sugar off the faces of the cabinets and the ceiling with sponges but they did it too lightly, swiping and laughing, like the flirting main characters in a romantic comedy. In the night, Bernie woke to the sound of scrubbing.

Leah's voice: Need help?

Then Alex's: OK. But this doesn't absolve you of anything.

Jigger made the rounds, knocking at each housemate's door in turn by shoving her supple black-and-pink paw pads into the wide gaps between where the door stopped and the floor began. The supplies of black beans, blocks of white cheddar cheese, and full-fat yogurt dwindled and everyone was confused as to whose turn it was to go to Sam's Club, since Bernie and Leah had thrown things off-kilter both emotionally and logistically. Activating the house group text felt too charged. Alex overcompensated for everyone, doing all her own regularly assigned chores and most of other people's too. She transferred the empty yogurt containers that had piled up on top of the fridge to a new silver wire shelf in the pantry. She vacuumed all the time so that no one's words of sympathy could be heard over the device's loud whine.

Meena was the only one who could reasonably call for a house meeting at this point, and so she went from person to person, telling, not suggesting, an appointed time.

This is bad, Meena said, when they were all assembled again around the oval dining table. This house feels bad.

Obviously, Violet said.

Jigger jumped on the table and Meena picked her up and held her captive.

Purr purr, Jigger said, making biscuits in the air.

The answer is simple, Alex said. I'll move out.

No, Leah said, please don't. I'll move out.

No one is moving out, Meena said.

Well someone could move out, said Lucy Vincent, whose presence had until then gone unnoticed. She sat not at the dining room table with the rest of them but on the smaller of the two living room couches, only the shiny top of her head visible.

Technically, and we should really amend this, as far as the house contract is concerned, Alex said, Bernie and Leah didn't break any rules. Ethically, yes. But housing-wise, no.

There's a house contract? Bernie asked.

Yeah, Meena said. We must have forgotten to give it to you.

We got lazy, Violet said.

Yes, Meena said. We all bear some responsibility here. Except Alex. But isn't violating ethical rules enough?

Alex shrugged, actually lifted her shoulders and let them fall.

You could have a trial, Lucy Vincent called from her couch. Decide if what they did qualifies as a housemate kick-outable offense.

Interesting, Violet said. But who would sit on the jury? It can't be us.

Yeah, Meena said. Too much conflict of interest. Not impartial.

You could get community members, Leah said. Friends? Post on that neighborhood group?

This is absurd, Alex said. We're not having a trial.

Well, Meena said, I guess we could just ask where everyone is at. Do you want to move out, Alex?

Not really, Alex said. But I would.

OK. Do you want to move out, Leah?

Not really, Leah said. But I could.

How about you, Bernie?

Leave her out of this, Leah said.

Aww, Lucy Vincent said.

Bernie watched Alex's face. She was behaving well, Bernie thought. Under the circumstances. What would she, Bernie, do if someone went away on a road trip and stole her girlfriend? She would not be sitting here, at this meeting, looking directly at the stealing party. Alex was brave, Bernie saw then, a kind of brave that she, Bernie, was not, and might not be for a long time.

What do you want, Alex? Bernie asked. We'll do what you want.

Alex looked at Bernie. In terms of this situation, I don't know yet, Alex said. I'll let you know when I do. But in terms of this moment, I'd like this to stop. I'd like to do something where we don't have to talk. Stare at a screen. Watch a movie.

By yourself or together? Meena asked.

I don't care, Alex said.

They all waited.

OK, Alex said. Together.

Violet hung a white sheet over the big front window with a staple gun and Leah and Meena pushed around the couches and put down blankets and they all settled into the various soft surfaces. Bernie and Leah sat on different couches, but looked at each other as Violet killed the lights. Alex lay by herself on the floor, propped up on an elbow. Meena sat next to Leah, loudly cracking pistachio shells.

What? Meena said when Leah looked at her. They're a good source of protein.

The movie Lucy Vincent had chosen—research for a part, what part no one asked—was about a little girl, good with horses, who was being raised by a mean aunt in a bleached Dust Bowl town but dreamed of going to Atlantic City where her life could begin. Having been thrown out by the aunt, she made it to Atlantic City where she got mixed up with a grumpy old man who wore a white leather beaded Native American jacket and his hot son who had an act in which a woman and a horse leap off a high tower into a deep tank of water. By displaying her horsemanship, the girl, now not so little, managed to become the understudy diving girl and soon the main diving girl, rejuvenating the act in collaboration with the hot son and taking the traveling outfit from basically washed-up to in high demand by summer state fairs and all-season carnivals.

But one fateful day, an overzealous brass band member banged his cymbals too loudly, spooking the horse the girl was riding down into the pool of water, and the horse reared and the girl hit the water with her eyes open. Despite her protestations that she was fine and her insistence that her developing eye issues were just temporary, the truth remained: she was blind. The hot son, who had since become her boyfriend and who loved her, told her that her days as a diving girl were over. But, in an act of boyfriend trickery and a dark-of-night horse training montage in which she learned to anticipate the approach of the horse using her ears and extrasensory perception, the girl was able to resume diving. She dove horses while blind. No one wanted to pay to see a blind girl kill herself, said a doubtful act booker when he realized what was going on. But he was wrong. They did. She dove, blind, and did not die. Lived.

As the credits rolled, no one moved. Alex had fallen asleep, lightly and with no snoring. Lucy Vincent was crying softly and Violet was petting her hair.

Meena gathered her pistachio shells in the hem of her tank top. But why do you think she wanted to keep diving even after she went blind? Like she got the guy, she got the life, she didn't need to keep doing it. Plus the danger, jeez.

She just liked it I guess, Leah said.

Loved it, Bernie said.

WHEN ALEX DID ACTUALLY MOVE out, suddenly and with no notice at all (she was spared any recriminations; the sympathies of the house lay with her as the injured party), to attend a residential organizer training in Chicago—no harm in seeing if I can't be both a journalist *and* an organizer she'd said—no one, including the new young housemate found quickly to replace her, maintained the Tupperware organizational system and soon the yogurt containers were interspersed again with the other containers and divided between the top of the fridge, the cabinet under the sink, and Meena's roof, where she used them as both watering cans and planters for her smallest tomato plants. The station wagon they'd taken on their trip and Jigger stayed behind.

Please, Alex said to Leah. Please keep them. I can't take either where I'm going and Jigger loves you so much.

Alright, Leah said. As long as you're sure. I'll pay you for the car of course.

I'm sure, Alex said. Maybe later. But for now, it's on loan. You'll need it. So what will you do now? Will you keep working for the paper?

No, Leah said. I don't think so.

Refocus on school?

No, Leah said. Not that either. Though I won't drop out, not yet.

Then what?

I don't know exactly, Leah said. But I think I found what I'm supposed to do, where I'm supposed to do it. It's whatever Bernie is doing. Wherever Bernie is doing it. I'm sorry.

It's OK, Alex said. I mean, it's not. But you know what I mean.

I do.

How will you get by? Money-wise I mean?

I'm not sure, Leah said. I still have my stipend from school, and a little savings.

You'll run through that in no time if you're supporting Bernie too.

Jeez Alex, what is this? I can look after myself you know.

Can you?

Yes. I think so. Are you sad?

No. Not about us.

Ouch.

I'm sorry. I just mean. I worry, is all. Bernie is talented, it's obvious, and she's charismatic, sure. But she's also impulsive, selfish, withholding, a teller of half-truths, and always broke. She'll be a hard road, I'm afraid, both in the long game and on the day to day. I just want to know that you'll be OK.

I will be.

Only a few people know that it was Alex who suggested that if they were going to call the project *Changing Pennsylvania,* it was positively offensive to not include some element of "tangible social change labor."

Like what? Leah asked. If you tell me you want us to give people cameras so they can document their lives, I'll kill you.

I don't know, Alex said. Not my job anymore to help you figure it out. Give your knowledge away maybe.

No academia, Leah said. No MFA. It's all just selling a dream that doesn't exist.

Then make your own school, Alex said. Offer free classes. Like for the community.

It was not a bad idea.

THE MAIL SORTING SYSTEM ALSO began to fail, the mail collecting in Alex's now-vacant mailbox instead of being distributed into the proper box of each housemate, though Meena tried. One Sunday while she was sorting for the first time in months, she received a notice of a job offer as an aide to the Pennsylvania senator in his office in Washington, D.C., (the email notification had gotten lost somehow, in her spam folder). The mail remained half-sorted as Meena wandered away, first to the living room and then upstairs to her own room, reading the words and pondering their meaning. D.C. was an easier city to lure Kate to than Philly. It was winter, and by the following spring, Meena was gone.

With help from Meena's replacement, Bernie and Leah dragged the dining room table out to the curb one Thursday night before trash day and replaced it with a rectangular one with four even legs. When Leah broke one of the gray IKEA plates, Bernie, a little high, suggested taking the rest out to the backyard to smash, and Leah, also high, agreed. The noise they made: the most sound an ear could hear followed by the least. Leah bought them new plates: green glass.

Bernie and Leah started sleeping together in Bernie's room, which was bigger and got better light, so they pried the slab of insulation from Bernie's wall and opened the door between their two rooms, making Leah's old room into an office with a desk for each of them. Bernie, on her way home from the library one day, picked up several wooden crates on the street and mounted them in a pleasing arrangement on what used to be the wall behind Leah's headboard to store their books. Instead, one of the boxes mostly stored Jigger, snoozing as they worked, Leah typing up her notes from the trip while Bernie unloaded the film in the changing tent, putting the sheets back into their yellow boxes and then carefully sealing them up with black gaffer's tape so no light got in.

One day at Bernie's work, the librarian left early to pick up her kid and a man wandered in and fell asleep in an undersized chair made for a child, his head on his arms like how Bernie used to sleep. But then he began to make noises—gurgling, choking. His body began to twitch a little and then went slack.

Terry, the security guard, came over. Buddy, Terry said, shaking the man, but he did not move. Hey! Terry said again, lightly slapping the man's face. The man's face was white and his lips were going blue. Fuck, Terry said.

Bernie knew that the librarian kept the Narcan in the top left drawer of her desk and she went for it, ripping the thick plastic packaging open and letting it fall to the ground as she ran across the quiet, sunny room. When she placed the white spritz bottle in the man's nostril and pressed the little red trigger, as she had seen the librarian do, the man didn't move at first, but then he sputtered awake.

What? the man said, over and over again, as if he could not hear Bernie.

Can I call someone for you? she asked. Can I take you somewhere?

What? the man said. What?

Eventually he stood and ambled out, pushing into the library's glass door with his shoulder until it opened. Bernie thought about him all the way home and into bed with Leah.

That night, Bernie read about the history of Kensington and the chemical process that made Narcan work and about a group of library employees who did free trainings on how to administer Narcan, in need of volunteers. She sent an email and received one back. Who had Bernie been waiting for to magically step in? It was people, just ordinary people like Bernie, who did what needed to be done.

Bits of the kitchen brick wall continued to come unstuck and fall to the floor, and one day while Violet was sweeping them together into a pile by the refrigerator and the sun was coming in hot and they were worrying about whether Lucy Vincent would throw them over for the new man starring opposite her in *Oklahoma!*—her first production that would give her points toward her Equity card—Violet swept up a piece of red Solo cup from Leah's long-ago twenty-fifth birthday party and stopped cold. Bernie and Leah were together, Meena had gone to D.C. and Kate had joined her, and Alex had overhauled her life. The housemates, as they had been, were gone; everything had changed.

Violet had been staying at Lucy Vincent's in South Philadelphia most nights anyway, so what was the difference? It took them months to move out, which they did in small increments, carload by carload in Lucy Vincent's blue Mini Cooper, but when the last slat of their IKEA bed was located in a closet and their last sex toy was washed and dried with a dirty washcloth and stuffed into Lucy Vincent's wide Joan Didion tote bag, there was nothing to say to Bernie and Leah but goodbye.

Come visit us, Violet said.

It's not like you're moving cross-country, Leah said. We'll see you.

They should replace Violet with a third new housemate, on this Bernie and Leah agreed that night, in their office room, as they pored over the processed negatives, which had come back from the lab—a different one that Bernie found on the internet, not Daniel Dunn's guy—tucked neatly, four to a sheet, in their special clear archival plastic. They'd exhausted Leah's grant, but Leah had picked up the negatives and paid the bill, and also for Bernie's new home light box—only $59.99 from the everything website. Bernie needed another way to pay for the hours, fifty dollars per, she'd need to rent the special Imacon scanner, making sure each photograph looked just right, though she knew Leah would find a way to pay for this too if asked. There was always her parents.

For the December holidays, Leah went back to New York, leaving Bernie behind in the house. It's just gone, Leah said now, when people asked her where she was from. It was so gone that you could go and stand on the corner where she had grown up and try to find anything that had been there when she was a kid. The exterior substance of the building, its brick and stone and windows that she had pushed open and pulled closed with a chain remained the same. But that was it.

She walked around the block several times. In Leah's childhood memories, the block had an Irish bar, a deli where she bought tuna sandwiches wrapped in white paper and pints of ice cream, a cheap hair salon where Leah and Evan could hang out if their mom had to go somewhere, a store that sold mannequins without faces, a BDSM leather store, and an empty storefront manned by a guy and his green parrot which Leah's father believed was a front for the mob. They could always get a cab because of the gas station across the street where the cabbies hung out, greeting each other and smoking.

During the years that Leah's family lived there, her childhood neighborhood had transformed from an area described as "run-down" in the 1980s to one of the wealthiest zip codes in Manhattan. Now, where the hair salon had once been there was a delicate lingerie boutique that sold bras that would cover perhaps a quarter of one of Leah's breasts for $189. A popular gay nightclub where beautiful men in luxurious brown leather moccasins loitered had replaced the empty storefront, and the corporate headquarters of an international luxury clothing brand stood where the leather store had once been. The mannequin store was now a pottery studio where affluent straights and gays alike went on third dates. The gas station was a sprawling CVS.

Evan came over to the apartment for dinner. He lived in Jersey City now with his wife, an Israeli woman he'd met at Brandeis, though the excuse given for her absence was nausea—she was pregnant. Evan was still fat but less so; he'd gotten into hiking and didn't eat anything that wouldn't have been available in caveman times. There was an awkwardness in the air between him and Leah, a politeness that could turn electric at the drop of certain words. Evan's wife posted anti-trans articles to the original social media app. Leah posted *Free Palestine* memes to the photo-sharing one.

Standing over the cracked wooden cheese board which

was spread with apricots and nuts and cheddars and mozzarellas, Evan announced that he'd recently been promoted to VP (of what, no one knew) and that he'd changed his party affiliation from Independent to Republican and was planning to vote for Trump.

But why? Leah's mother said, leaning against the broom closet, white cheddar on a cracker halfway to her mouth.

Yes, in God's name, why? Leah's father said. He stood at the stove stirring a sauce.

In God's name, exactly, Evan said. He's the only one of them who cares about Israel, who is willing to protect us.

Us, Leah said. Hahaha.

Evan lifted his tie and threw it over his shoulder, preparing to eat a cluster of apricots and almonds held between two fingers. He regarded his family with a look in his eyes that might have been fear, or might have been something else entirely. Then he spoke again.

I feel sorry for all of you, he said. He had slicked his hair back with gel but now a piece was falling out and down into his eyes.

Honey, Leah's mother said. I don't want to fight.

It must be so exhausting, Evan continued, to make fun of what everyone else believes in when you don't have anything that you believe in yourself.

Leah's father opened his mouth, triggering a festival of sounds, but Leah fled the room before the fight could lift off, followed by her parents' newest thin dog, Beatrice. In the TV room, she munched her cheese and crackers in peace and flipped channels with Beatrice by her feet until she reached one where people were singing. If a group of crows is called a murder, what do you call one hundred young, clean-cut blond men? She watched the men sing, standing in a semicircle, as BRIGHAM YOUNG MEN'S CHORUS flashed underneath. They finished a Christmas song and began a new number about a green mountain where small white flowers grow in the summer. Their voices resonated and blended, rose and fell, extended and stopped suddenly. There was skill there, yes, and there was leaping too.

For leaping, Leah saw then, requires release, surrender, trust, openness; things that, as it turns out, may be the opposite of knowledge.

Leah stopped chewing. She had tears in her eyes.

Not you too, Leah's father said, standing in the doorway.

Leah's mother came in behind him and ducked under his arm. What are we watching?

Singing, Leah said. The three of them watched and listened. On the screen, the boys sang about a place beyond the river where the air was cool and the sky had stars.

Look at their silly faces, Leah's mother said. Look at their haircuts.

Hideous, Leah's father said. Makes my skin crawl.

Leah got up then and returned to the kitchen where Evan was sitting at the table, site of so much wretchedness, alone now with the cheese board, which he picked at while looking at his phone.

If, to a father, a daughter is his heart with feet, walking around in the world, what to a little sister is an older brother? A tether, a satellite, a mirror, a fact-checker, a mentor and a mentee? When Leah was little, she and Evan had played a game where they would try to keep the other under a blanket for as long as possible. While she had held the blanket down with all her might no matter how much Evan swore and yelled, at the slightest squawk from her, Evan would whip the blanket off, releasing her, asking if she was alright.

Evan looked up from his phone and set it down on the table.

I just came to see if you were alright, Leah said. She pulled out one of the light aluminum metal chairs, and sat down in it.

I am, he said. Thanks.

And Hava? Leah said. And the baby? Everyone is, healthy?

They're fine too, he said. Thanks for asking.

Good, Leah said.

And you?

I'm actually seeing someone new.

Oh? he said. No more Alex?

Leah shook her head.

I'm surprised. I hope it works out for you though.

Evan lifted up a cracker, used it as a shovel to pick up a large piece of herbed goat cheese, and put it in his mouth.

Fuck that's good, he said.

Oh I know, Leah said, taking her own hunk of cheese. Creamy. Melts in the mouth.

It's like, Evan said, taking another piece of cheese with his fingers, sort of savory and sweet at the same time?

Tastes fatty, Leah said.

It does, Evan said. In a good way.

IV.

BERNIE DIDN'T MOVE, DIDN'T TURN HER HEAD, JUST KEPT LOOKing at the big negatives on her light box.

Leah stood in the doorway, waiting for some sign of love.

I'm working, Bernie said, at last.

And I'm here to work with you, Leah said.

No, Bernie said. I'm working on my own.

Oh, Leah said. But I need to know what you're doing for what I'm doing to make sense.

An hour, Bernie said. That's all I need.

So what are you thinking? Leah asked, returning exactly an hour later. The photo-sharing app with captions? The photos blown up huge with text on walls?

Slow your roll, Bernie said. We don't know what we're doing yet. How it all comes together.

OK, Leah said. How does it come together for you?

I want it to feel like an experience, Bernie said. Like something people have to stop their lives to do. Something you can't look away from.

Experiences are always exclusive, Leah said. Ticket prices. Travel. If you show it at night, only certain people can come.

Unless it was an experience you could do at home, anytime, anywhere you wanted.

How would you do that?

I don't know, Bernie said. Some kind of video I guess. But the apps on a phone will be too small, won't give the kind of impact, won't show all the detail of the photographs.

You're always looking for problems. You don't really want to put them out there, do you? Leah asked. You're content just having the work, never showing it to anyone.

That's not true, Bernie said. I just want it to be perfect.

What if we never find the perfect way? Leah said. What then?

Bernie didn't answer. Then we wait, she wanted to say. But she knew what Leah would say back: you'll be waiting forever.

Leah got up and went to bed, withdrawing her book of fairy tales.

I'm going out, Bernie said.

BERNIE SAT AT THE BAR at Jaffa looking for trouble, but no trouble found her. The man was there again, drinking his seltzer and doing his crossword.

Don't bite this frog, eight letters, the man said to the bartender.

Beats me, the bartender said.

She looked especially good that night and Bernie tried to make eye contact, but the bartender looked over Bernie's head, passing the drink in its plastic cup to a tall girl in a snapback. When would Bernie's eyes stop looking, stop *wandering*, as people liked to say? Never, never, never.

Cane toad, Bernie said, the clue having rung some very old bell. I think that's what they're called. The ones where whatever bites or licks them dies because they're toxic.

That works, the guy said. Thanks.

Bernie bowed her head in acknowledgment. She hadn't thought about those toads in years, but she thought about them now and how she too might be such a toad. Whatever licked or bit her was bound, eventually, to perish. It was silly really and strange that she felt that way, but she did. The idea spoke to her on some deep level, felt profoundly, if illogically, true. A delicious but deadly snack, the internet wrote of these toads. Tough and highly adaptable. Multiplied like crazy. "Blasted" their way across continents. "Invaded." Caused species extinctions. Didn't need much water. Ate almost anything.

And yet, when she got into bed that night, Leah rolled toward her. Leah pulled Bernie to her hot belly, hot from sleep, and then pushed Bernie's hair up and onto the pillow so she could kiss Bernie there. Leah was not afraid to touch her sharp shoulder blades, her dry skin with its bumps of bone.

When Jigger got fleas and then gave them to the red velvet chair, the chair was replaced with a round yellow one. A rug was procured from the marketplace of the original social media app; Bernie went to pick it up and after a long conversation with the owner of a vintage rug store ended up bringing home four new dining room chairs too, swapping out all but two of the old ones, which Bernie and Leah pushed to the wall unless they were having extra people over, a thing that almost never happened anymore when COVID came. At first Bernie and Leah and the new housemates, who occupied the third floor, were slow, steady, respectful. A lot of jigsaw puzzles and tea and texting about hand sanitizer and the details of one of the two new housemates' poly arrangement. But soon both housemates, students at the University, in the absence of in-person classes, absconded to their families of origin, leaving Bernie and Leah—beautifully? terrifyingly?—alone.

And what to do now? One afternoon, having watched and read everything imaginable and fucked several times, they opted to spring-clean. They removed the plastic sheeting from the windows in what had once been Alex's room; they pulled back the bed frame from the wall to reveal a treasure trove of brunette bobby pins glinting in the light, which Leah remembered aloud that Alex would remove before bed. Leah, with some love left, swept up the pile of bobby pins, and Bernie, on the small stepladder, washed and dusted the windows and by nightfall Leah had carried up a second nightstand and Bernie's lamp into Alex's room. Now they slept and used the bathroom on the third floor and worked haphazardly all over the second, Bernie moving her cameras and equipment into what had been Violet's room, while Leah stayed in her little office, warm and cozy as a hovel, with Jigger.

Many things were forgotten, many directions for movement fell through, many ideas no longer made sense, were no longer resonant in this new context. Things move too fast for art to keep up. Would *Changing Pennsylvania* still matter when the world had been hurled into even more fear and uncertainty and so many people were dying? Maybe yes. But maybe no. The photographs they had made on that first trip were about something else than the world was about now, Bernie began to feel, as she looked at them on the light box. They had been made by someone she no longer was.

Let's go out again, Bernie said.

Go where? Leah said.

Like before, Bernie said. But here, just around the city.

Leah went and got her driver's license, and with this, she was much more useful. It was on these smaller trips around Philadelphia that they talked constantly about how to do it.

But where can we do it? Bernie asked.

Outside. It would have to be outside, Leah answered.

Who will come?

I don't know. Whoever comes to see art? It will tell the story of our first trip, from you, your childhood, where you're from, to Dunn and his shed, to us and then incorporate more recent images, bringing the viewer up to the now. I'll be speaking live. I'll pull out certain words, phrases. But how will we make sure people aren't missing the photos, their quality?

We'll leave them up on the screen a long time. Much longer than you normally would for a slideshow. An uncomfortably long time.

Yeah. And then we'll put the whole show up online too?

Yeah, I guess. On a website.

And you can teach people about the big camera.

Me teach?

Yes. You'd be great at it. They ask you questions and you answer.

Teaching is more than that.

Obviously. But you'd start there. Then, one day, we open the community art school. We can use the first floor, downstairs, to hold the classes when it's safe again. Use the third floor kitchen for our meals. Until then, the porch.

Who will the classes be for? Bernie asked. The world has enough men photographers.

What about people in the neighborhood though, Leah

said. Like people who are from the neighborhood, from the city.

OK, Bernie said. Them too.

We'll need cameras, Leah said.

I know, Bernie said.

One day in June, the sky above the house filled with helicopters and they watched their own neighborhood on TV, watched tan military tanks meant for warfare roll past the Foot Locker at 52nd and Market Streets. Leah was among the protestors that day who walked from the art museum to city hall and got trapped on 676, the city's central highway. But Bernie was not.

Are you coming? Leah had asked as she was leaving, a bandana around her mouth and a backpack full of water.

No, Bernie said, standing in front of a big mock-up they'd made of *Changing Pennsylvania* on a whiteboard screwed into the wall. I'm working.

You can't stay in here, Leah said. Bring the camera.

And she had been right. Bernie set up the camera on the steps of the art museum and on a hill looking down at 676, hunching under the dark cloth and looking at the mass of bodies, moving slowly, upside down. Leah was down there, among the people, and she was still down there when Philadelphia police officers, who had received orders from the city to tear-gas its own people, began to do it. Bernie picked up the camera and ran back with everyone else, a safe distance away. When they finally reunited at home, Leah's eyes were purple-red and blotchy. Bernie blinked and blinked as she held the bag of ice to Leah's face.

WHEN THE HEAT COMES THAT summer, two years out from their road trip, they go to the beach, as the house still does not have air-conditioning.

They go to the Jersey shore, in joyful configurations of fours and fives and sixes. After they've showered they come back to Bernie's studio on the second floor and stand, moving around shoddily printed photographs and pages of text and Post-it notes.

Shelves break, pieces of the kitchen island chip away, paint comes unpeeled. Small pieces of wood that once were attached to windowsills become small pieces of wood that now hold windows ajar from windowsills. Leah spills a chocolate milkshake on the upholstered couch in a moment of sexual communion, and Bernie, falling asleep with the glass in her hand, spills red wine on the footstool, and so these too are discarded.

The gladness of seeing the other's face every day does not fade, the gladness of making breakfast, moving around the island to the toaster, from the toaster to the sink, moving the plates from the kitchen to the dining room (Bernie hangs new red curtains with tassels), coming downstairs for lunch and then again for dinner, these things are good, even very good. Bernie never does take up piano, but Leah has taken up basketball, playing in a small league that happens on a court a few blocks' walk from the house, and the satisfaction of dribbling, crossing over from right to left, faking out an opponent with her eyes, and launching a ball through a hoop—swish—also never gets old. Her body looks the same on the outside, but inside it feels different, changed. There is less hateful yelling when she looks at herself in the mirror, turns to the side, turns back to face front. When she listens now, there is only a hum—not like a sweet tune but not like a bitter one either.

At the very end of that season, on the last possible beach day, windy but still warm enough, Violet and Lucy Vincent invite them to a big day at the gay beach, closer to New York than it is to Philadelphia, and while Leah is tired from how late they have been staying up to work on *Changing Pennsylvania*, Bernie insists they go.

Lucy Vincent is radiant in a hot-pink bathing suit that laces up the back and Violet crawls through the sand on their hands and knees to talk to Bernie and Leah on their blanket. To Bernie's eye, Violet is just as beautiful as ever, but they look different—less cleanly barbered, bonier, dark purple patches around their eyes. Lockdown has taken a toll on everyone's bodies, but Violet seems to have been maximally affected, a little woozy and wobbling. Bernie can see now that their beauty, their physical form, what it gave them and what it took away, is not some lottery they won but rather something they will have to contend with, forever.

Violet says that they quit their job with the migrant workers organization and have instead been making dumplings and bao buns since the start of the pandemic. They can't stop, they say, and plan to open a restaurant and finance it themselves though that makes no sense ever, but especially now, when restaurants are closing left and right. They say Lucy Vincent has been depressed, has been suicidal since the shuttering of her show and no new parts on the horizon, and that feeding her with literal food has become their life's purpose and they've never been happier. Both Violet and Lucy Vincent have many people with whom they go on dates, and their life is messier and more complicated and better now than it has ever been.

I'm happy for you, Leah says.

Thanks man, Violet says. And you all?

Bernie and Leah tell Violet, vaguely, about their project.

We're still figuring it out of course, the logistics, et cetera, Bernie says. Like for people who don't feel safe enough to come in person.

Live broadcast it, Violet says, so people can watch at home, or anywhere around the world for that matter.

Huh, Leah says. Not a bad idea.

Bernie and Leah fall asleep side by side, but it is only Leah, so fair-skinned, who burns.

On the drive home to West Philadelphia, their legs and crotches are scratchy with sand and the sun is going down directly in front of them, due west.

Leah is driving and Bernie is looking out the window with her eyes and with her little 35mm camera.

Do you forgive Violet? Leah asks.

For what?

Breaking your heart.

They didn't, Bernie says.

After a few miles, Bernie speaks again. Yes, she says. I forgive them.

I think maybe you were more open to me because of Violet, Leah says.

Maybe, Bernie says.

And do Bernie and Leah feel together with each other then? It changes, I think they would say, moment by moment. In this moment, I think they would say yes.

THE HOUSE'S FRIDGE BREAKS AND the owner, via the rental company, refuses to install a new one for several days, so Bernie and Leah go out every night to eat in Jaffa's courtyard. They are walking to dinner on the third night when Benjamin Pogden calls again.

Everyone, me included, thought that Bernie's decision to leave Daniel Dunn's stuff where it lay in his shed was complete and final, and though hard and twisty, ultimately right. But in truth the decision not to become the steward of Dunn's work is a decision Bernie will make over and over again, in many small ways (by email, by phone, by DM on every platform) and though Bernie mostly maintains this decision, at a few important moments like this one, she does not.

They are standing on the avenue just outside the organic food co-op and many people they know a little bit are walking by in both directions.

Uh huh, Bernie says, again and again. She wanders away to stand on the grocery store's ramp as Leah chats with passersby.

Here is what Pogden tells her: Some Brazilian man who bought an $11.2 million house in Los Angeles wants to impress a client who loved Daniel Dunn and won't stop calling Pogden about Dunn's diner photograph, won't take no for an answer. The gallery would take their cut and there would be taxes but Bernie would receive $417,000.

It's interesting, Pogden says. What you did, by abandoning the shed and all the negatives. You made Dunn's prints that already existed so rare, so valuable.

I didn't mean to, Bernie says.

I know, Pogden says. But you did.

How different would everything be if Bernie didn't have to worry about money, if she could take that one heavy thing off her plate, not forever but for a while? What could she do with three years, or five? Who might she be? She could be, if she wanted, Leah.

He wants me to accept custody of the diner photograph, Bernie tells Leah, once the call has ended. The one I loved in college.

Why? Leah asks, and Bernie tells her.

And? Leah asks.

And I said no, Bernie says.

Leah says nothing.

What? Bernie says. That's the decision I made. You were there, remember?

I remember, Leah says. But things are different. Think of what you could do with that money now.

You're not serious, Bernie says. You're the one who said it was a trap.

I never said that. Plus, that was a long time ago, Leah says.

Two years, Bernie says.

Feels like longer, Leah says. We could start the school. We could buy cameras for people.

Bernie is aware in this moment and Leah will soon be, too, that money has always been a part of their relationship, and that if Bernie has her own, something between them will shift. Also, Bernie has lied—she already told Benjamin Pogden yes.

I'll be tied to him again, Bernie says.

It's just one photograph, Leah says.

There will be times in the years that follow when Bernie will look at the photograph in the room that had once been Violet's, of the interior of Daniel Dunn's shed, which was indeed demolished along with his house, the land sold, and she will think, what a waste, what a terrible waste, how young I was and how dumb. And there would be other times, particularly when an article comes out, *Lauded Interdisciplinary Community Art Project* Changing Pennsylvania *Funded by Known Sexual Abuser Daniel Dunn,* when she will feel the same thing, but about taking the money.

The Housemate was always poorer than I even though she had the good teaching job and I didn't. She didn't come from money and felt that the smell of poverty followed her. She was always making bad money decisions and I'd find her up at night worrying over her checkbook. The house was always in my name.

Can poverty cause cancer? I don't know. All I know is that money is partly what killed her, her and many others, and what might she have written if someone had given her $417,000, enough to stop churning, digging, thrashing around for a while. Money is one thing that may be exactly the same for Bernie and Leah as it was for The Housemate and me, if not worse.

All of this is to say that when people talk about Bernie and Leah taking this money, when people accuse them of hypocrisy and weakness, as people are wont to do, I defend Bernie. I don't blame her for wanting what she never had. I don't blame Leah either. But I do not defend her.

WE'RE READY, LEAH SAYS THAT fall.

We're not, Bernie says.

We're ready, Leah says again.

They print the flyers. They tape them up to light poles around the neighborhood with clear packing tape. They buy the dinky projector and the speaker and the microphone. They rehearse the script.

I think you should let the first photo sit longer before you come in, Bernie says.

I think you should make, not force, but strongly encourage, people to go under the dark cloth and look at the ground glass, Leah says. They need to see what it's like under there. It's part of the experience.

For the first few showings, like the one I went to, no one comes—three or four people, mostly their friends. By the fifth or sixth, a few neighbors and people who are sitting in the park come over to watch. For the tenth, a hyperlocal online magazine has written them up, so a small crowd of mostly parents and children come, and one kid sticks a squished M&M to the camera's lens. On the twelfth, the man that always sits at Jaffa drinking seltzer and doing the crossword puzzle comes. He goes politely under the dark cloth when Bernie offers and leaves exactly at the forty-five minute concluding mark, but the following week they receive a call from a *Philadelphia Inquirer* fact-checker and then the stylish first-person article runs: *What Abbott's photographs, with the help of McCausland's captions, achieve is nothing less than a re-seeing of our troubled, troubling state. A strange, impossible to describe masterpiece. For all those tired of feeling depressed and uninspired in your houses, go see it for yourself and feel alive again.*

Holy shit, Bernie says. They are sitting on the porch couch with coffee, reading it.

Captions? Leah says. He called them captions.

Oh they don't know what words to use, Bernie says.

But it keeps happening. It is the photographs people love. The text too, yes. But they tend to forget. *Screening this Saturday night in Rittenhouse Square is the photographic/performance art piece that your coolest friend has likely already told you about,* writes Stephanie, the managing editor for the paper where Leah once worked, *consisting of photographs from a young local talent named Bernie Abbott taken in a painstakingly antiquated process, digitized, and paired with words and sounds. And you don't even have to leave the house to take it in if you don't want to.*

They didn't even print my name, Leah says.

They're idiots, Bernie says. As you well know.

Once their live shows have concluded, Leah's old cohort colleague Anya, who has dropped out of the PhD program and does something techy and mysterious, uploads a short excerpt of the show to the video-sharing platform which is not new, but is newly used for things beyond synchronized dance videos.

From then on, Leah can't remember the order of things, nor where one thing ends and the next begins. The calls, emails, and texts. Them bringing the camera to the convention center and making picture after picture and Leah writing and making sound memos on their phone as people dance and yell and shove and wait and people they know stand inside counting the ballots. The offers of sponsorships, gallery representation, literary representation, space, time, use of a darkroom in Center City. The space and the time and the darkroom they say yes to, all the rest must be refused.

We cannot become hawkers of goods or products for money, Leah says.

I agree, Bernie says, a little ruefully. But a gallery could be nice. And don't you want a book?

Leah does want it. Oh how they still want it all! They feel ill, nauseous. But there is another voice there, that other voice again, that seems to come from somewhere else. The past, or maybe the future. *That way madness lies,* says the voice.

It was my voice.

Can't, Leah says, their stomach nearly ripping apart in the answering. The galleries, the publishing houses, they're too big, too powerful, too tempting. They'll eat us alive, I think. Tear us apart. Pit us against each other. We have to stay, I don't know. Together. We own our own work and don't depend on anything we don't own. I think that should be the rule.

OK, Bernie says, after a long time. I can agree to that. I can agree to try for that. Together. But, she points out, they don't own the video-sharing platform.

That's true, Leah says.

That night, Leah calls Anya and arranges for her to create a website for them where the images and videos can live instead.

They begin work on the second installment of *Changing Pennsylvania,* which will be about what it felt like to live through this time in Philadelphia. They now have a small team of people, overseen by Anya, queers who Bernie and Leah hire themselves who are only a few years younger than them, but decidedly different, decidedly Gen Z instead of millennials, whose fingers race across the little keys and whose laptops bear stickers that say IT WAS CAPITALISM ALL ALONG.

Changing Pennsylvania Part 2 comes out as before, but with fancier equipment and in much bigger parks. A ten-city tour with many more screens so people can get close, each screen with its own speaker but Leah still speaking live. Sometimes, when the whole project team is all in a van together, or sitting around in a rented room, Bernie laughingly calls them "the housemates."

But they're not, Leah says. They go home.

I know, Bernie says. I was only kidding.

But a worried look crosses Leah's face then. The feeling of something trying to get through, something trying to be heard has not eased for Leah. If anything, the feeling has been blown up, gotten louder, magnified. What they once thought was enough is no longer enough; their ambition and doubt has only grown. They will, it seems, never be satisfied. Where for Bernie, the reviews are satisfying and the requests to speak and collaborate and take on new projects for money make sense, are a service you provide based on the money offered, money Bernie deposits into the account they share equally for *Changing Pennsylvania,* Leah is not sure. At any moment, Leah feels, something could happen that could undermine the whole enterprise, compromise it ethically or artistically. Could they be doing more? Thinking more complexly? Reaching more people? Plus, Leah is cranky that people call more often for Bernie than for them and that their name is often mentioned after Bernie's.

What does it matter? Bernie says. We're doing what we said we'd do.

Easy for you to say, Leah says. But then several hours later, after they have thought about it, they will come back, apologetic, and ready to kiss and fuck and dream about the next project. I was thinking, Leah says, about the community art school. I think we'll be ready to start classes this spring. Imagine. Imagine it.

ON HER FIRST DAY OF teaching the free classes, Bernie is slapped by the enormity, the weight of what it is to stand at the front of a classroom and look out at the big beautiful faces staring back at her. They are afraid to touch the cameras. Distributed in a U shape around the first floor of the house, the students, young people and old, of all genders, Black, white, brown, and Asian, one by one tell her that they are there to study photography because they saw a photograph once that changed their life, because they think there is nothing cooler than making pictures, because they want to do something like *Changing Pennsylvania* but with the place where they are from, with Delaware, California, Atlantic City, Kensington.

Teaching? When it's good? A marvel. A fucking miracle. They live, and then they turn to you to tell you about it. It's as if no one has ever seen before, the way they talk about it. It's like this painting, they say, this song, this book. They want to chop up the words of the poets they admire and tattoo them on their arms. Bernie can't remember what it felt like to respect artists that much, in that faraway way, now that she talks to them all the time, and eats with them and is privy to the petty bullshit, the jostling for power, the pay to play. There are so many artists, she thinks, that if some of them died to make room for her students, that would be alright.

They want to hear what she has to say. If she likes something, they like it, or disagree with it so vociferously that it's clear they also kind of like it. If she makes fun of something, they laugh. They write down what she says to reread later. Sometimes she says something that's useful to one of her students and they are able to see something that they didn't before and then they use it in their own work and then other people can see it too. It's like making photographs, but exponentially. Good teaching is like making a work of art that then goes out and makes other works of art, and so on, forever.

And when it's bad? She tries to stuff too much in, or covers up her insecurity with rules, or she makes social and human mistakes, and her students temporarily hate her. They hate her like she is their mother or their father. They hate her because she has hurt them, offended them, abandoned them, taken them only so far but not far enough.

One boy, from Kensington, a former addict, he's said, who wants to do a project about his neighborhood and fellow addicts, stays after class to show her some photos he's taken with a Polaroid camera. What do you think? he asks. What do you really think? Do I have it? Do I have what it takes?

I don't know, Bernie answers honestly. Don't ask me. I am not the one who gets to say. But, she says, I hope you will come back.

And what does Bernie feel, once they are all gone? Standing in that classroom which was once the dining room, she feels she has lived longer than she ever planned to. Things that were once very painful are less so. Things that she thought would work out have not worked out, and the reverse. Her brother is still alive, though sick with COVID (he had not been vaccinated, but again, not because he is Trumpy but because he is so free). Her mother lives on in Baltimore, having moved in recently with housemates, and has been calling. Could they get together? How was Bernie doing? Could she finally meet this Leah? Bernie and Leah have enough money for perhaps three more years of making new segments of *Changing Pennsylvania* and doing the community art school but money will have to be raised after that, or new work found. Invented. The future seems so blank it's not just white but see-through, there isn't even a wall it seems, to tack it to.

Yet, upstairs on the third floor Leah is making lunch, opening the fridge, closing it. Bernie can hear it. They are cutting cheese now, slicing tomatoes. Now they are putting butter in the pan. Now they are turning on the flame.

V.

HERE IS MY OPINION: IT IS NEVER EQUAL. IT IS NOT EQUAL in natural ability, or in opportunities given, in time, in effort, in struggle, or in risk. Not in money or groceries or sleep or orgasms or teaching jobs or cat care or miles driven, dinners cooked or ordered in, meetings skipped, notes taken, 1099-MISCs or W-2s filled out for oneself or for them, time spent listening to a problem, time spent being summoned to read an email over their shoulder and offering your thoughts on how they should respond, time spent answering back when they call out asking how to spell acceptance which they can never remember, time spent finding and then sending articles on power imbalances and white supremacy in the classroom when they are (correctly) accused of being racist by a student, time spent scheduling their dentist appointments and submitting their therapy superbills to insurance for reimbursement and going to parties and talking up their work instead of your own. They've been down as of late, you might say. They could really use an ego boost.

Whether you can accept this inequality, whether Leah can, today, tomorrow, ten or twenty or fifty years from now, depends on a great many things. I do not believe that there is only ever one main character in a story but I do believe that some people have to try harder than others to achieve the same result and that some people are able to live their lives with their eyes slightly more open.

It depends also on things that no one, not one person, can control, a truth we wouldn't change even if it could be. Moments of being in the center of the action cannot, do not, last forever. One day people are calling, knocking, begging to be heard, and the next they are not. One day the ideas are knocking and it is hot and good. It is fire, it is electricity. But then something happens, someone interrupts. Your cat gets sick say, and needs a tedious series of injections to her plump pouch and the vials must be picked up at a highly specific and inconvenient time of day and injected at another extremely specific and inconvenient time of day that conflicts with when you do your best thinking. Or the world changes and things that were once exciting no longer are, ideas that were once unthinkable can now be thought.

Or, say, perhaps, time just passes and things just change with the person you love best. They are different, older and a heavier drinker, but it is not really about these things. Say it is not because you have always felt a little apart from them, a little tempted to run, but rather because you now feel together, so very together. Their arms are always wrapped around you in the night, and their ideas are inextricable from yours. If you think a thought in the morning, by afternoon they are telling you about it, as if the thought left your head and traveled down the stairs without your permission.

Say then that the person you love best gets sick, very sick and suddenly, and their best friend Paul flies in with his wife from Santa Fe to help out but is constantly reading out loud from the paper. Listen to this, listen to this, he is saying, but he isn't waiting for anyone's reply to see if you actually want to hear it, he is just going ahead and telling you. Suddenly you can't bear to be there in the room with them, not one moment, not one second longer, not with Paul's incessant speaking and his wife's knitting needles clacking and The Housemate's coughing—why did you let her smoke all those cigarettes for years, for years you watched her light the tip over and over again and breathe and breathe until the tip glowed even brighter each time? Go now, someone is saying. Go today. It is you who is saying it.

So you go. You go to Maine. You always loved the water. But instead of ocean, all you find is a lake, a lake where people come at dusk to fish, fish that the state restocks every year because they do not regenerate naturally. The loons eat them. There is only one place to stay in the town you've chosen, which is the first or last—depending on the direction of travel—stop before or after the one-hundred-mile wilderness stretch of the Appalachian Trail, so thru-hikers are always appearing exhausted and famished or else jittery with anxiety at the hotel's restaurant. You buy them beers, ask them to tell you about themselves, and when they're gone, you wonder what is wrong with you, why you can care for these strangers when you cannot care for The Housemate. At night, the loons—plump from eating fish in the lake but with strange beady red eyes—call out and call out.

When the call comes, you are at the hotel restaurant. You are masticating lobster with clarified butter when Paul tells you that The Housemate has died and it becomes real to you only then that you will have to imagine a house, a life, a world without her in it, and then you will have to live there. It is as if all your life you have been pushing against the closed door of a small room from the inside while someone pushes against the same door from the outside and then one day the force exerted from the outside is just gone. But you are still pushing against the door. You find yourself in a large empty hallway then, having fallen to the ground, and unable to stand up.

It may be, I am thinking now, that whoever seems, on first blush, like the one who is the beloved is actually the lover. Whoever seems to love less, actually loves more, needs more love.

People say that art will save your life and I know this to be as true a statement as any, but I also know that during the many years after The Housemate died but before I met Bernie and Leah, when I lay alone in the dark with the weight of the air sitting just above my chest waiting for art to save my life I could have kept on waiting a long time.

And yet, I admit that when I hear through the grapevine that a glossy national magazine is doing a story on Bernie and Leah and looking for a Philly-based photographer to shoot them, I work every connection I have left. My friend is surprised.

All these years and you finally want to work again because of two kids with a social media account? she says.

It's more than that, I say.

Suit yourself, she says. I'll make some inquiries.

In the end, the contract is mine and the shoot is scheduled for a gray Friday afternoon. Leah meets me outside on the house's porch wearing a Canadian tuxedo—blue denim pants, and a blue denim button-down shirt with pearl cowboy snap buttons.

Bernie will be down soon, they say. Or at least I hope she will. Get you anything?

I decline. We wait, on a new wicker porch couch that's replaced the old one.

It's nice to see you again, Leah says. How have you been?

I decide to answer honestly. Not good, I say. But I'm getting better.

I'm sorry to hear that, Leah says, though I think they think I'm talking physically, or maybe globally.

Congratulations to you both, I say. On everything.

Thank you, they say. It's been quite a year. I mean in the world, a very bad year of course. But for us, for me personally and professionally, a very good year. Which is weird.

Sure, I say. Sometimes it happens that way.

Does it? they say. Did it ever happen like that for you?

I can see then in a way I haven't before that what makes Leah a disarming interviewer and a good writer is their warmth, which sits right up against their sadness. They wear both lightly like a lotion or a cologne, both radiating off them, positively wafting, in a way that makes you want to say something, anything, that will decrease their sadness by some small degree and tip the balance. You want to share something of yourself that will make them happy, which is a strange reason to tell the truth.

Yes, I want to say. The center of the action and the center of your life are never really aligned and if they are, you are doing something very wrong.

It's getting late, I say instead. Should we check on Bernie?

I'm sorry, Bernie says, when she finally appears, following Leah, face splotched red, on the porch. She wears black wide-legged pants that are too short yet somehow look just right on her, nicely worn-in narrow black leather boots, and a thick white scarf looped strangely around her neck. No earrings. Her bangs have grown out and she keeps smoothing her hair behind her ears, which are pink and small. Closes her mouth over her teeth. Doesn't smile.

I have Leah sit on a top step and Bernie stand below, but the effect looks off, odd, as if Leah is the whole picture and Bernie just their wisp of an attendant. Bernie's body doesn't naturally take up space, lacks organic presence, I'm noticing now.

Could you come closer in? I ask Bernie, and she scooches toward Leah.

Good, I say. Could you touch her, sorry their, shoulder. Could you touch their shoulder almost like you're leaning on it but you're not really? Nice. And could you toss one side of the scarf over—may I?

Yeah.

I stand in front of Bernie and untie her scarf from where it is knotted tightly around her throat. I take one of the ends and pull it long and drape it over Bernie's shoulder so that the end that remains is very short, its fringe resting on the flat of her turtlenecked chest.

I don't know, Bernie says, what to do with my other hand.

How about if you put it in your butt pocket? I suggest.

No pockets in these pants, Bernie says.

Rest it in the waistband? I say. Fake it?

Oh, Bernie says. OK.

She breathes heavily, audibly, like she's just been exercising.

You OK? I hear Leah ask softly, after I do a batch in that pose.

No, Bernie says. Can we take a break?

We can. We do. Leah goes into the house to fetch me a beer and when they return, the three of us stand around on the sidewalk drinking from our green bottles. I feel almost young again.

It's just weird, Bernie says, to have my picture taken by someone else. I'm sure you understand.

I won't do you dirty, I say.

I don't want to be pretty, she says. But I don't want to be ugly either.

OK, I say. What then?

She chugs from her beer and I see one of the problems between them: as soon as Bernie came onto the porch, I forgot Leah. I could see Leah clearly when Bernie was not there, but when she was, Leah became impossible to find. I look around for Leah now, and find them, to my left, already done with their beer and peeling at its label.

I don't know, Bernie says.

Scary, Leah says. She'd like to be scarier.

Bernie smiles. Exactly.

And you? I ask Leah.

I know I'm fat, Leah says, and I'm not asking to be thinner. No good angles, no tricks. Just make me look as I am.

OK, I say.

Also, I'd like to look dignified, Leah says. Not silly. Like someone serious. Talented. Worthy of respect.

We try another setup, this time they sit side by side on the steps, shoulders touching but knees not and I get out my little stepladder and shoot them from slightly above.

I am pretty sure I've got the shot, but I don't want to let them go. I know that as soon as I do, both of them, but Bernie especially, will race away from me back inside the house. Leah might linger for a moment to be polite, but then they too would be gone. I'd see both of them again from time to time after that, around the neighborhood in three dimensions and on my phone and computer in two. But they wouldn't be mine anymore.

Are we done yet? Bernie asks, shading her eyes from the setting sun.

Leah too is shifting, checking their phone, ready to get back to work.

Not yet, I say. Maybe I want them to release me, to tell me it's time for me to go. Maybe I want them to ask me to move in.

Not just yet, I say. Soon.

ACKNOWLEDGMENTS

This book was touched by four brilliant editors, who all made it better at crucial junctures: Alexis Washam, Jillian Buckley, Annie Chagnot, and Parisa Ebrahimi. Thank you. My gratitude to everyone at Hogarth and the Random House group who championed *Housemates* over the long haul: David Ebershoff, Jaylen Lopez, Andy Ward, and many more whose labor is never seen. And of course, to my agent, Jin Auh, who makes all things possible.

Hilary Leichter and Denne Michele Norris, thank you for articulating Bernie and Leah so clearly in their earliest forms, a kind of seeing that became my true north, and for all the kvetching and voice memos. Annie Liontas and Piyali Bhattacharya provided essential editorial insight in *Housemates'* final season, and my Philly writer's group, the Claw, as a whole kept me going with pep talks and camaraderie and cheese. Sections of this novel were written with support from Millay Arts, Lighthouse Works, and Monson Arts.

The mechanics of large-format photography and production, as well as many of the insights into large-format photographic art making, come from hours of shadowing and texting with Jade Doskow, a photographer whose work at Freshkills Park in Staten Island and elsewhere I admire enormously. I drew also from writings by and about Berenice Abbott, Eugène Atget, Margaret Bourke-White, Nan Goldin, Baldwin Lee, Annie Leibovitz, Stephen Shore, and others. Elizabeth McCausland's criticism on a wide range of subjects was enormously impactful.

I did not write a historical novel of Abbott and McCausland in part because it already exists—*The Realist* by Sarah Coleman. Julia Van Haaften's biography *Berenice Abbott: A Life in Photography* was an indispensable resource, without which this book never would have been born. The scholars and writers Ariel Goldberg, Sarah Miller, Bonnie Yochelson, Susan Noyes Platt, Susan Dodge-Peters Daiss, Tirza True Latimer, and Rowena Kennedy-Epstein shared essential papers, archival documents, and knowledge about Abbott and McCausland or pointed me in the right direction. Thank you to Ken Fox for several important days at the George Eastman Museum library and archives in Rochester, New York.

The line about a man's daughter being his heart with feet walking around in the world comes from Mat Johnson's novel *Loving Day*. Bernie's sense that her drawings of horses look like sausages owes a debt of gratitude to family friend Terry Allen's song "The Beautiful Waitress." The idea that any parent's fears come back around to take revenge on them through their children came from a conversation with the writer Rachel Heng. The facts of Rebecca Wight's murder in the Michaux State Forest come from Claudia Brenner's memoir, *Eight Bullets: One Woman's Story of Surviving Anti-Gay Violence*.

Big gratitude to Anna Krieger, Rosie Guerin, and Sonia

Williams-Joseph for your insights into having an older brother and to Joshua Demaree for bringing me into central Pennsylvania over the years and suggesting I read Galway Kinnell's *The Book of Nightmares*.

Mom and Mollie: I love you, I appreciate you, thank you for being my family.

Art: I'm grateful for too much to name. Thank you for your love, for being my consultant on what it feels like to put a toe into film photography and fall, and for the loan of your belly to Leah.

My dad, Alan Eisenberg (April 15, 1935–October 7, 2023), did not go all the way with this book, but he was there when it counted. I write and re-write because of him.

I celebrate and mourn the lives of the queer ancestors who came before me, artists whose names the world knows as well as those who died unrecognized for their contributions. May their memories be a blessing.

ABOUT THE AUTHOR

EMMA COPLEY EISENBERG is a queer writer of fiction and nonfiction. Her first book, *The Third Rainbow Girl: The Long Life of a Double Murder in Appalachia,* was named a *New York Times* Notable Book and was nominated for an Edgar Award, a Lambda Literary Award, and an Anthony Award, among other honors. Her fiction has appeared in *Granta, McSweeney's, VQR, American Short Fiction,* and other publications. Raised in New York City, she lives in Philadelphia, where she cofounded Blue Stoop, a community hub for the literary arts.

emmacopleyeisenberg.com
X: @frumpenberg
Instagram: @frumpenberg
TikTok: @frumpenberg

ABOUT THE TYPE

This book was set in Fairfield, the first typeface from the hand of the distinguished American artist and engraver Rudolph Ruzicka (1883–1978). Ruzicka was born in Bohemia (in the present-day Czech Republic) and came to America in 1894. He set up his own shop, devoted to wood engraving and printing, in New York in 1913 after a varied career working as a wood engraver, in photoengraving and banknote printing plants, and as an art director and freelance artist. He designed and illustrated many books, and was the creator of a considerable list of individual prints—wood engravings, line engravings on copper, and aquatints.